ACCLAIM FOR

Everybody Has Everything

A GLOBE AND MAIL 100 BEST BOOK OF 2012

A NOW MAGAZINE TOP 10 BOOK OF 2012

"Katrina Onstad's beautiful new novel is a clear-eyed look at an ordinary marriage under extraordinary pressure. EVERYBODY HAS EVERYTHING is about many things—family, friendship, responsibility, loss—but at its heart, it's about what happens when the person you love suddenly veers off in another direction. It is unflinching yet tender, gripping, and lyrical and devastating. I can't stop thinking about it."

—Lauren Fox, author of *Friends Like Us* and *Still Life with Husband*

"Ambitious and assured... Onstad's timely new novel examines how and why adults choose to be parents, and what happens when you don't have that much choice in the matter... Ana and James are thoroughly convincing and their agony and triumphs compelling."

—*Globe and Mail* (Canada)

"A literary excursion into the poignancy and murkiness of loss, parenting, and marriage...impressive...intelligent, ambitious, and unsettling."

—*Winnipeg Free Press*

"Unsparingly honest...Never sentimental but always compassionate, this compelling book is hard to put down."

—*Hello* magazine

"Everyone will recognize the all too common yearnings and failings of two people trying to figure out what will make them happy."

—*Chatelaine* magazine

"This new book is very good, to get that out of the way: Onstad's writing is always vigorous, funny, and mean-because-it's-true...Onstad perfectly gets at her characters."

—*National Post* (Canada)

"Revelations are both joyous and heartbreaking, and Onstad handles both aspects well...The characters' motivations, self-revelations, and discoveries are carefully elucidated, such that the reader is able to form connections not just with Ana and James, but with the supporting characters as well...Onstad delicately builds up layers and peels them away."

—*Quill & Quire*

"With a keen eye for details of the contemporary good life, Katrina Onstad precisely delineates the crack in the vase of what appears to be a happy marriage. This is a book that challenges conventional wisdom about love and parenting and rising to the occasion in a crisis. And there is no way to predict the next turn of its events, which makes it a delicious read."

—Carol Anshaw, *New York Times* bestselling author of *Carry the One*

"What an interesting, vivid, utterly modern novel Katrina Onstad has written. I love how intelligently and precisely she explores James's and Ana's emotions around marriage, love, sex, work, ambition, and parenthood. EVERYBODY HAS EVERYTHING made me both think and feel differently about my own life."

—Margot Livesey, author of *The Flight of Gemma Hardy* and *The House on Fortune Street*

"I inhaled every page, feeling gut-punched by a writer willing to tackle such taboo subjects as the ambivalence of motherhood, the catalytic nature of children, and the restlessness of marriage. There are no unearned tears, when I laughed or cried, it was always for the same reason: painful recognition. I loved this book."

—Lisa Gabriele, author of *Tempting Faith DiNapoli* and *The Almost Archer Sisters*

Everybody Has Everything

Everybody Has Everything

Katrina Onstad

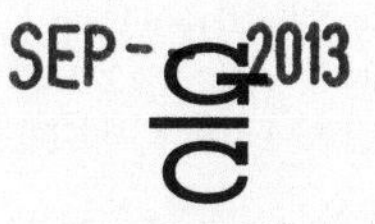

GRAND CENTRAL
PUBLISHING

NEW YORK BOSTON

This book is a work of fiction. Names, characters, places, and incidents are the product of the author's imagination or are used fictitiously. Any resemblance to actual events, locales, or persons, living or dead, is coincidental.

Grand Central Publishing
Hachette Book Group
237 Park Avenue
New York, NY 10017

www.HachetteBookGroup.com

Printed in the United States of America

RRD-C

First Edition: June 2013
10 9 8 7 6 5 4 3 2

Grand Central Publishing is a division of Hachette Book Group, Inc.
The Grand Central Publishing name and logo is a trademark of Hachette Book Group, Inc.

Library of Congress Cataloging-in-Publication Data
Onstad, Katrina.
Everybody Has Everything / Katrina Onstad. —First Edition.
pages cm
ISBN 978-1-4555-2292-7 (trade pbk.) —ISBN 978-1-4555-2293-4 (ebook)
1. Marriage—Fiction. 2. Conflict of interest—Fiction. I. Title.
PR9199.4.O67E94 2013
813'.6—dc23

2012040785

To Julian and Judah and Mia

Somebody loves us all.

—from "Filling Station"
by Elizabeth Bishop

The Day After Labor Day

IN THE END, it took Ana and James only an hour to become parents.

James arrived first, stumbling toward a police officer sitting on a chair by a door marked MORGUE. He felt his eyes ballooning, growing too big for his face. He tried, but could not blink. *You are awake,* he thought. *This is happening.*

"My name is James Ridgemore," he said to the policeman, who stood up quickly, as if caught in the act. James noticed he was short, or shorter than James. "My name is James Ridgemore."

"Just a moment," and the policeman went into the room, leaving James in an empty hallway, sniffing at alcohol and something he couldn't identify: Fire? Burning hair? It was freezing down here, devoid of heat. The second finger on his left hand turned white at the tip.

The policeman reappeared, holding open the door. When James entered, the contents of the room dropped away. All that was left was a body covered with a sheet hovering in bottomless space. But in fact, the tray jutted out of the wall. A matchbox sleeve. James could not tell if the thing upon it was male or female. Other people were there (he would remember that: the chatter, the grocery store dullness of all crowds), uttering words he knew from television shows about coroners and death reports. No voices were lowered.

A woman pulled back the sheet. She wore clear rubber gloves that left her wedding band visible.

James looked down and recognized Marcus, the check-mark scar beneath his bottom lip. His black hair was matted with tar. *Why would that be? Who closed his eyes?* James ran rapid-fire through questions but silently, his mouth too dry to speak. *Why does he look so different? Is it only the difference between the living and the dead?*

Then he realized that the difference, the strangeness, came down to something simple: Marcus was almost always smiling. James had never seen his lips so straight. There was no peace about him, no angel in repose, no release, no calm. He looked agitated, unsettled, as if he'd just been annoyed by a telemarketer.

"Yes, it's him," said James, though no one had asked a question. His legs felt hollow, swirling with smoke. But he did not feel ill. He was not repulsed or disgusted. He did not find it hard to look upon the body. Then the tray slid back into its cabinet and was sealed with a heavy handle.

The woman in the rubber gloves smiled at him ruefully. *Well-worn, this smile,* thought James.

On his way upstairs in the elevator, she stayed with him. She had removed her gloves, staring straight ahead as she did it. She was tiny. Everyone seemed small that day.

"You have a strange job," James told her. She pecked a nod. "You're so little. How do you lift the bodies? Is it hard?"

Then there was a roaring in his ears, the sound of steel twisting, a train exploding off its rails. He leaned against the wall and closed his eyes, heard a stream of sound pour forth from the tiny woman's mouth, but he was unable to distinguish one word from the next.

The elevator stopped, and the woman put her hand under his elbow. She guided him out on his empty legs, past green walls, his feet on different-colored footprints stenciled on the floor. She appeared to be following the line of purple footprints, and so James did, too, pulled along as if riding a skateboard, past elevators, around corners. At first there were a few patients walking here and there. Someone with his papery ass hanging out in the open air, pushing an IV. But as the other colored footprints disappeared, the corridors grew quieter, more deserted. Though he knew it already, James was reminded that what was coming next was serious; not as serious as the basement, as Marcus frozen in a drawer, but serious.

At Room 5117, they stopped before a closed door. The woman propped up James against the wall and entered the room alone, a bellhop doing one last pass before opening the door to a guest. When the door opened for him at last, James saw a body on the bed; it was cleaner than Marcus, its face bloated, the head held to the body by a large collar. Tubes snaked from the fingers, and white bandages soaked with deep brown circles covered the head. A plastic hose hung from the open mouth like something being expelled. Her eyes were closed, but the sounds of the machines clapping and whirring were like a language, the body announcing itself to this room, singing its name: Sarah.

This room. James glanced around at all the people who emerged then, slowly, in full relief. Unfamiliar faces and, in the middle, a male nurse cradling a bundle of sheets in his arms. Out of the sheets, dangling in the air, was a foot encased in a small white running shoe. James moved then, fast toward the sheets, which were not sheets at all, but a boy, and not a boy, but Finn. Marcus and Sarah's Finn. It was the longest walk James had ever taken, those six steps through a room of strangers, his arms out, his body trembling.

"Give him to me," he whispered hoarsely, angry at the time between the now and the boy he needed to put to his chest, angry that no one had given him over sooner. He grabbed the bundle, and my God, it was still warm, which meant he was alive—didn't it? And then something happened that was not of this earth, that was transporting, undenied. The bundle shook to life, let loose a howl never heard before, a howl from a place in the boy of all knowing, of the mines beneath the beneath, a sound of despair that rolled like a boulder over James. He held the boy closer, the boy who would soon be too big for this kind of holding, his legs dangling from James's torso. There was a sneaker on one foot, a dirty sock on the other, as if he had been running. The sticky black tar was not tar, James recognized finally, but blood. Blood in Finn's blond hair that James was weeping into, keening along with him but holding on, holding him, the unbreakable, undroppable boy.

Ana became a mother during a conference call.

Staring out the window, she had just finished leaning into her desk phone, explaining two weeks' worth of research that she'd delivered that morning in bound copies and via e-mail. The air outside was bluest blue, and a surprise burst of early autumn warmth wrapped gold around the city. Her cell phone shook on her desk. She ignored it.

"Mark? Any thoughts?" Rick Saliman's voice always sounded clearest. He had a more expensive conferencing phone in his office, three floors up.

Ana listened as the men turned over the information,

searching its crevices for a way to save their client, a multimillion-dollar tech company that had behaved like a shoplifting teenager tucking a piece of cutting-edge technology in his pants and scurrying out of the office the day before a merger.

A text message appeared: *Come home. Urgent. Accident. J.* Instantly, lightly, Ana stood up, dropping a pen from her hand and leaving it to roll off her desk.

"If you're done with me, I have to take another call," she said, and hit the button to disconnect.

She must have grabbed her things, but only in the elevator did she notice she was holding her bag. She tried to call James, but he didn't answer. Then, with a boneless finger, she speed-dialed her mother's nursing home.

"I'm looking for Lise Laframbroise," she said. "I'm her daughter."

"She's at lunch. Do you want me to page her?"

Ana hung up, put her hand, that same jelly hand, up in the air until a cab pulled over. She instructed the driver to take her home, and he began plowing through thick traffic.

"I'll take University," he said, and Ana noted the dots of sweat lined up like a smile at the base of his bald head.

Even as it was happening, she was aware that she would remember that ride forever: the rising heat outside; the traffic on Spadina; the cyclist in her skirt, hiked up a little too far so that a dangerous flash of white underwear revealed itself with each push of the leg.

The third number she tried was Sarah's. No answer.

She texted James: *I'm coming.*

And a response, instantaneous beeping: *University Hospital, Room 5117,* which was approaching in the distance, an odd, jarring coincidence. The wide boulevard the driver had chosen held several hospitals. Patients wandered the sidewalks slowly, in hospital gowns. A man smoked, leaning on an IV drip.

"I'm sorry, can you take me to University Hospital instead, please?"

The taxi swung across three lanes, setting off honking. The driver stuck his fist out the window.

Ana felt that if she were in a movie, she would grab a twenty and fling it at him for the eleven-dollar ride. But that kind of drama wasn't in her, and she paid him thirteen dollars exactly and waited for the receipt.

She rushed, sincerely, up the stairs, stopping for another stolen moment to use the hand sanitizer.

The man at reception acted as if he had been waiting for her: "Yes, yes," he said. "Third bank of elevators, north side."

Ana continued rubbing her hands after the sanitizer had evaporated. Up she rode in the elevator until her ears gently popped.

She saw James immediately, or the back of him, through the glass window of a cordoned-off waiting room. He faced a panel of three white coats, as if taking an oral exam. The three doctors weren't talking but nodding and listening to James. Though the glass prevented her from hearing his words, from the stabbing and flapping of his hands, Ana knew that James was holding court.

She opened the door.

"They want information," James said to her once the tides of introduction had receded and they'd all sat down.

"We are trying to establish a medical history," said the young doctor, an Asian woman rescued from her adolescent looks by painfully thin eyebrows. Next to her sat a stout Indian doctor, bored and fuller-browed. "Your husband thought you might know if Ms. Weiss had any history of high blood pressure? Diabetes mellitus? Kidney problems?"

Ana stared at the Asian doctor's blank face.

"What are you talking about?"

"Oh, Christ," said James, who had been bobbing up high in his shock, caught in its currents. "You don't know what happened."

"How would I know? I was on a call and I got a message—" The unspeaking doctor looked at her watch.

"There was a car accident. On the Lakeshore. Some kind of debris in the road, and Marcus swerved—" James spoke without any emphasis, a witness giving a police report. "No other cars were involved, but Marcus's car went headfirst into a retaining wall. Finn's okay, but Marcus—he died." The last two words sounded like a book clapping shut.

Ana put her hands together, and they rose to her mouth, touched her lips, then moved to the bridge of her nose and stayed there. She closed her eyes, bowed her head, and tasted the information. She felt James's hand on her back and shrugged it off quickly, her whole body in thrall to a sensation of bugs crawling and burrowing. Then she realized what she had done, the quick and urgent rejection of her husband's kindness, and felt upon her that pettiness, and on top of that, the awful loneliness of what had happened. She saw, bright and burning in her head, a red station wagon crumpled like a rolled toothpaste tube up against a concrete wall. She felt the hopelessness of flesh between car and cement. And she dizzied and reached quickly for James, for his arm, his shoulder, clasping his left hand, finally, to her right.

As all of this was happening, the doctor explained that Sarah had hit her head. "We stopped the bleeding," she said, and the other doctor perked up with pride.

"Where is the bleeding?" asked Ana.

"A good question. In the frontal lobe, so focal processes are affected."

"Wait—her brain?" The muted phrase "hit her head" had tripped up Ana. She hadn't considered the brain inside that head, somehow picturing an external cut to the scalp, like a nick from shaving.

"Most people wake up from a coma within a few days or weeks, but hers is a severe trauma."

"Coma!" Ana said.

The doctor ignored her incredulousness. "We're waiting to hear from her GP, but it would help us to know her medical history. James said she has no living relatives."

"No parents. She's an only child," said Ana, scanning her memory for cousins, aunts, uncles. "She's—she was—very healthy. I don't know. There's a lot I didn't know. Don't know." James squeezed her hand.

"Neither of us have heard her talk about taking medications," he said suddenly. Ana wondered, just for a moment, how he could speak with such authority.

"Wait—" Ana shook her head. "Why did you call us?"

"We're the emergency contact, remember?"

"We are?"

"I'm the executor."

"The executioner?"

James stared at her. "What?"

Ana rubbed her forehead. The conversation had occurred a few months ago, in a wine haze. It came to her now, lightly, faded. *"We're in such an unusual situation—would you guys consider—if something happened to us—"* Flattery and consent.

"Do you know if she's allergic to penicillin?"

Everyone looked at Ana, as if women shared all such intimacies—pedicures, and Pap smears.

"No," she said. And then James remembered when he had last set foot in this hospital. It was the day after Finn's birth.

"She had her son here," said James. "There must be records...."

The silent, bored doctor suddenly stood up and left without a word. James hated her for a moment. He knew the type: young, overachieving, and indifferent. A straight-A suck-up.

The remaining doctor said they now had to wait. Sarah was too swollen for an accurate reading of the depths of her sleep. To James, waiting seemed like a euphemism for futility, but the doctor went on, painting a picture of a future in which Sarah could be better, where she might move a little, then a lot, and one day, snap to. But then that happy picture was snatched back by the phrase "potential persistent vegetative state."

"We have her on a cocktail, if you're wondering about the IV."

"Cocktail?" said Ana, and she glanced at James, whose mouth began to twitch.

"Vitamins and glucose and—"

From her husband's mouth, a small laugh, which Ana caught and returned.

"I need a cocktail, too," said James, wishing it didn't bother him that the doctor didn't crack a smile.

* * *

Two days later, they arrived at an unadorned apartment building, the rectangular shape of proletariat Russia, one of several jutting out of the cement, circled by parking lots.

Earlier that morning, Marcus's lawyer had called about something called "direct cremation." This request was in the will. James gave the lawyer his Visa number to cover the $1,600 cost and scribbled instructions on an envelope about recovering the money through the insurance policy. James marveled at Marcus's foresight. He couldn't even plan lunch.

James negotiated the buzzer and doors of greasy glass. Ana held his hand, gripping him in a way she almost never did.

"Did you eat anything?" he asked her, as they walked up the stairs to the third floor, obeying the OUT OF SERVICE sign on the elevator.

"No," said Ana.

"Me neither. Maybe we can take him for some food after."
Ana nodded.

The hall smelled like burned wax, which Ana identified as sesame oil. In places, the carpet curled up at the edges, as if trying not to touch the walls. On the door to the apartment, someone had hung a little straw heart with a stuffed red bird dangling in the center.

The door opened to reveal a short, heavyset black woman. Her breasts were half her body, it seemed to Ana. "Hello," said the woman matter-of-factly, as if they were there to sell her something she might or might not want to buy. "Come in."

But the apartment was sunny and clean—Ana felt relief. A stack of children's books sat by the sliding door that led to a tiny balcony where a child could slip through the bars, dropping to the parking lot below, James thought.

A tall, stoop-shouldered woman stood up from the couch

and offered her hand. "I'm Ann Silvan, Finn's caseworker, and this is Mrs. Bailey," she said.

Mrs. Bailey had moved over to stand by a makeshift mantel, a shelf right above where a fireplace might go, and a row of thumb-size glass animals. Above that, along the wall in matching gold frames, were dozens of photographs of children and babies, brothers and sisters leaning into one another, smiling.

James turned around and around, searching.

"Where is he?"

"The boy needs to nap," said Mrs. Bailey, revealing a thick Jamaican accent.

"I'm Ana," said Ana, extending a hand first to Mrs. Bailey, then to Ann Silvan.

"We have the same name," said the social worker. Ana smiled and nodded, even though she had never felt like an Ann, letting her mother correct every bureaucrat and schoolteacher: "It's On-na," her mother would say, "as in: 'On a moon.' "

"Mrs. Bailey is one of our best foster parents," said Ann Silvan, smoothing her skirt, which had a prominent wrinkle down the front, Ana noted. "She's been with us for sixteen years and worked with more than eighty children. Is that number about right, Mrs. Bailey?"

Mrs. Bailey nodded. James wondered about the use of the honorific, if the foster mother had requested it, a grasp at a kind of authority. They were sitting now, Ana and James in oversize armchairs, Mrs. Bailey and the social worker on the couch. James felt a strange urge to lean back and kick out the footrest he knew would appear at his ankles.

"I have three of my own, but they're gone now." Mrs. Bailey gestured to a triptych of photos, three teenagers in their graduation caps. "Each one has gone on to university." Finally, she smiled.

"So there's much to discuss," said Ann Silvan. "How are you feeling?"

Ana felt like spitting, all of a sudden.

"Our lawyer told us the will wasn't being contested," said James.

"It's not, but there are checks and balances." A strange phrase, thought Ana, a phrase to connote democracy, as if there were choice in this room. Ann Silvan continued to talk about Children's Aid and home visits, leafing through papers.

"You're not working right now, Mr. Ridgemore?"

"I'm writing a book."

"What's it about?" asked Mrs. Bailey, raising a penciled eyebrow. Ana was curious, too; she hadn't been able to ask about this herself since James had been fired. All three women tilted toward him.

"It's nonfiction. It's about terrorism," said James, his voice thinning. It was a little bit true that if anything had been written, it might have been on terrorism.

Ann Silvan wrote on her pad of paper.

"So you'll be at home with Finn, then? Or will you be taking time off, Ana?"

Ana shook her head. "Maybe a couple of days. I—my work is quite unforgiving." She felt this statement take hold in the room. It stuck like neglect.

"It will be something of a transition." Ann Silvan continued to talk, and Ana piped in from time to time, working from a list of questions that she had researched. There was money to be released. There was a court date pending. There was suddenly a fleet of people in their home, in their bank accounts, her office. Ana had begun to feel like a criminal, as if she were trying to steal this boy who had, in fact, been given to her, shockingly, without her request, even her knowledge. Between lunch and dinner, Ana and James had become the stewards of a human being.

"Did you know we were the guardians?" Ana had asked, her head in her hands in their living room. "I thought we were just executors. I don't remember agreeing to guardianship."

"I think we did," said James. "I don't know." He felt guilty somehow. He hadn't told Ana about his visits with Finn, the ones that had filled up so many afternoons lately. Maybe they had meant more than he'd realized. Now James could never tell Ana about those visits, though he had been waiting to tell her about them, searching for the right moment. But suddenly his relationship with Finn had taken on new significance, and he couldn't explain it to Ana, just as he knew that, with Sarah in her hospital bed, there was no one to expose him to her.

But he hadn't done anything wrong, had he? This had been for James, privately, the summer of Finn. He remembered their last visit in the park: He held a miniature soccer ball and a bag of graham crackers while Finn ran in circles, over and over, until he collapsed. Finn wore a plush panda suit, his face peering out from below the ears, his wrists and ankles exposed, a pair of white sneakers on his feet. It was still hot, but according to Sarah, his panda suit obsession was nonnegotiable, and she had decided not to fight it.

Finn got up, arms out, and ran in a small circle until he collapsed again. James laughed, crouched down on the grass, irritated by the cigarette butts, the stupidity of people who smash beer bottles where children play. A tall hipster walked by, smoking a cigarette, wearing sunglasses as big as the front window of a car. James felt a surge of hatred toward the guy's skinny legs, his huge headphones, probably playing something electronic. He picked up an old cigarette butt and tossed it at the guy's back, narrowly missing him as he trotted along, oblivious. Even though James still had four or five cigarettes a day, around Finn he became a virulent nonsmoker.

James and Finn had already been to the museum that week to look at the dinosaur bones. The week before, they had taken the ferry out to Toronto Island, and James had steered a paddleboat with Finn at his side. Sarah said she was thrilled to get a break, that she could finally get some time to herself to work on her photography, to sleep.

"I can't go back to teaching," she had told James. "But I can't always be around him, either." James was impressed with how efficiently Sarah sliced and packaged time. Three days a week, Finn was in day care, but only until two. Marcus often didn't get home until seven or eight, when Finn was in bed. The daycare mornings were catch-up time for chores, household management. Sarah needed just one afternoon a week to herself, open time. James was happy to take Finn. He liked the idea of saving someone.

When James was with Finn, he felt useful again, which he hadn't in the months since he'd been fired. He got a different response from people when he entered a store or rode the streetcar with Finn than he did when he was alone and suspiciously present during the city's working hours. But with Finn, the world was a gigantic welcome mat. People hummed a low, inviting note that only parents could hear, that James had never known existed. It reminded him of when he would walk with his black friend, Kyle, and Kyle would exchange a little nod with every other black person who went by. James had considered researching this phenomenon for the show, but when he took a pretty black intern to lunch to covertly test his theory, she just looked straight ahead and never glanced at anyone.

"Finny, do you want to get a croissant?" asked James.

"Oh yes please I do!" cried Finn, and he began to run toward Queen Street, a two-and-a-half-year-old who knew the way to the city's best croissants. James wondered if he could work that into his unwritten novel.

While they sat on the bench eating croissants, James asked Finn questions.

"What did you do at daycare yesterday?"

"Panda suit."

"How's it going with the panda suit, then?"

"I like croissant." James pulled out his ears and made a silly face at Finn, and Finn laughed and laughed, little pieces of croissant stuck to his chin, a strange bearded panda.

Marcus was waiting on the porch when they arrived back at Finn's house. His feet rested on a broken tricycle, and his laptop was open on his knees. His briefcase balanced on a scabby paint tin.

"There he is," he shouted. Finn dropped James's hand and ran up the walk toward his father. Finn curled into Marcus's body. Marcus pushed back the head of the panda suit and kissed the boy's hair, smiling. James shuffled back and forth, halfway up the walk, feeling found out.

"Thanks for taking him, James," said Marcus.

"You're home early," said James, and the wifeliness of the comment immediately struck him.

"Such a beautiful day. I wanted to take him to the park."

"Yeah! Park!" said Finn, as if they hadn't just come from there.

The two men nodded at each other, caught in the silence of a meeting without women.

"Definitely a day for the park," said James. "I've got to get going, so..." He began to back away.

"Do you want to come in? Grab a beer?"

"No, no," said James, who suddenly remembered where he'd had this feeling of barging in on intimacy before: walking into his old apartment to find his roommates clothed but disheveled in the kitchen, gazing awkwardly at each other, mouths swollen. "I've got—stuff—I should—but thanks. See you soon, Finny, okay?"

"Bye, James!"

"Hey, man," said Marcus, rising with Finn still barnacled to his chest. "Really: Thanks for helping out. It's hard for Sarah, being home all the time. You're saving her sanity."

Those were the last words James had heard him say.

Finally, a moan swelled from behind a nearby door. Mrs. Bailey rose, opened the door, and shut it immediately behind her. Ann Silvan talked on while James stared at the closed door. This was the moment, the shedding of all that came before, and he was alert to it, waiting.

When the door opened, Finn walked out slowly, one arm around Mrs. Bailey's wide leg.

Ana watched as he let go and ran immediately to James. She saw Ann Silvan writing again, probably describing how Finn had bypassed her. She shouldn't be hurt. She believed that at some point, she couldn't recall when, she and Finn had agreed to shared indifference. Sarah always had to prod him into acknowledging her: "Say hi to Ana, Finny." And politely, in that cartoon voice: "Hi, Ana."

James murmured: "How are you, Finny? How's it going?"

"Good." He looked around the room, at all the women and James.

Ann Silvan said: "The most important thing is structure, routine. Try not to disrupt his life too much."

"Should we take him to visit"—Ana stopped, leaned in—"the hospital? Does he know about the hospital?"

"He knows his mommy is very sick, and his daddy isn't coming back."

James frowned. "You guys told him that? You don't think that might have been better coming from someone who knows him?" he said. He was slumped in the chair. Ana noticed that he was often draped across furniture lately, boneless and large.

Finn had gravitated toward the books and sat with his legs like a swami, opening and closing a pop-up book. Up rose the bus; down. Up, down.

Ann Silvan's face tightened. "He had questions. We're trained in these matters." She reached into her briefcase and handed Ana a sheaf of photocopies.

"There's a wait list for counseling, but Finn's on it," she said. "You should get a call in four to six months."

"Efficient," muttered James.

Ana skimmed the pages: *Toddler can sense when a significant person is missing... Presence of new people... No understanding of death... Absorbs emotions of others around her/him... May show signs of irritability... May exhibit changes in eating, crying, and in bowel and bladder movements...*

James, looking over her shoulder, whispered in Ana's ear: "That could be a description of me." She didn't smile, caught on the last line: *Bowel movements.* Ana wondered where they would put all the used diapers, the wads of wipes, if they would need to buy one of those pneumatic tube garbage cans. One time at Sarah's there had been a perfect ball of a dirty diaper in the center of the living room for the entire duration of Ana's visit, distracting her, crying out for disposal. Finally, when Sarah left the room for a moment, Ana grabbed it. She had stuffed the slick mass in the kitchen garbage, then scrubbed her hands at the sink like a surgeon.

"We need to stop at the store," said Ana, suddenly, to no one.

James was putting shiny black running shoes on Finn's feet. They looked new and cheap. Finn opened and closed the bus pop-up book, happy to let James Velcro him in.

"Finn take book home?" he asked. Mrs. Bailey crouched down and enveloped him in her arms, his body sinking into her endless chest. The word "home" rippled through every person in the room.

"Yes, sweetie. You take it."

She stood, handing Ana a shopping bag. "A few clothes I had lying around."

James and Ana backed out the door, murmuring thank-yous. Finn slipped between their bodies and ran down the hall quickly. Then, at the far end of the corridor where the light was dimmest, he stopped and looked back. His eyes scanned Ana, then James, taking in their nervous smiles. He looked, for a moment, as if he might back away, but he waited, puzzled and patient, until they caught up to him.

James put the car seat in the back while Finn walked around

Ana's legs, ducking through them from time to time, not laughing but with a great sense of purpose. She looked around uneasily. A group of black teenage boys leaned on the hood of a Honda sedan, talking loudly, laughing. One tossed a basketball back and forth in his hands. A woman in a hijab with a plastic grocery bag lightly banged against Ana and mumbled, eyes on the ground.

Suddenly, Finn sprinted into the parking lot, toward the group of boys. *That car is coming too fast,* thought Ana. She looked first for James, who was bent over the backseat. *James, solve it,* she thought, but there was no time to say it before she was running, and as she ran, the tallest of the teenagers looked up, saw two things: a blond boy running toward him, and the car aloft, somehow silent and soundless, Finn too small to be seen by the driver, the exact tiny size to fit between two wheels. The teenager, the stranger, stepped out into the path of the car, put his fingers in his mouth, and whistled like a train. Others were shouting: "Stop! Man! Slow the fuck down! Fucking slow down!" And it did, the car slowed down, the sun too bright to see the eyes of the driver, just as Ana was upon Finn, had him by the shoulders, shaking him.

"Don't do that! You can't run away!" She was shouting. Finn looked up at her, his lips vibrating.

"Lady, you okay?" called one of the boys. She had Finn in front of her, her arms straight out, gripping his shoulders.

"Basketball," he said, and started crying.

"Thank you," called Ana, nodding to the boys, hoisting Finn to her hip. The boys watched her. One bounced the ball.

"I think it's in," announced James, uncoiling from the car, his forehead shining.

He rose to a puzzling image, Ana with the child clinging to

her neck, crossing the parking lot, shadowed by a slow-moving silver car.

"What happened?" asked James. Ana shook her head, passed him Finn, who relaxed instantly into James's arms, ceased his sobbing, shifting into a low purr.

Ana's hands fluttered as she buckled herself in. In the back, James was cursing, trying to connect straps.

"Do you know how this works, Finny?" he asked. "What do you say? Can you help me?"

Ana gripped the dashboard.

"Can we go, please? Can we just go?"

James clicked the final latch and patted Finn's head.

They drove out of the parking lot, under the collective glance of the teenage boys, Ana hating herself for her judgment, her fear. She blamed her own parents, their willful ignorance about adulthood, how they chose anything else over it whenever they could. "I love you, kiddo," said her father once when she returned from the park, eager to show him a dirty dollar bill she'd dug out of the sand. "But man, I wish I could go to India." And so he had gone, without Ana or her mother, and he'd never really come back.

In the car, James looked at Ana, coiled in silence. He wondered how long her absence would last.

Finn yammered in the backseat, incomprehensible words that James attempted to interpret, responding in a range of theatrical voices. He could make Finn laugh easily, a sound that rang the bells of James's own pride and moved along the knots of Ana's spine with a tentacled, creeping dread.

At the north end of the street stood a house that Ana felt certain was a brothel. Its thin, yellow-brown curtains were always shut, even though it was still light at night, and the front yard was dotted with cigarette butts and smeared, discarded plastic bags.

One by one, over their seven years on the street, Ana and James had watched the old Portuguese and Italian couples die off. Sometimes their children moved in, plumbers and contractors who got up before the sun rose, slammed truck doors, and sped off to rebuild houses belonging to people like Ana and James, houses like the rest of the houses on the block. But most of the time, the houses were sold and the Dumpsters arrived. Then came the couples and their children, and the mother eager to meet Ana and James, until the discovery, so soon, that no, they didn't have kids. Yes, the schools around here were supposed to be good. Yes, it was a big house for two.

The Victorian facades remained, though often painted witty crayon box colors. But inside, walls were coming down.

Ana could see the lack of walls as they drove through the neighborhood. Through large front windows, the uniformity of these renovations revealed itself: the broad loft-like space imposed on the skinny Victorian bones, the pot lights, the marble kitchens at the back looking out onto tiny gardens kept by gardeners. The tacit, unspoken agreement about what was beautiful.

Then there was the brothel, a squatter house than the others, shutterless and plain; the only other detached house on the block besides James and Ana's.

Last winter, when the city was sunk in snow, she had seen a young woman walk out of the house late at night wearing a gossamer T-shirt and leggings, arms wrapped around her torso, her feet hanging over the heels of her slippers. Her hair was blond and thin, a wild aureole about her head. She had spied

Ana, coming home late from work with her attaché case in her hand, the remnants of coffee in a thermos mug in the other. The girl's eyes were scooped out, set as far back in her head as a blind person's. She had scowled at Ana and scurried away, out of the streetlight shadow.

This was almost a year ago, in the dead cold, and Ana had seen no other sign of activity from the place.

"We're home," said James. "A parking space!"

Ana turned to look at Finn, who was staring out the window, nodding lightly.

James did the unstrapping, and when he pulled Finn out of the back door, holding him to his chest, he saw that Ana had already gone up the street and into the house.

Inside, James placed Finn high up on a barstool at the island in the kitchen. He swung his feet, smiling. Ana's back was to them both as she flipped the cheese sandwich grilling on the stove.

"Maybe we should sit in the dining room. It seems like he might fall off," said James.

"But the rug in the—" said Ana, then withdrew. "Whatever you think."

"Finn stay up!" he cried when James went to lift him. "No! Want to stay here!"

James set him back on the stool, where he wobbled in all directions. Finn picked up the grilled cheese sandwich Ana had cooked for him, taking mouse bites around the edges. Ana and James stood side by side, staring across the island at the boy as if he were a hostage, and any minute the authorities might bang down the door.

Ana began to unpack the groceries. Animal crackers; organic macaroni and cheese; miniature applesauces. All things she had seen at Sarah's, empty boxes and sticky half-filled containers for Ana to step around. Where should they go? She pulled open drawers and cupboards, finally stuffing the boxes next to the white balsamic, moving aside the olive oil from a trip last spring to Umbria.

"Finish," said Finn, dropping his sandwich and pulling himself to standing. Within a second, he had his arms high, a diver preparing for his descent. Ana let out a yelping sound, and James rushed toward the boy. Ana breathed quickly; the danger Finn brought with him felt all-encompassing, like the three of them had been submerged together in a water tank of sharks.

She glanced at the hole in the backyard, abandoned again by the workers. The winter before last, old clay pipes had cracked in the depths beneath the back lawn, and the repairs had dragged on and on. Workmen came for a few days and then vanished. Piles of limestone wrapped in cellophane crushed the plants on the perimeter.

"Can you call the guys about the yard?" said Ana.

Finn wandered through the kitchen, opening every cupboard at his eye level.

"What's in there?" he asked each time. Ana answered: "Oh, I don't know. Pots..."

"What's in there?"

"Umm...pipes, from the sink." She found it difficult to focus on unpacking the groceries with the noise, each question punctuated by a slammed cupboard.

"What's in there?"

She didn't answer, macaroni in hand, trying to unravel the question in her head: *Should the macaroni and cheese box go by the oil? Really?*

"What's in there?" asked Finn, loudly. "What's in there?"

Ana turned quickly and snapped: "Just look, Finn. Figure it out."

"Ana—" said James, but when he saw her face, flashing fury and then trembling into fear, he didn't say what he'd been about to. "I think it's probably his bedtime."

Ana placed the macaroni in the cupboard and closed her eyes. When she opened them, the clock by the garden door said 8:34.

"Is it? Is this when he goes to bed?"

James shrugged. *"Aucune idée,"* he said.

James walked Finn upstairs, holding his hand. He drew the bath, his finger under the tap, trying to determine the right temperature. Finn sat on the white-tiled ground, removing his small T-shirt, then his sweatpants. Standing only in his diaper, he did a small jump.

"Ana! Is this too hot?" called James, but she couldn't hear him over her own scrubbing and the sound of the water. "How hot should it be?" James called downstairs. Still no answer. James turned on the cold.

Finn's plump hands gripped the edge of the tub, his toes lifting off the ground.

"Wait, wait!" The diaper looked like it was barely hanging on, sagging like a smile along his backside. James tore the fasteners and the diaper fell free, relieved, into his hand. It was full of dark shit, round and heavy as a miniature medicine ball. James was embarrassed: *Why didn't I notice? Why did we have him for hours and never think about the diaper?*

"Ana!" This time, she appeared, eyes immediately upon the diaper in his hand.

"Okay, okay," she said. "Don't move!" She could see Finn, his bum smeared with feces, giggling and moving like an inmate in a Victorian asylum toward the white walls and white towels. "Don't let him move!"

Ana raced down the stairs, while James held Finn by the hands, but far away from him. She rooted in the cloth grocery bags for wipes, the kind Sarah always had—hypoallergenic, biodegradable, chlorine-free, unscented. Ana grabbed the diapers, too, number 5s, as Mrs. Bailey had told them, and a garbage bag. She sprinted upstairs, a medic attending to the injured, dropping all the gear on the white bathroom floor. Finn and James were still locked in their strange dance, far from the walls. Finn's toddler penis hung (uncircumcised, noted Ana; quite large, noted James, who thought, then, of Marcus and wondered), a strangely mannish thing out of place on his child's body.

"We have a shituation here," said James, as Ana pulled out wipe after wipe. She managed a small laugh, passing the packet to James. James wiped and cleaned, folding each used cloth into the next, then stuffing the ball into the dirty diaper, expertly. He enjoyed a moment of satisfaction, held back his shoulders at his accomplishment, and then looked at his wife, hovering in the doorframe.

"I'm not sure what to do now," she said.

"Why don't you get his bed ready while I give him the bath?"

Ana nodded, and James turned to the boy, lifting him gently into the tub. "Let's get clean, right? Let's get clean." James wiped the washcloth with Ana's French milled soap, then rubbed it up and down his back.

"Where toys?" asked Finn.

James looked around the bathroom. Stainless steel soap pump. A small vase with a white daisy in it. The uselessness of the room struck him: Two years ago, they had knocked out walls and installed a sitting area in the bathroom. It contained a large black cane chair and a table holding magazines that had never been touched. James sat in the chair only once, the day it arrived, declaring it not uncomfortable.

Under the sink, James discovered an old blue plastic water cup—something of his from a long-ago apartment. With the cup, Finn began to bail the tub back into the tub; dip and pour, dip and pour, while James sang a Jonathan Richman song that had lingered, waiting for use, in the back of his head for twenty-some years: "'What do I now hear, hark, hark? Is it really leprechauns, and have they come back to rock 'n' roll?'" Finn was oblivious to the song—dip and pour—but James kept going, pleased with himself, repeating the chorus: "Ba-doom ba da da da da, da da..." James reached for Ana's shampoo, also French, with the price tag still on it.

He said to Finn: "Twenty-two dollars? Who pays twenty-two dollars for shampoo?" He made Finn's foamy hair into a gigantic spike, still chanting. At the end of the song, Finn splashed a gentle sprinkle on James's face and looked at him expectantly. James reached into the tub and flicked a bit at Finn, and for a moment, it looked like the boy was going to cry; his face gathered, as if preparing to come apart—*oh God no,* thought James. *Oh no.* But it suddenly ceased, and Finn laughed, picking up the blue cup, dipping and pouring.

Ana returned with a green fluffy towel that she sniffed before handing it over—verbena. James lifted Finn out, and as he held his gleaming wet body up in the air, Ana saw in her mind's eye James's hands slipping, and Finn, falling fast, cracking his head on the bathtub, leaving the white tile veined with blood.

But then Finn was on the bath mat, grinning. Both of them scanned his body for cuts and bruises, markers of what had befallen his family. He was perfectly clear, just as the doctor at the hospital had said. Not a freckle, not a mole. No evidence.

James wrapped him in the towel.

"I'm a burrito!" cried Finn. "Tighter! Like Mama make it!" The words knocked James. He looked into the boy's face, his little teeth far apart, all of him without mourning. James tightened the towel until Finn resembled a long green onion, blond hair spiking through the top. Finn giggled at his immobility, trying to walk and falling on his back, laughing and laughing.

James scooped him up, carried him to the guest room. Ana had made up the bed with honey-colored linens. *It isn't a child's room,* thought James, dropping the towel on the leather love seat. There was no whimsy anywhere in the house. They didn't speak of this guest room as a future nursery anymore, though a nursery with a view of the garden had been a selling point, hadn't it? He was sure it had.

"Help me," said Ana. James looked at her and realized she meant the bed. Together, they moved it to the wall.

"Watch TV!" cried Finn, jumping on the bed, while James tried to pull a pajama top over his head. Blue, with a monster's face: "Veddy scary!" The fabric was nubby and worn, another item from Mrs. Bailey's. James tried not to imagine what horrors had been witnessed by all the foster children who had worn these pajamas.

"No TV. We'll do a book," said James, then looked at Ana, who hovered again in the doorframe. "Wait, do we have any books?"

"We left the bus book in the car," said Ana, watching James expertly stick the diaper, pull on the monster pants.

About the absence of books, James said: "Shit."

Finn went still. "You say shit," he whispered.

Ana, roused to James's defense, said: "You said it, too."

"I know. You're right. It's a bad word," said James. He turned to Ana: "Can you see if there's anything for him to read? Maybe a graphic novel or something."

"I don't know if Robert Crumb is appropriate," said Ana, but she headed toward their bedroom and the basket of magazines next to her bedside table.

Finn folded into James's lap, letting James brush his hair, his face turning sleepy.

"Maybe the cartoons in here?" Ana asked, returning with an old *New Yorker* that Sarah had lent her months ago. James laughed. Ana sat down on the bed next to James, as if she, too, was awaiting story time. He flipped through the magazine, James asking Finn what animals were in the cartoons, what sounds they made; James telling him stories about vultures and dogs. Both Ana and James were acutely aware of what this looked like from a distance. James pulled up the quilt to Finn's chin.

Ana placed throw cushions on the floor at the side of the bed, a circumference, like a ring of lye outside a village hut used to keep away the witches. James leaned down, and small hands circled his neck. Ana patted Finn's leg, his body a tiny bump, lost on the big bed.

"Sing light," said Finn.

"Leave the light on?" asked James.

"No! Sing it! Sing it!"

Ana raised a single finger to her temple and began to rub, as if it would help her to draw understanding out of her skull.

"Light? A song about light?" she said, feeling like she had walked into a game of charades.

"Yes! Sing it!"

"Can you sing it, Finn?"

"No, Mama sing it," he said. James and Ana went still, wondering what would happen next. Finn looked at them, waiting.

James said, "I'm sorry, Finn, we don't know it. Do you want to hear the leprechaun song again?"

Finn considered this, let out a very adult sigh, as if he had expected no less incompetence from these so-called caregivers.

"Okay."

James sang it again, and Ana looked away. But James wasn't self-conscious, almost never was he self-conscious, and especially not now, having seen how his song rescued the boy from the edge, pulled him back from the churning waters of sadness. He smiled again, laughed even as James sang the last line: "'They come back to rock 'n' roll.'"

"Good night," said Ana, leaving James to do the final kiss and tuck. She found herself in the hallway, with her hand on the wall, closing her eyes.

"Good night," she heard her husband say.

James was in bed first, looking from his laptop to Ana as she moved through the room in her long white nightgown. She straightened an angled jewelry box, then carefully hooked her belt on a belt rack, her blazer in the section of the closet reserved for blazers.

"I didn't put my shoes away," he said, as she picked up his sneakers from the middle of the floor and placed them, toes out, in the closet.

"How about: *Sorry,* I didn't put my shoes away." She moved like a machete hacking the reeds, clearing, clearing, clearing.

"Okay, sorry," said James, just a touch of sarcasm. "It says here the ideal bedtime for a two-year-old is seven p.m."

"Mmm," said Ana.

"It also says we should get baby soap. He could get eczema."

Ana was lost in her movements, saying nothing. James used to joke about the tidying. When they left her apartment to go out, James would help, putting the clean dishes in the cupboards and emptying the food trap in the sink. Then he'd stand at the door waiting and announce: "All locked down, Cappy!" In those days, Ana had smiled and laughed and, in doing so, admitted this need as eccentricity. *There's no shame in it anymore,* thought James. *And God knows, no comedy.*

She finally climbed into bed next to him, propped up by pillows. James threw several to the ground. He placed his computer on the table and leaned to face Ana, but she was up much higher than he was, and he could see only fragments of her, smell the crook of her arm. The pillows made them silly.

"We didn't brush his teeth," said James.

Ana answered with a question. "What do we do tomorrow?"

"Daycare, I guess. They said to keep the routine, and it's Monday."

"God, is today Sunday?" Ana felt stuffed with questions, as if they would tumble out and fill the room if she dared open her mouth, a fisherman's net releasing question marks. What she wanted was an explanation, but for what? She could sense James getting sentimental next to her, curling closer, trying to hold her hand, which lay limp above the covers.

She was waiting for the softness, the cool white space. Ana had invented this state of being when she was a child, lying in bed during the loudest parties, the doors slamming and the accelerated roar of her mother's nightlife. Or even on a quiet night, alone with her mother, watching her shape shift over the course of the evening, the ice cubes clattering in the tray, and the bottles ringing in the garbage against the other bottles—then, *poof*. Ana could vanish. She thought of the white space as a destination, a place she had to get to in order to block the noise. Now the noise came from the social worker: "And Ana, what kind of hours do you work?" The voice hungry for judgment.

And then the social worker was silenced by Sarah's light laughter, ringing gently. Ana squeezed her eyes shut.

"Where were they going?" Ana asked. "Were they going to get groceries? What was the point?"

"I don't know," said James. Ana opened her eyes and frowned.

"It's going to be okay," said James. Abruptly, Ana reached for the light, sliding down past the pillows onto her back, so that not even her head was elevated. Now James was too high, looking down at her.

Ana pictured Sarah alone in her own bed, suspended from tubes, that yellow sunflower bruise across her eye, the black stitches slicing her face. A goalie's mask glowing in a dark hospital room.

James had his own vision: Marcus in the drawer. A life-size doll of Marcus.

"What's happening?" she asked, strangled, and James went down to her so they were face to face. He stroked her hair, murmuring. She let him. She gave that to him until, somewhere in the middle, it felt like something she wanted, too.

* * *

Two years before, on a spring morning, side by side in narrow chairs, Ana and James had received the third opinion, which was the same as the first two.

The specialist was young and well known in certain parts of the city. As he delivered the news, his features puckered and aged with a sadness that struck Ana as suspect.

"Okay, then," said Ana, gathering to go, wanting to escape the sensation that she should comfort this celebrity doctor.

After, across from the subway station on the gravel path that cut through an orderly church lawn, Ana held James. He did not weep exactly, but pulsed evenly on her shoulder—in and out—his face buried in her wool coat. A mechanical sound. Ana pictured a bright silver electronic heart held aloft by a surgeon and then—*plunk*—dropped into James's open chest.

Above him, she raised her head and looked up at the flat blue sky.

What to make of this sudden calmness that wiped her down, erasing the faint, pulling panic she had lived with for two years? It was the relief of shutting the hotel room door after a day in a New York mob. It was the feeling she used to get when she was totally alone at the end of a long, loud evening out, sitting on her couch in the old apartment that only she lived in.

"Then we can look into adoption," James said, pulling apart, wiping his face on his sleeve.

Ana nodded.

"Or surrogacy," he said.

Ana nodded again, then turned back to the sky.

"They have great weather," she said.

A streetcar slid by, noisily, and Ana couldn't hear, but saw James's mouth move: "What?"

"Great weather for the wedding."

James looked at her, and she could see him thinking: *This is how she copes.* It was likely that he had read an article or written a segment for his show on how to comfort her in the event of this confirmation that they were indeed in that select statistical sliver for whom treatments were useless.

"Do they care about the weather? It's indoors, isn't it?" He touched her hair. She reached up and took his hand.

"We should get ready."

"Whatever you need."

Ana dropped his hand, deciding that not holding it was what she needed.

She was surprised to have been invited to the wedding. Sarah and Marcus were new friends. The four of them were tentative around one another still, counting on the wine to pull them through.

James followed Ana through the church gardens. She stooped to pick up a half-empty McDonald's cup of Coke. James watched her: her foot popping ever so slightly out of the arch of those black shoes that looked like ballet slippers. He didn't think about her beauty, but her lightness, the sense of upward motion in her body at all times, the ever-present possibility that she might bend her knees, push off, and float up and away from him.

"Just leave it."

"It's too pretty here for all this garbage."

This wasn't true. Ana was projecting a month into the future, when the famous gardens would be in bloom. At the time she received the referral, she had been pleased that the doctor's office was so close to the church, picturing bougainvillea and tulips bracketing each visit. But her timing had been off. Their first appointment had been in winter, when snow blanketed the grounds. Now the gardens were just dirt beds, thawing, and the grass was patchy, defeated. And they wouldn't be back for the bougainvillea. They were done.

Ana carried the cup in front of her, arm straight, thumb and pointer finger just skimming the rim, the other fingers curled into her palm like a TV dad confronting his first dirty diaper.

Ana deposited the cup in a garbage bin. Following, James glanced over the bin's edge. Soda everywhere, soaking old newspapers and fried chicken bones and dog shit and a single needle.

He walked behind her to the parking lot. He knew that he cried too easily, and the crying acted like a defenseman's shoulder check, sent her flying. But still he hoped, just a little, that she might break. Then he could be wonderful.

"Give me a second," he said.

Ana sat in the car while James lit a cigarette, leaning on the hood, frowning. In the sky, a flag appeared. Wind must have loosed it from a pole, and now it flapped above James's head, moving closer, as if preparing to drop and cover him. And then the flag revealed itself to be, in fact, a flock of birds, diving down in a solid, waving page.

He flicked his cigarette butt into the garden.

In the car, Ana had a small white mint in her hand. As she held it out to him, James remembered all the women who had held out a hand to him over the years, uncurling a palm to reveal a joint, an ecstasy tab, a condom, a ZIP drive.

"Let's go," said Ana.

* * *

At 2:47, a sound, deep and dark. A moan, gathering strength as it awoke, fattening into a full scream.

James got up first, running down the hall in his boxer shorts, turning on lights, trying to flood it out. Ana was behind, walking quickly, arms around her torso.

"Finny, Finny," said James. He could hear him but not see him, his eyes scanning the room, the empty bed, the quilt on the ground. And then he saw the boy, limp and piled in a corner on the floor, his head next to a bookshelf. The sound had returned to a moan by then, gaining momentum, like a police car getting closer.

"Finny," said James. He gathered him up off the floor. His body softened in James's arms.

The moan became a whimper, and then the whimper silenced.

Ana put the quilt on the bed and turned back the top in a triangle.

Slowly, James placed Finn on the bed. Instantly, the boy flopped toward him, hands up, the moan returned. James sat on the bed, rubbed his hand along Finn's back, feeling his spine through the thin material of the borrowed pajamas. The boy quieted again, his breathing slowed.

James felt like he knew exactly what Finn was seeing, because he was seeing it, too: the wall coming toward him, the stupid thump of bodies on a dashboard, the shattered glass. Or maybe it was just a kid's monster, a purple one with bony knees. Finn didn't have the language. There was no way in.

"I'm going to stay here for a while," James whispered.

Ana nodded, useless again. She straightened the cushions on the floor surrounding the bed, then left them alone.

Finn ran up ahead of James, stopping at the fence enclosing the playground. James glanced down at the piece of paper in his hand with the address on it and then up at the sign: FAMILY PLACE DAYCARE. He had walked by the gray stone building, a former elementary school, many times and never considered who was inside. So Finn was changing the city for him, too. James remembered that when he finally bought a car, auto body shops seemed to suddenly spring up everywhere, tucked between the buildings in the neighborhood where he lived, previously unneeded and therefore invisible.

Early in the morning, when the sun was just rising and Ana and Finn still lay sleeping in their separate rooms, James had walked to Sarah and Marcus's. He had a key, and implicit permission, but a neighbor appeared immediately on her porch next door, peering at him. They had met before—James remembered that she was a teacher, like Sarah, and Marcus complained that while she was going through her divorce, she whaled on some kind of brass instrument at all hours of the night. The neighbor informed him that she was looking after the cat (*There was a cat!* thought James, stung by all he couldn't remember) and had put a lamp on a timer. "I suppose you'll be taking care of the rest," she said.

James nodded weakly.

Inside, the one lamp made everything seem darker. James felt criminal. He couldn't bear to look around. He would find the address of the daycare only and leave the rest to Ana. He tiptoed through the domestic scramble of dishes and strewn clothes. On the fridge he found a handwritten list of phone numbers: M at Work, M: cell, S: cell, Dr. Garfield, and Family Place Daycare. He took the paper, picturing himself on some future day carrying Finn, hot with fever, into the office of this Dr. Garfield.

Now, at the gate of the daycare, James looked around: So this was where Finn spent his three days a week away from Sarah.

"James open gate?" Finn called. The cheap black sneakers from the social worker looked gigantic and theoretical on his feet, an idea of sneakers sketched in a factory by someone who had never seen them.

Finn led James inside the building by the hand, toward a hook marked with the name FINN in a laminate square. Finn had already removed his red hoodie and dropped it on the floor, then his baseball hat, a breadcrumb trail behind him as he ran down the hallway in a race with a smaller black-haired girl. James was a beat behind, picking up after Finn, putting the coat and hat on the hook, walking quickly to keep up.

A woman did the same, collecting her daughter's droppings. James glanced at her hair; it must have been a style at one point, but now it was just a shape, a rectangle. Her eyes were padded with exhaustion. James turned on a smile and tried to catch her eye, hoping to share a moment of parental chaos. But she looked straight ahead and strode away, putting distance between them.

The classroom was a whorl of sound, high-pitched. One wall was covered in paper plates painted different colors: some splattered, some entirely solid, one or two with just a brushstroke. James moved closer, scanning for Finn's name like he would at a gallery opening.

"You must be with Finn," said a voice next to him, a man with two gold hoops in his ears and a glowing bald head. He held out his hand: "I'm Bruce, one of the educators in the preschool room."

"I'm James," he said, surprised by the man's strong grip. "Finn's—" They looked at each other, waiting. "Guardian, I suppose."

Bruce nodded knowingly and ushered James to the sink, out of range of the children.

"We heard what happened from the social worker, and we're all so unbelievably, unbelievably sorry," he said.

"Oh, I believe you're sorry," said James with an awkward laugh. He became glib when nervous. But Bruce was not the kind of person to be hindered by other people's responses. He continued.

"I want you to know that I personally have taken a training seminar in children's grief, and everyone is on alert," said Bruce. "Sad to say, but it's not the first time we've had a child lose a parent." James glanced at the circle of kids sitting cross-legged on a blue carpet, eyes upon a young woman reading a book out loud: "Olivia likes to try on *everything*!" Their size was incompatible with Bruce's admission; how could these children possibly contain such sadness? Where would it go?

"Where do you take that kind of seminar?" asked James. At the five-minute mark, he had learned that Bruce had a B.A. in social work, and an Early Childhood Education Certificate. He hated the caseload as a social worker and always wanted to run a daycare, but it's unusual for men to work with children in this day and age with all the suspicion, and on and on and on.

Oh, how much people will share. James saw Bruce naked in

animal form, snarling and crouched in waiting, praying to be asked to spring upright and grunt out a story.

"How is Sarah doing, anyway?" asked Bruce, laying a hand on James's forearm.

James was struck by guilt: He had not been thinking of Sarah. He had considered the situation decided.

"We have to wait. The prognosis is still vague."

Bruce nodded. "Just keep us informed."

"Same here," he said, gesturing toward Finn, who had separated himself from the circle of readers and was stacking plastic animals: a bear riding a tiger; a hippopotamus astride a dinosaur.

"I'd like to live in that world," said James.

"Pardon me?"

"A world where a tiger gives a ride to a bear. You know, everyone helping one another out." He was joking, but Bruce lit up.

"If only!" he said.

James turned to find Finn, anticipating his first public send-off. But the boy was captivated by the stacking animals, frowning as each pair toppled.

Suddenly, Bruce let out a chirp: "You know, James, I remember you from TV, right? Aren't you on TV?"

"I used to be."

Bruce clapped his hands together.

"Ha! I knew it! You know, we have a lot of famous people at this daycare. Ruby's mom wrote that cookbook, the one about organic baby food? And in the kindergarten room, there's a little boy named Luke whose mom was in that miniseries, the one about the hockey wives?"

James clucked his interest, but he did not appreciate being in this particular lineup.

James leaned into Finn's line of vision, tried to catch his attention. He felt Bruce watching as he blew him a kiss that went uncaught.

James crossed the street, glancing back at the daycare.

As he did at least once a week, James walked back to the TV station where he used to work and sat facing the building on his favorite bench. He thought of these visits as a kind of crime-scene reenactment, as if by going back again and again to the site of his firing, he could make sense of it. He lit a cigarette.

The day James got fired had not been the worst day of his life. He was as still as a man Tasered to the ground and he contemplated this calmness as Sly—his old friend, his boss—sat across from him, slick with sweat, panting, saying what they both knew was coming. "This kind of television isn't resonating in our research.... It's not you, we think the world of you, it's the genre... the demographic... the economy... the Internet..."

James's mind was a jumble of all the things that made this moment not so bad: the unwritten novel, the untapped potential, the upcoming summer.

He had suddenly thought of a parlor game he and Ana had played in the early years of their marriage. "Who are you? Four things only." James, when he read aloud his own list, was always: "Husband, journalist, hockey player, future novelist." He thought that listing his marital status first would flatter Ana, but she saw through it. When Ana did James, she put journalist first. But now what he had written had come true: He was mostly her husband.

Ana would know what to ask. Severance package. Legal loopholes. He got into her head, tried to emulate her thinking, as ordered as a plastic binder divided by tabs. James said some adult-sounding things, and Sly gave answers. Sly even lowered his accent to something kind of Cockney for the occasion, as if they were a couple of British coal miners at a union meeting in the Thatcher years. Then, when Sly had wrung out every cliché, he leaned in, as if about to go for a hug: "I'm so sorry, mate." He reached out a hand. James thought: *I've never heard him use the word "mate" in my life.* He noticed that Sly's hand was shaking, and he felt bad for him. James had never had a job that required him to fire anyone.

A thought crept into his head, surprisingly, of his old favorite childhood thing, the rock tumbler—and how he would sit for hours in his bedroom watching the rocks go up and down the tiny conveyor belt, growing smoother and more similar to one another—and then he thought of his wife, of Ana's ass, particularly, turned toward him in bed. *The first thing I will do is my wife.* And the ass image faded to be replaced by a face, that of the intern Emma. Emma: a name no one used to have, but now there were three Emmas working on his show.

This Emma's face in his head was all lips, red, which of course meant baboon ass, and soon James was thinking about the fact that he was an animal and marveling at how base it was to be a man, waking up his goaty longing.

It was Emma who brought in a stack of collapsed cardboard boxes.

"At my last job, they, like, escorted this guy from the building. They didn't even let him take his pictures or turn off his computer," she said, standing near the open door. Her voice was shrill, pointed. It corrupted a unique silkiness in her body.

James had nodded. He took a framed picture of Ana from the desk and put it into the empty box, facedown.

"So you know, they obviously like you here," said Emma. She was wearing all black—black T-shirt, a tight black skirt, black boots. But she looked naked to James. He could barely stand to look at her, the curve of her breast, her dark skin. What was she? Was she black? Asian? Some modern hybrid.

If she knew what he was thinking, he'd be called a racist, on top of being a sexual harasser. It was as if, by being fired, he was able to see new shapes in the picture, to really look at this woman without the echoes of workplace propriety seminars and interoffice "plain language" memos. He felt like a priest who had been handed civilian clothes.

"I don't think I'm unliked, I just feel—" James paused. "Obsolete." Before the word was out, he realized he had potentially bricked a wall between them. It was a word that drew attention to his age, which was about fifteen years worse than hers. But the repulsion he anticipated didn't happen: Instead, she made a clucking, *aww*-ing sound, like she was tickling Finn under his chin. Then she turned and shut the door, faced him again in the sealed room. She walked toward the desk, smoothing her skirt at her hips. It was a surprising gesture, and it amplified for James the sensation that, with his firing, a range of previously unthinkable things could now occur.

"Can I say something to you?" she asked. She was quite close to him, eye to eye, with only the desk between, at the level of her crotch.

A peep escaped James's throat. He nodded.

"I really love what you do," she said. He tried to smell her, but his nose was useless from smoking. "I think it's really important. Like, seriously, no one else is going to do the stuff you do. That piece you did on the Inuit film collective? I totally loved that. I think they're making a huge mistake." She stepped back, shook her body a little, relieved to have unburdened herself.

James wanted to lean over, curve a finger, and say: *Come here.* He wanted to make her climb across the desk on her knees, put his hand between her legs. He wanted to shake her for her feeble attempts at consolation. He loathed her inexperience and her boots that were too pointy for walking. Then he loathed himself, too, the never-ending stream of hateful thoughts like these. A lifetime of images of women glorious and grotesque trotted beneath his eyelids, unfulfilled, ungrabbed hands and fists never inserted, things that occupied his mind, filled him up, kept him dumb. He wished she would leave.

"Thanks for saying that," said James. She stood there, as if waiting for something.

James doubted she was waiting for the same thing he was. Without looking at the title, he pulled a book from the shelf and handed it to her.

"You should have this." She flipped it this way and that, like she had never touched a book before.

"Thanks." She held it out to him: "Could you write your number in there?" James hesitated: It was the phrasing. "Could" he? Well, he could. And so he did, his cell phone number in red ink, right on the title page, like an author's autograph under the title: *Televisuality: Style, Crisis and Authority in American Television.* It was the first time he'd cracked its spine.

James had walked home with the box of books dragging down his arms, his back moaning. He had decided to carry the box because it was the first really, truly nice afternoon of the year, the kind of day when he would usually leave early anyway. He walked with purpose, wondering if anyone in the windows of the cubic building where he'd worked for years was watching him go. Perhaps there was someone standing at a revolving door, under the propaganda-size posters of the network's news anchors, head shaking sadly: *Glad it's not me.* James was almost certain this was not happening, but still, he couldn't bring himself to look back.

When he was far away, and standing in a grassy area near the art college, he dropped the books and smoked a cigarette. Then he called Ana on his cell phone. He left a message: "It's just me."

James heaved the box back into his arms, felt the sweat at his forehead. He had not gotten fat yet, but it was coming. Oh, he was old, old, old. He still couldn't fathom that he was forty-two. He felt seventeen, always, expected to see seventeen every single time he looked in the mirror.

The sweat trickled down his forehead, needled him in the eye. His arms weren't free to rub so he squinted, shook his head. He deduced that he looked crazy. The students walked around him, giving him space.

He liked to cut through this campus, wondering if the art school girls mistook him for a hip young professor. Academia was one of the few professions where forty-two seemed relatively young, he thought. In television, even public television, it was ancient. Why did this suddenly come as a revelation to him? Why had he never prepared for this moment? It occurred to James that he might be in shock.

He put the box of books down on a bench and sat next to it, breathing heavily. A mother—squat, rigid with anger—walked by quickly, dragging a toddler by the wrist. Both of them were silent, the mother staring straight ahead and the boy blank, inert. They had just exited a fight and were moving fast through its plume. The boy wore a backpack with the tail of a lion poking out of the bottom.

James walked in the opposite direction from the pair, carrying his box through the fish gutter chaos of Chinatown. The crowds thickened and thinned as he passed McDonald's and the hospital. A new organic chocolate store had opened up where a Chinese grocer had been.

James's arms were aching by the time he reached the bottom of the street. He passed the two-in-one semidetached houses, his neighbors joined at the hips, with shared yards and little fences between.

He knew that Ana would be home soon, and he was pleased to see a parking space right in front of their lawn. Ana had taken the car to work so she could grocery shop after, and she would need a place to park.

The neighborhood was permit-only and in the throes of what James had labeled, in his letters to the city, a "parking crisis." He had considered pitching a piece to his producers on the absurd parking situation in the city (There was no logic to it! No system! No grand vision!), but couldn't figure out the right angle. And it was too blatantly antienvironment for Sly. Who had sympathy for drivers these days?

But James loved the car, a leased black Jetta. He wished it were here right now. He would get Ana to pack one of her wondrous picnic lunches with the white cloth napkins, a glass bowl of green grapes, her chicken sandwiches. He would drive her anywhere she wanted to go, out of the gridlock, maybe to Niagara Falls to look for barrels, suicides, get a drink in a horrible restaurant with gigantic plastic menus and cream sauce on everything.

This was, he realized, a memory from their twenties.

Suddenly, a silver SUV pulled into the space directly in front of James's house, a space James presently thought of as Ana's. Now where would she park?

James hated the silver SUV. It was a bully. The cars on the other side of the street had garages and no reason to take up perfectly good parking spaces that were meant to be used by those on James's side of the street, where there were no garages, just small gardens backing on to other small gardens. But this particular guy—a loud, brickish Portuguese construction owner whom James called Chuckles to his friends—used his garage as a woodworking shop and cannery, and paid for permit parking (James had done some sneaking around the lane to figure this out). He had a large van, too, which often had two-by-fours sticking out the back, taking up even more spaces. All of this infuriated James, who loved rules when they worked to his advantage but was otherwise an anarchist. Ana had pointed out that he might be a libertarian, but James bristled, picturing people in mountains with war-painted faces arming themselves against immigrants.

Chuckles got out of the car, pulled up his pants over his hips. He had a Bluetooth clipped to his ear and was gesticulating, but James couldn't make out the words. When James got closer, and Chuckles disappeared into his house across the street, James saw that, of course, he had taken up nearly three parking spaces, parking smack in the gravitational center between two cars, leaving emptiness on either end much too big to be acceptable, much too small for anything but motorcycles. Now Ana would probably have to park a block over, which meant it would take her longer to get back and comfort him, and also the extra walk with groceries would be hard for her after a long day.

James staggered up onto to his porch and dropped the box of books. He unlocked the door to the smell of cut lilies and last night's olive oil. He threw his jacket on the ground. In the kitchen, he found a black marker and, in the recycling bin, an old photocopied flyer for a maid service. On the back of the flyer, he wrote:

WE HAVE A PARKING CRISIS ON THIS STREET.
PLEASE RESPECT YOUR NEIGHBORS AND PARK
NOSE TO TAIL —YOU ARE TAKING UP SEVERAL
SPACES.

James wrote fast, wetting the paper, letting the ink leak through onto the countertop.

He paused.

YOU HAVE A GARAGE—WHY DON'T YOU USE IT,
YOU FAT FUCK

He looked at the paper. *More?* He added punctuation:

YOU FAT FUCK!

James stood beside the car, humming profanity under his breath. He placed the note under the windshield wiper and went inside, sat on the white club chair facing the window, and waited. Soon, surprising himself, he fell into a deep sleep. When he woke up, darkness had come to the room. His cell phone beeped from somewhere. He had missed a call from Ana, who was on her way home. She had texted: *Anything else from the store?*

He looked out at the SUV, the flyer paper flapping in the breeze, and a deep pull of panic set in his stomach. No, no, no! In his stocking feet, he got up and ran to the door, down the stairs, looking both ways, wondering if the fat man would appear, or Ana, or—this was the worst image—both at the same time. Both of them, dots far away coming into focus, rolling in from two different directions: Ana's puzzled face as the fat man pulls the paper off the car; Ana, looking up at James in the window as the fat man shows her his handwriting—

James grabbed the paper from the windshield and ran to the porch. But then he saw the box of books there, and remembered his day. He looked at the paper and tore off the bottom part, crumpling "YOU HAVE A GARAGE...YOU FAT FUCK!" and sticking that portion in his pocket. Then he walked back to the car, calmer now, and placed the rest of the note, the part he told himself was neighborly, on the windshield.

Then he went into the house and waited for his wife.

The firing didn't seem to gut him today, James noticed. There wasn't the same pleasurable pain in reliving it, and he left his bench.

At a café, James drank his second Americano of the day. Bruce had suggested that he update Finn's enrollment, "considering the circumstances." James felt like he was applying to grad school, filling in the sheaf of forms: phone numbers and work schedules, dietary restrictions, religious practices. He signed in the space marked "Parent/Guardian." He circled the latter. Below his and Ana's numbers, he put his mother's as the emergency contact.

"Is there any information that would help us get to know your child better?" James considered writing: "Mother in a coma; father in a drawer." He didn't, but smiled at the possibility, then accepted the sorrow on the other side of the smile.

The door of the café opened, and a red stroller appeared. It stuck in the door, then jiggled this way and that until, finally, a seated young man clicked shut his laptop, pulled out his earbuds, and loped over to pull it through. A flushed woman on the other end thanked him, and then immediately behind her, another red stroller stuck in the doorway. The young guy pulled that one through, too, and accepted the thanks. And then, finally, a third one appeared, this time green. The women laughed loudly. Chairs scraped, and tables banged. James relinquished an extra chair. The young man packed up his laptop and left. When finally this swell of bodies settled, the room's tininess had lost its charm. James was now wedged too close to the espresso machine, which stopped and started with a go-cart revving in his ear. He attempted to finish his papers while the women talked. There was such panic in their voices, such urgency, as if they had just had duct tape stripped from their mouths. It seemed to James that there was nothing linear in this talking, no distinguishing one voice from the other, no call and response, just call.

"The thing is, if you don't want me in your store, then fine, I won't go in your store—"

"Right, right—"

"But then, you don't get my business—"

"Right, right—"

"And what is this contempt, then? Right? What's the expectation? What are we supposed to do, stay in the goddamn house all day and watch the tampon channel? Like, sorry, I'm not—"

"Giving up everything—"

"Right. You're the same person. You have a right to—"

"Theo says: 'Just stay home.' But what the hell does he know? I mean, he comes in at eight—"

"And he never gave up anything. He doesn't know what it's like. No one tells you what—"

Then, atop the symphony of exigency, a baby began to moan. Then another set free a wail. Soon, all three had shaken off their flannel blankets and uncoiled from their baskets to lie across their mothers' bodies. The sounds of soothing were as loud as the babies' cries. Plastic toys were shaken. Songs and murmurs. Breasts appeared from sweaters.

All those years that James had been in his office, women had been having this conversation. It came to him as a major revelation that the city was lived in all the hours of the day, and often not by him. He felt strangely left out, as if the city had been duplicitous, a disloyal friend. Borrowed. He had never really known it after all.

James put on his jacket and stepped into the day. The sidewalks were clean, crowded with sunlight.

James tried to imagine what Finn was doing at that moment. He knew there would be a nap at some point, and he liked that idea: all the little cots laid out on the floor, a shuttered room, dark and silent, in the middle of the workday. He felt a little envious of all they were permitted.

James walked until he was in the mall, which he had covered on the show once, gleefully, as a kind of Ellis Island of shopping. Turbans, saris, burkas, baseball caps backward on the heads of brown boys, their underwear waistbands exposed. A celebration of the interstice of commerce and immigration. Or something like that.

James headed toward the most expensive corner of the mall, a children's store with fall displays: kids in rainboots with animal snouts on the toes; umbrellas resembling frogs. He grabbed a basket. After staring at the labels for several minutes, he realized that the child's age determined the size. Finn was two and a half, so he piled size threes in the basket. James thought, *Wouldn't it be great if the size were still the age? Give me the forty-twos, please.*

He selected carefully: nothing with slogans, nothing overly sporty. But it was difficult to find anything without baseballs or soccer balls or team numbers emblazoned across the chest. He thought of Sarah and her pride over secondhand bargains. What would she make of this? James found a pair of sneakers hipper than the ones Finn had been given by the social worker. Blue Adidas with a seventies retro stripe, but tiny.

The clerk ringing through his purchases was blowsy, overly effusive.

"These are sooooo cute," she said, folding a pair of jeans. "Totally popular for fall."

The credit card had his name on it, but it was Ana's account; would this piece of information have made the saleswoman less solicitous?

Only when she dropped Finn's new shoes into the bag did James realize that if he swapped his laces for Velcro straps, he'd be wearing exactly the same pair.

Arrival

ANA AND JAMES and Sarah and Marcus had become friends slowly at first, and then suddenly. Within months of meeting, they were at the forefront of each other's lives. It happened when Finn was a baby, the friendship springing to life alongside his own brand-new existence, month upon month.

It had started at the wedding.

The bride was eight months pregnant and could not stop laughing. James had a few, and he started laughing, too, until everyone between the rose walls of the hotel ballroom was laughing so hard that the justice of the peace, a tent of a woman, held up her hands.

"People! Come on, now! We have work to do! It's supposed to be serious when you straight people get married!"

James and Ana were surprised to find that they had been seated at a table with the bride and groom. They had known the couple only a few months, though technically, James had known Sarah years ago, in college before Ana. He'd made the first mention of her in the winter.

"This woman I sort of remember invited us to dinner." Ana was emptying the dishwasher. "I forgot to tell you."

"Who is it?" Ana ran through a mental list of all the women James had known before her.

James frowned. "Odd. I don't remember her name."

Ana held a clean mixing bowl in her hand. She rubbed its glass belly with a dishtowel.

James typed on his BlackBerry, bent thumbs clicking. He didn't even keep it in a pocket anymore; it had become an extension of his hand, a beeping carbuncle. "It's here. Sarah. Her name's Sarah."

"Can you help me put these away?"

He said: "Why are you drying dishes that are already dry?"

Ana told Sarah that she looked beautiful, and she meant it. Sarah's dress was a divable sea green, and this fishy aspect continued with her cropped, glossy black hair.

"Are you appalled by the wedding-ness of this wedding? I think I am." Sarah pointed at a string of white Christmas lights winding around the windows overhead. They were in a basement ballroom; the small rectangular windows sat up high, near the ceiling, peeking out into bushes. Their shape and secret location near the ground—windows she would notice only if she stopped to tie her shoe—made Ana think of an old-fashioned prison on a main street in a small town. She expected to see ankles and feet pass by outside, through the shrubbery.

Sarah patted Ana's knee and grinned. Of all the people here, Sarah had chosen her to lean into. Ana felt cozy.

"Something comes over you when you plan a wedding." Sarah pretended to whisper her confession. "You start giving a shit about things you absolutely should not give a shit about."

Ana laughed and told Sarah about the night before her own wedding, when she stayed up until 3 a.m. tying bags of tea with white ribbon because the wedding favor CD that James had made seemed suddenly inadequate.

"Okay, that's pretty bad. You've made me feel better," said

Sarah, rubbing her hand over her stomach, which jutted out in front of her in a perfect circle, like a prosthetic. Ana did not flinch. She decided that she liked this loud, pregnant woman, a conclusion she hadn't quite reached over the prior few weeks. Ana needed a new friend.

Across the table, James was face to face with Marcus, the groom. James did most of the talking, arms and hands punching. He sensed Ana watching him and looked over, gave her a quick smile midsentence, then turned back to it.

"Did you think it was strange that no one walked me down the aisle?"

"Oh," said Ana. "I didn't—"

"We're orphans, Marcus and I. My parents are dead, and his are fuckwits." Sarah chewed ice out of a water glass. "Usually, it's totally fine, but today, I did mind. I feel like I can say that to you." Ana nodded.

"Most of these people are work friends. Nice people. We haven't lived here that long, really, when I think about it. It's all pretty new."

Now Ana recognized what was strange about the small crowd: Barely anyone in the room looked older than fifty. Ana remembered the old schoolhouse where she had been married, with James's great-aunts and -uncles in their wheelchairs in locked positions tucked away in the corners like umbrellas.

On the edges of the empty dance floor, a small child swayed by himself, wearing a rock 'n' roll T-shirt—ABCD split by a lightning bolt, like the logo for the band AC/DC—with a blazer over it, hair hanging in his eyes. How old? Ana had no idea.

She had seen the boy earlier, in the bathroom. As Ana stood at the automatic dryer, his little hands had suddenly brushed against hers, grabbing at the warm air, his body up against her skirt.

"Oliver, don't be rude!" The boy's mother had appeared, pulling him away. Ana smiled, shrugging lightly. "I'm so sorry," said the mother, unfolding a soft towel from the stack by the sink. She rubbed furiously at the boy's hands. He looked at Ana quizzically, silent. "Were you smart enough to leave yours at home?"

Ana sighed internally, knowing what she'd find at the next step of this conversation. "I don't have kids."

And so it came: the pause and the nervous rebound. "Right, I get that, absolutely," and the exaggerated eye roll at the small, wet child. It surprised Ana how often mothers played up their misery, as if she would find it comforting to pretend they would switch places with her.

Eighties pop rock blasted from the speakers. In daytime, this room would probably be used for a conference, a PowerPoint presentation to bored executives trying to keep their tortoise necks from snapping down to sleep. Ana attended these kinds of meetings and had occasionally led them. She knew the closed air of this kind of room, the scent of boredom, the water glasses and pens lined up next to blank tablets of paper. She didn't like to think of Sarah's wedding shadowed by the ordinary in this way.

"You forget all about the wedding when you realize you're in a marriage," said Ana, her eyes now on James, who was still talking.

"I know. We've been together so long, I'm not sure why it mattered at all to Marcus. His traditional side appeared as soon as I showed him the pee stick."

Then came the sound of knives clinking on glasses and a small cheer. Sarah rolled her eyes at Ana with a smile that discredited the eye roll. Marcus leaned across the table and gave his bride a kiss, so deep and certain that Ana looked away. James did not. He let out a whoop.

When Ana turned back, Sarah was beaming and cackling, her big sound bouncing below the DJ's music like an extra track. The cake appeared, carried by two sweating women in manly black vests and white dress shirts. Three tiers of white buttercream icing, ribbons of chocolate down the side. A round of applause. There were no figurines on top. Ana remembered picking her bride and groom: James thought it would be funny to use two black people, or a pair of women. In the end, he let her pick, and she panicked and chose two that were so small her mother drunkenly asked if they were children.

The women placed the cake directly in front of Ana, which set off fireworks of flashing cameras.

"Oh, no, no. I'm not—" said Ana, sliding her chair closer to James, out of the way of Sarah and Marcus and all the years that this photo would exist in computer in-boxes and dresser drawers.

The sound in the room was beginning to bother her. A thrumming filled her skull, and her body craved the cool of the sheets waiting for her at home. The edges of her eyes blurred.

James saw Ana cringe a little and knew what was happening. He put his arm around her, and she leaned into it. She tried to stem his worry.

They were equal now. All that work to clear the tubes of their nests of cysts, and it didn't matter: According to the celebrity doctor, Ana had an "inhospitable" uterus—no visitors allowed. Its walls were thin as onionskin, unable to support anything. And James's sperm had low motility. They were too lethargic to broach those walls anyway.

Now they had the information, the perfectly balanced failure. A year ago, they had agreed upon the circumstances under which the long, gruesome trail of appointments and injections would end, and today they had kept their covenant. No more stirrups and pills. No more bloody syringes and bruised thighs. No more electronic wands.

James had a new plan now. Even as he was explaining to the table why vegetarianism was an untenable ethical position, the other part of his brain had him sweeping into Rwanda. He had been there once, during the rebuilding. He had opened the door to a church, and children came tumbling out like jelly beans from a machine. He imagined himself on an airplane back from Africa. Finally he'd be one of those dads he always got seated behind. But he would be bouncing and expertly soothing the new baby, a baby with no one besides them. Ana was in the seat next to him, holding a baby bottle. They could do that. It would be good for everyone.

But then, there were risks: trauma; fetal alcohol syndrome; the stigma of being a racial outsider...He glanced at Sarah's swollen stomach. Maybe they could borrow a healthy uterus for a while and grow their own.

Ana did not know what thoughts were racing through James's mind or why his eyes on her smiled sadly. She wanted to show him that she was all right, to let him know that it was possible to be happy for someone else. She gave him a small kiss on the neck. She was trying to remind him of something that she herself was working hard to remember.

A year later, Ana watched James through the kitchen window, open for the first time in months. He looked medium. His brown hair had thinned at the top of his head to reveal a little gleaming planet that hoped not to be discovered. When he turned sideways, the silhouette of a small belly emerged from his untucked shirt, surprising her.

Ana rapped on the window. James waved. She pointed to her wristwatch. He nodded.

Ana had discovered the pipes had broken when a smell led her to the basement, where shreds of toilet paper and purple-black sludge coated the drain in one corner. James had handled it, which meant that when Ana came home from work the next afternoon, there were three men in her frozen, broken yard, and James, too, each of them drinking a beer out of the bottle. James had gloves on; the men did not. One was Romanian and two Italian, though they considered themselves Sicilian, really, James informed her later, in the bathroom, his mouth filled with toothpaste. The tinier the country, the more divided, James noted. (Ana thought: *What about Andorra?* But she didn't say it out loud.) He prided himself on always knowing something significant about everyone within eleven minutes of introductions.

The pipes had been replaced, but the yard remained ripped apart. James and Ana had decided to leave it until spring, and now it was spring and James stood in the very center of the frozen lawn like a spoon in a bowl of hardened pudding, with two rolls of sod at his feet. James knew a little about gardening—he had interviewed some organic farmers in

California who discovered ammonium sulphate in their fertilizer—but not enough to save the lawn.

Ana surveyed the kitchen. The risotto ingredients were lined up in small ceramic bowls as if waiting for a cooking show close-up. Ana wore an apron James had sewn years ago in his high school home economics class: WOK WITH JAMES, it said in black iron-on letters across the chest, a reference to a popular TV show Ana had never seen.

James slammed the back door, letting in a gust of cool air.

"How can you not be wearing a coat?" asked Ana.

He leaned over her three-ring binder, reading the recipe in its plastic sleeve.

"This looks great." Then: "I'm not cold. That apron is still fucking hilarious."

He plugged his iPod into the dock in the next room and returned midsentence, speaking over the music, telling Ana about the band, which included a tuba player. This enthusiasm reminded Ana of a time during their courtship when James would arrive at her apartment in the middle of the night—3 or 4 a.m.—just as the black crust of the sky was breaking. He had a key by then, and wouldn't wake her, but would stand for a moment at the side of Ana's bed. She would press her eyelids closed, feigning sleep. After a few minutes of heavy breathing, if he was still there, she would open her eyes. James never went out at night in those days without the paramedic's shirt he'd bought at a second-hand store in Kensington market. It had blue crosses on the shoulders and a polyester sheen made Day-Glo by James's sweat.

"How did it go?" Ana would ask, watching him vibrating with eagerness to tell her what had happened to him and what she had missed with her early-to-bed rhythm, her morning-person status.

"Excellent," he'd grin, his tongue broad with drink. "I got right to the front around midnight."

James would wear the shirt to cut through the crowd, calling: "Excuse me, excuse me! Paramedic coming through! Medical! Injured woman!" He did this when the lights were low, timing it perfectly so the music was just beginning, and the crowd was distracted but not drunk enough to be ugly. Oh, man, it was miraculous: The fans parted for this compassionate professional.

Ana was charmed when she heard the story the first time, and laughed. But later, she came to identify the gag as a piece of a bigger problem. James got older, but his great sense of entitlement stayed around: the stacks of unpaid parking tickets; his clear conscience over buying a shirt, wearing it, and then returning it to the store a day later. He had many theories, rationalizations about Dada and culture jamming and upending a system that was inherently disadvantageous to... well, not him, maybe, but people who didn't even recognize they were disadvantaged. Somehow, it was his duty to get the best of the world. After a while, Ana tuned out that particular strain of James, the yammering of the kid from the suburbs justifying why his hand was reaching for the last piece of cake.

But back in the beginning, it intoxicated her to be with someone who handled everything, everyone. This was new to Ana, who had paid her mother's bills at nine, worked after school at the doughnut shop at thirteen, wiping the drink fridge clean of broken juice bottle shards and bugs entombed in gelatinous substances.

In the beginning, she wanted to curl up inside James's certainty. She loved him, she loved him, and how he fell into bed next to her those late nights. His slick skin, sweat and beer. The lean muscle of his thigh flung open on the sheets. She pulled him closer in his paramedic shirt.

From the window, Ana watched James outside in the yard. He stared up at the darkening sky, which was much too light for stars. But she took note of the fact that he looked anyway. He was hopeful. She felt something shift inside her, as if, to make room for all this love, she would have to rearrange her insides. James was gigantic that way. When she wanted him, she wanted all of him. When she didn't, he felt murderous, unstoppable. A superhero gone mad on a busy downtown street. It had been a while, Ana realized, since she had experienced the scope of her love.

Not wanting to linger on this absence, she turned to her vegetables. While James showered, Ana walked through the house, placing small glass pots of candles on the mantel, on ledges. She turned down the lights, put a single bloodred gerbera in a white vase in the center of the table. Her hand moved across the place mats and linen napkins. In the living room, as she half lowered the blinds, a man walked by, his hair softly blowing, his spine curved, hands in pockets. He looked up, and their eyes locked. Ana marveled that while he was a grown man, he was still far too young for her to romance, to have sex with, even to know. At thirty-nine, she was too old not just for boys but for full-fledged adults. A male temp at work had called her "ma'am" the other day.

But Ana knew also how she looked through the window: "good for her age." Attempting a moment of private flipness, she thought: *My body has not been ruined by childbirth.* She savored it, then abandoned the thought as too cruel.

Ana turned her head to a flattering angle, but when she glanced sideways, the man had already walked on. All she could see was concrete and an old oak tree that threw moving shadows across the line of parked cars.

The baby was in a blue-checked sling across Sarah's body like something worn by a contestant in a beauty pageant.

"Hands-free," Sarah joked, waving her glass of wine. The baby nursed covertly. Only the extra crescent of Sarah's pale chest peeking out of the sling confirmed to everyone in the room that there was a naked breast close by, and a mouth upon it. Each discomfort provoked by this was unique to its owner.

It had grown late, but Ana did not want them to leave. These dinners, which Sarah and Marcus protested over in the beginning, had become regular Friday night gatherings, always at Ana and James's house, with the excuse that they were all working together to break Sarah's maternal isolation. Sarah complained about the "mommy circuit," as she called it. She liked to mock the neighborhood mothers with their fear of strangling stroller straps and sudden infant death syndrome and uneducational toys. They bored her. She described a kind of narrowing that happens to women when they have children, a trivializing. Ana listened, rapt, to the traveler returned with her tales. She had a colleague, Elspeth, with secret children. She hid them away from the men in the firm, like Jews in attics. Occasionally she confided in Ana, usually when complaining about the nannies.

But the mothers Sarah knew existed entirely in public. They

met in the daylight in coffee shops and at baby yoga classes, speaking of nothing but their children. The mothers had left their jobs and were shrinking, hunkering down, backing into their stalls. At first, during these litanies, James cast concerned glances at Ana that she could feel, though she refused to meet his eye.

"I like it," she told him later. "Sarah knows about us. I like that she doesn't treat me like an outsider." And so he was relieved to be able to enjoy it, too, this refracted life that might have been theirs (that might still be theirs, she reminded herself).

Tonight, Marcus and James were talking about Jesus. James had recently finished a segment for his show about a new church that gathered in movie theaters downtown. James was bulimic when in possession of fresh information; as soon as it came in, it had to come out.

"Jesus is back in vogue. These kids relate to Jesus like he's straight out of Japanese anime."

"Yes, but at the end of the day, you have to see it as completely fictional, right? You can enjoy the fairy tale, but it's sad, isn't it, to see grown people subscribing?" asked Marcus, in his question mark–inflected way. James's own sentences were stubby and leached of doubt.

"And dangerous," added Sarah. "I had a horrible incident in my class just before the baby. I was hugely pregnant and I actually told a student: 'You can wear your hijab in here, but know that it changes nothing about your fate.'"

"Wow," said Ana. James laughed, slapping his knee.

"I was so hormonal!" said Sarah. "But this girl is impudent, truly. She's a total bitch. She makes fun of nerds."

"Is she popular?" asked Ana. These were the only terms

through which she could understand high school: popular and unpopular. When her mother had settled them down long enough, Ana had often been popular and felt guilty for it.

Sarah didn't answer, because James had moved into the space. "Diehard secularism is just as dangerous as institutionalized religion." Ana knew this speech. "Secularism becomes religious, then you have Stalinism, all the iconography of religious faith in a secular package."

"What are you saying?" Marcus was smiling, always smiling. This placidity was broken only by a small, angry scar below his lower lip in the shape of check mark, a hint of past violence. He seemed to take great pleasure in James, which surprised Ana, and was a relief to her, too. James's verbal girth had become less appealing to people over the years. Ana didn't say this to Sarah. She didn't want to draw attention to her petty worries. She was sure that the smallness of her inner life would appall Sarah, that this was not how Sarah wanted to think of her new friends. She often got Ana to talk about her life with her mother, her itinerant upbringing among the downtown artists and drunks. These stories made Sarah red with excitement, and they woke up Ana, too. She felt breathless sometimes to talk about herself in this way, as if she were recounting the racy chapters in a book she had read. But there were details Ana would not share, because she knew they would sour the bohemian fantasy. She didn't tell Sarah about the famous blues musician who breathed cigarette smoke onto her hair and ran a finger under the collar of her sweatshirt when she was eleven years old, stopping there only because her mother entered the kitchen. That time, her mother did something: She slapped his hand away. A week later, they moved again.

"We need to take it back to Jesus," said James.

"You propose living by Jesus's doctrine?" asked Marcus.

"Well, I mean, *I* can't, but even people who reject Christianity dig Jesus. Who's not down with Jesus?"

Sarah shifted and unstuck the baby, who emerged endlessly out of the sling. A magician pulling a toy snake out of a hat.

"He's a long guy," said James.

Finn made a hissing sound, then burped. Sarah patted his back, and he flopped over her shoulder. James saw the baby's reflection in the living room window, his head bobbing. He looked like Casper the Friendly Ghost, this bald kid. James wondered if anyone would be offended if he made this observation out loud. Marcus was easygoing, but it was hard to know for sure; the women were the ones bonding in this foursome. They went for lunch when James was on the road for work. What did they talk about? James tried to imagine Ana talking about him, their sex life, his balding head.

James wondered if Marcus possessed a less genial side. He couldn't figure out where to place him yet, if he should invite him to play hockey or take him to a lecture. He couldn't quite see a future with Marcus in it. Marcus didn't smoke.

"Does anyone want to hold him? I'm pretending to ask politely, but I'm actually begging," said Sarah.

"I will." James rarely saw his nephew and nieces, though they lived only a half hour from his home. Holding his nephew as a baby, he had felt that he was holding a mewing, grotesquely small version of his brother. He kept expecting the baby to sit up and say: "So, Jimmy. I made an awesome trade today! Markets are up!" The boy bucked and twisted in his arms. But when held by his mother, as if to make a point, he softened, even cooed. This had seemed to James to indicate a future mean streak. He had kept his distance since.

But Finn was more of a public concern. Happy in all arms, he seemed to belong to everyone. Finn sat propped in James's lap, facing outward with his legs straight in front, shaking a plastic cup. "Ba," he said. "Babababa."

"Exactly," said James. James had developed an unspoken narrative in which he and Finn had a special bond. He did not tell Ana how it made him feel, this warm bag of socks over his shoulder, the pleasure he got when Finn moved his penny-shaped mouth.

He was certain that Ana was still heartbroken, as sick inside now as after the third miscarriage, when she vanished for four days, leaving only one voice mail. She returned in the same clothes she'd left in, walked past James in the foyer, and straight into the bathroom. While she showered, James looked in her purse and found nothing, until, at the bottom, his fingertips touched a layer of sand. Sand! She had driven all the way to Lake Superior, she finally told him, her hair wrapped in a white bath sheet, seated on the edge of the white duvet. She had gone to see the rock in the shape of the old woman, and she'd slept in a motel with a sanitation sash across the toilet and a hundred channels. Those were the only details she shared.

She felt better, she told him, and she was sorry.

James stood outside the door to the bathroom as she showered, wondering if he should get angry, wondering if this great writhing hatred within was visible to her. He did not want to find out, so he brought her tea, rubbed her back as she fell asleep on the new sheets he'd bought to replace the ones she'd bled into, the ones onto which she had leaked their lost child.

* * *

James watched her, carrying in an apple green lacquered Asian serving tray with a pot of decaf coffee, four mugs. Finn giggled while Ana poured the coffee.

"Oh, Ana, it's always perfect here," said Sarah, leaning back with her coffee, one hand stroking a forest green silk throw cushion.

"It really is great," said Marcus. "It's like a hotel."

"Tell me about work. Tell me about the crazies," said Sarah.

Ana pictured Christian. He was junior but she had worked with him on several cases, most recently researching a patent infringement. He appeared at her office door far too often, breaking the silence of the fifteenth floor, where Ana and her fellow neck-bowed research lawyers clicked away. Christian brought with him his litigator chatter, his unmet high-fives and golf scores.

Ana described how Christian insisted on using a billfold instead of a wallet, and the way he demonstrated this characteristic constantly. He played off the partners' vanities, researching their past successes and bringing them up in meetings, wide-eyed: "Oh, wow, I studied that case in first year. You killed! Oh, wow!" And the men above her adored it. Even as they shushed him for his obviousness, their bodies inflated before her eyes, their cheeks reddened with pride.

Ana was surrounded by men all day, and had been for years, but she didn't understand them, really, their shimmery foreheads, their noise, their presumption.

Sarah listened, asked Ana questions that no one else asked her about intellectual property. "What's the infringement?"

"Oh—it's nothing. It's a tech company suing another tech

company over storage device interfaces." Sarah nodded lightly, her mouth pursed in listening. "I give the opinion. They ask for it, I give it."

The men drifted off into a separate conversation about hockey. James talked from down on the rug with Finn, who attempted to pull himself along the edge of the coffee table. Every few minutes, James would grab him and make farting sounds on the baby's belly, and the boy squealed with delight.

Ana's certainty that she was dull was offset by the wine, which had the effect of speeding her up. So she told Sarah how there was a new young temp on her floor, a meek young woman merging documents for special projects.

"Special projects!" said Sarah. "I love that. Makes me think of birthday parties for handicapped people."

This girl, Ruth, was off-putting. She hovered with a half smile, hoping someone would talk to her. The other day, her cardigan was buttoned wrong, and it dangled lopsided off her torso.

"I didn't know if I should pull her aside and tell her."

"What did you do?" Sarah asked. "I know what I'd do." (Only later did this aside come back to Ana. In the night, she jolted awake: What would Sarah do? Why does she know so easily?)

"I did tell her, but late in the day. Around three. She was mortified, too, and since then, she's seemed kind of angry with me. She walked right by me yesterday, and not even the office nod."

"That's fucked," said James. Ana startled. She hadn't known he was listening.

"Is it? She's the youngest woman on our floor, she's not even a lawyer, and I criticize how she looks. Doesn't that affirm a certain currency for her?" Ana frowned. "Maybe I did it because I'm threatened."

"But you were trying to help her," said Marcus.

"But I only drew attention to her. I didn't help."

No one said anything, and in that silence, Finn grew frustrated, unable to walk more than a few steps along the coffee table without falling. He sputtered: "Bababa! Ba!"

"Oh no!" said James, grabbing Finn under the armpits. James held him out for the pass, and both Sarah and Marcus stood up quickly, extending their arms.

"Oh!" said James, holding Finn under the armpits, jokingly waving the baby back and forth between his parents. "Who loves me more? Who loves me more?"

"Here," said Sarah, stepping forward, blocking Marcus with her body. Ana tried to find Marcus's face, offer a small smile to diffuse the puff of humiliation in the air, but he was looking to the side, and Ana was stuck with it, this unreceived grin.

A stuffed bear and several blankets were gathered, the baby placed inside his jacket, all with great efficiency. Ana offered a Tupperware container of leftovers, which Sarah at first resisted, and then slipped into the bottom of the stroller.

At the foot of Ana and James's walk, a group of young people appeared out of the darkness, the girls with bare legs and metallic purses. Cell phones bulged from the boys' hip pockets. Their loud directionless voices crisscrossed one another.

The two couples watched them from the porch.

"It's nice that there are still students around here," said Sarah.

"Except they don't know when to take out the garbage," said Ana.

"And they play their shit music all night," said James.

"If it was better music, would you mind?" asked Marcus, laughing.

"It doesn't even have words," said James.

"Jazz doesn't have words," said Ana.

Marcus lifted the stroller with Finn tucked inside, moving down the path toward the sidewalk. Sarah followed him. The students remained, their talking elevated to yelling. They did not move to make way.

"Right on!" shouted a boy into his phone. It was a signal to go; plans had been made. They passed through Sarah and Marcus and the baby like ghosts walking through walls.

Marcus put his hands up to his shoulders, palms out, and shrugged.

Sarah and Marcus waved as they walked away, pushing the stroller, calling thank-yous behind them as Ana and James stood on the porch, James's arm protectively around his wife, wondering if anyone else had noticed that Ana had never once held the baby.

September

ANA STARED OUT the window at another tower just like hers. She looked at her watch: Finn would be at daycare, still. But James would be picking him up soon, and they would leave together, hand in hand, she was certain. She let that feeling push itself across her chest.

For a while, there had been a blond woman about Ana's age in the office across the way. One day they were wearing the same navy polka-dotted blouse—an unusual blouse, expensive—and Ana laughed at the mirror image. The next time it happened, Ana spontaneously waved at the woman, gesturing to their matching shirts. But the woman didn't respond, kept typing, her head bowed in a willful manner. When Ana returned from the bathroom, the woman had drawn her blinds. Embarrassed, Ana did the same.

Now the office was occupied by a man who sat with his back to the window, his curly hair somehow childlike over the collar of his shirt. That choice, to turn one's back to the window, seemed obscene to Ana.

"Ana?"

She started, spinning her chair toward the door.

"Having a moment to yourself?" asked Christian. Everything he said came off like he wasn't so much talking to her as gathering information for a dossier he was preparing about her faults.

"What do you need?" she asked.

"An opinion," he said. "We need it fast, but I don't think it's complicated."

Ana wanted to say: *Now, why would I do that for you?* Instead, she said: "I'm quite busy right now."

"Looks like it," said Christian with a barking laugh. He behaved like a businessman from a movie, without one sincere gesture in his repertoire.

But, in fact, he had found her with an open space in her schedule, now that the servers trial had begun. She had been wondering what would come next. The impermanence was what she loved about being a research lawyer: the presentation of a problem, its resolution, and then a new problem. Litigation hadn't worked for her—all that noise and bluster—but up here, on the fifteenth floor, her inwardness was a virtue. She billed high and long; her bonuses arrived twice a year. But that wasn't why she loved it: She was vicious in her determination to make the law understood. She hacked problems into tiny pieces and spent hours on the computer, trawling databases until she had solved each question, wrapped it in understanding from every direction. Then she presented the finished product, the opinion, to the lawyers, who crowed and hollered. She was a costumier, arming them for battle.

But she preferred not to work with Christian. His officiousness, his white teeth. There were other research lawyers he could use, but he always came to her.

"What is it?"

"Biotech. That old chestnut..." He adopted the booming voice of a news anchor. "Should higher life-forms be patentable?" She knew the law, had mined it several times for several different cases: Humans couldn't be patented, but seeds could.

"For Emcor?"

"They're suing that farmer."

Ana had anticipated this. It had been in the news that Emcor, one of the firm's multimillion-dollar clients, had been knocking on the doors of farmers when their trademarked seeds, genetically modified to perfection, began to turn into crops on the fields of farmers who hadn't bought them. The farmers said they didn't know how it happened, blaming the wind. Intellectual property theft, the Emcor representatives called it. Ana pictured men in suits handing subpoenas over white picket fences to men in overalls.

"Soybeans," she said.

"Right. Those naughty farmers are infringing."

She couldn't tell if he was kidding or not.

"Really, Ana," he said, leaning in. "I need your wisdom. I'm in over my head, I think." He said it like it could never be true.

Ruth appeared in the doorway, looking tidier today, her hair pulled back, her skin clear. Ruth the Temp, but could she still be temporary? She had become a fixture, a shadow of slouch in the halls.

"Sorryinterrupt..."

"Leave the file," Ana said, and Christian gushed his thanks, blew her a kiss on his way out.

"What can I do for you, Ruth?" asked Ana.

Ruth sat down, pulling her skirt over her knees.

"I just wanted to see if, you know, you'd had a chance to talk to your husband." Ana cocked her head, blank. "Do you remember? When you said that about me maybe talking to him?"

Ana winced. The invitation. For a year, the girl had been silently waiting for Ana to set her up with James, to discuss her career path.

"I'm so sorry," Ana said. "James isn't even working in TV these days."

Ruth's mouth closed, and her face, which seemed as if it could fall no further, did so, reddening.

"We've had an intense few days," said Ana. Then she tried it on, saying it out loud for the first time, slowly: "A friend of ours died, and we're looking after his little boy." Where was Sarah in this version? She couldn't bring herself to say it; the mawkishness was overkill, the story unconvincing.

"What do you mean?"

It was not a response Ana had expected.

"Just what I said. So I'm unusually tired."

Ruth nodded. "My sister has two kids." Ana saw a flash of silver in mouth: a stud through her tongue. "Someone's always puking or throwing a shitfit or something. . . ."

Ana tried to picture Ruth at a job interview. No one in here possessed a sense of humor, so what was it that got her hired?

"Mmm," said Ana. Ruth rose, mumbling, and something in that incomprehensible sound prompted Ana to say: "I'll talk to him, though. Maybe next month you can come by. When we're more settled."

Ruth nodded, walked out, leaving Ana to her window. Then suddenly she reappeared: "I could, like, babysit for you or something if you needed it. You know, if you need any help or anything."

Ana smiled, surprised.

"Thanks, Ruth," she said. "That's very sweet."

Ana watched Ruth shuffle out into the hum of the office and wait for two people to pass. When there was enough space between them and her, she trailed behind like a footman, head bowed.

Ana remembered that she and Ruth had almost entered each other's lives once. Though it had occurred nearly a year ago, she could recall it vividly because it was one of those times when she and James had been clawing toward parenthood.

She had walked a long time that day, looking for a place to eat, past the smoky glass of Ki, glancing at its leather banquettes and ceiling of long, narrow lamps dangling like shining knives. She had recognized a group of associates, with Christian at the center. Usually they waited until after work. But she sensed in these younger ones a retro dream, a wish to return to the three-martini lunches and sharp suits of the old days. The corporate credit card that Ana kept tucked behind her driver's license, unused, was at the front of their wallets, ready for the draw.

She had gone farther than usual, away from Bay Street, rejecting the subterranean food courts, past the high-end sushi restaurant where the counter was surrounded by a river, and the sashimi rode past in a little boat, and you could reach out your hand and pluck whatever you wanted.

Off King Street, on a quieter one-way street crowded with delivery vans and bicycle couriers, a man approached. Noting his tank top, Ana thought: *Is it that warm out today?* But then she saw that he was muttering to himself, his face covered in deep, bloody acne, his fingernails running up and down his arm like he was doing scales. She tried to decide which way to go, and bobbed and weaved. He mirrored her and then stopped abruptly, face-to-face, smelling like urine. He shot her a fuck-you look.

Ana pulled her coat tight around her and walked away quickly. She felt the man's eyes on her back, watching her like she was a celebrity. She turned into the next restaurant she saw, a sushi place with a ring of half-dead Christmas lights around the window. As soon as she set foot inside, she knew it was a bad idea. The room was almost empty; only a couple of teenagers, possibly cutting school (undiscriminating diners; cheap), sat together in the window. A smell overwhelmed her, something chemical, treacherous. A waitress swarmed her with unidentifiable Asian chatter, ushered her to a table with a hand on Ana's back. Ana found herself seated in a booth, looking at a greasy menu, a dollop of something red crusted to the center of the photograph of a Hockey Sushi Box.

Ana tried to relax. She liked her lunch hour, waited for its arrival, mourned its conclusion. Most people in her office didn't take lunch. They ate out of Styrofoam boxes at their desks. But Ana went out a few days a week, speaking to no one, reveling in her anonymity. Often she would stop at the kitchen store or the storage store and peruse the towers of large plastic containers. She sometimes bought something small, the Portofino Office Storage Box in olive, with the faux-leather grained top. She had a stack of these boxes in different sizes and colors—chocolate, cranberry, pastel floral—in a wedding cake shape on a shelf next to her desk at work. Sometimes, while on the phone with other lawyers, she surprised herself by noticing that as she talked, she was stroking the boxes, so beautiful she couldn't bear to put anything inside them.

In the restaurant, she had pulled out an old issue of *The New Yorker* that Sarah had dug out for her. She was halfway through a story on Raymond Carver and his editor that Sarah had insisted she read, saying, "Oh, Ana, you would love this."

But as she read about Carver, too drunk to notice his editor thieving his words, she couldn't fathom why Sarah had recommended it. She often seemed to hold an image of Ana that was entirely foreign to Ana's own conception of herself. Sarah had told Ana when they first met that she thought Ana looked like a figure skater. Even James had no idea what this meant.

But Ana couldn't concentrate on the story. She had been pulled back to the meeting of the previous evening, and the blond, quivering woman in the Chinese slippers who had told them she would "set things in motion." Uncharacteristically, James had arranged the meeting, calling people who knew people for recommendations and booking the appointment. Ana rushed to be on time after a long meeting and met him outside the agency doors. She was still red-faced from her sprint when she learned that, yes, they were good candidates for international adoption. The white woman in the Chinese slippers told them this while sitting beneath a giant oil painting of the Great Wall of China. Now they had to find a social worker who would come by the house and interview them. Several meetings for several thousand dollars. And then, if they passed, it was back to the agency, and a series of courses on cultural sensitivity, and several thousand more dollars. And then their names at the bottom of a long scroll that could take years to wash up on the shores of China.

Ana drank tea and ate her flavorless sushi, prying apart the upcoming invasion. "It's bullshit," James had said. "But we have to do it." He was determined, and with James, that was significant. Still, it was Ana who had spent the years before being opened and scraped. Now she would have to do it again, but in her own house.

Ana had paid her bill and stepped outside.

As soon as she reentered the human stream on King Street, Ana recognized Ruth. She was smoking, walking slowly, her cardigan buttoned properly. If Ana walked as slowly as this girl, it would look like she was stalking her. She wanted to cross the street, to ignore her, to make her vanish, but it seemed impossible not to be found out. She walked at her normal pace and was quickly next to her. She said: "Hello, Ruth."

"Oh!" said Ruth, putting her cigarette behind her back, as if her mother had snuck up behind her at school.

"Did you have lunch out?"

Ruth shook her head. "I can't really afford it. I just went for a smoke."

Ana recognized the phrasing as something rural and coarse. She sounded like Ana's distant cousins, who said things like: "I'm going to the can."

"It is a nice day," said Ana. "How are you doing anyway? How do you find it in the office?" Ana had a flash of altruism, pictured herself as the kind of lawyer who might take the girl in, mentor her. She had been to a few of these events in the past, wearing a pink ribbon for charity and walking a few miles with other women lawyers. Everyone's legs looked pale in their shorts, and they all seemed embarrassed. Ana had not been able to stop herself from beginning to jog, slowly at first, and then running. The walking women were far behind when Ana finished the course before anyone else and left quickly.

Another time, at a luncheon called "Women Lawyers: A Dialogue About Transformative Leadership," she had sat at a table with a group of married associates, mother lawyers she had rarely seen on the fifteenth floor. They exchanged numbers about outsourcing: who delivers dry cleaning, emergency nanny agencies, car services that drive children to music lessons. At one point, one of them looked up from typing into her phone and said: "Okay, who do I hire to screw my husband?" Everybody laughed.

One statistic lodged in Ana's head from that afternoon: For every ten male lawyers at her firm, there was one-half a woman. Ana pictured that half-woman lawyer, sliming along the hallway on her stumpy torso.

On the street, Ana had asked again: "How's work?"

The girl looked straight ahead, put her cigarette between her lips a little defiantly. "I don't know. It's okay. It's not really what I want to do. I guess I'm not supposed to admit that to the boss."

"I'm not the boss," said Ana, so quickly that they both knew it to be false. "So what do you want to do, then?"

"I want to make movies. Maybe documentaries. About bands, maybe." Before she even finished the statement, her defiance drained away, as if this were the most unrealistic dream a person could hold. Her voice turned into a mumble. "I don't know."

It struck Ana as unlikely that this limp girl had some affinity for rhythm in her, that she liked back rooms, electric guitars. Maybe she was one of those girls who gets used. Maybe she stood at the front of the crowd and stared upward, inserted herself backstage, became a joke between a drummer and a bassist the next morning.

"My husband makes documentaries," said Ana. "For TV."

"Really?" Ruth looked at Ana sideways. Ana felt something: They didn't like each other. Ana tried to pull the girl back from the brink of this mutual realization, to distract her with kindness.

"He works in public television. You should come over some

night to meet him. Maybe he could help you out." Why had she said this? The thought of Ruth, in Ana's house in her mis-buttoned sweater, mumbling at James's feet. This was the type of girl who would love James, and James would be kind to her, would perform for her, tap dancing through his latest thought. It would be both excruciating and sweet, a combination that exhausted Ana.

She could not imagine this evening happening and knew they had entered a conversation that had no conclusion. Ruth would be checking in with her again and again, for months to come.

Inside the building, outside the door to her office, Ana did it first: "I'll throw some dates at James and get back to you."

Ruth looked up at her, and something surprising happened: Her face thawed. The blandness, the boredom, slid away. She was smiling, a huge, unyielding smile that revealed a heap of crooked teeth. The teeth made Ana remember the child's game with the hands piling up, each person pulling the one from the bottom, slapping it down on the other.

The door to Sarah and Marcus's house opened quickly, lightly, which surprised Ana. She had expected the creaking of Al Capone's vaults to match her sense of invasion. She drew the scattering of mail and flyers to her body.

Straightening, a grim old-lady smell washed over her, spiked by something sour, foul. Ana put down her briefcase and an empty suitcase on wheels. She made two tidy stacks of mail—urgent and not—and took off her heels. She moved quickly, glancing at the clutter of toys in the living room, the clothes and shoes strewn. That giant bag of cat food was still there, resting against the wall, though the cat was living next door now. Ana barely remembered the cat: black, maybe, and fat. Looking at the cat food, she regretted that she had never bothered to learn its name. She would take the bag to the neighbor later.

The kitchen was Pompeii: plates of half-eaten food, a booster chair covered in Cheerios and chunks of browned banana. She tracked down the smell to old milk gone solid in a blue plastic cup covered in cartoon bees, sitting on a counter.

Ana was filled by a rush of conquering energy. She marched into Sarah and Marcus's room, pulling open drawers until she found jeans, a T-shirt, both too big, but clean and folded tidily, which surprised her. Ana placed her skirt and blouse on hangers that she put over the doorknob, careful not to let her clothes touch the ground, which was covered in a thin layer of dust. Gray balls of fluff made space for her as Ana moved around the room in Sarah's clothes.

She rolled on a pair of Marcus's sweat socks. In this uniform, she set to it, opening windows, gathering dirty laundry, and tossing toys into wicker baskets.

And she worked, yellow gloves filling garbage bags, scrubbing soldered food from plates, keeping the kitchen sink filled to the rim with soapy bubbles. Draining the fat swirls and food chunks and refilling, over and over.

After a couple of hours, Ana noticed the silence, the noise of her breathing. She hit Play on the stereo (and dusted it, too). A familiar CD, a lament; spare guitar, the kind of music James used to play for Ana, tears in his eyes: "Hear this part? It really starts here...."

The music carried up to Finn's little room, which was like wandering into Sarah's force field, like hearing her calling:

This is how much I love him. The white curtains were covered with tiny embroidered trains. Red bunnies repeated on his bedspread, and the throw rug was a scurry of cuddly bugs. All these crowds of miniatures, thought Ana, stripping the bed, throwing scattered toys into a toy box. She should take some toys home, too.

She looked through a stack of books: *Tell the Time with Pooh, Olivia Saves the Circus, Scaredy Squirrel.* Which ones were right for Finn? Which were his favorites? All the information was locked away, irretrievable. Most of Finn's preferences resided elsewhere, with his parents, in the shadow world.

She pulled open Finn's dresser drawers. The underwear was folded into little boxes; Ana felt strange packing the suitcase, wondering how it would look if she somehow got caught—pulled over by a police officer for speeding and revealed as a grown woman with a suitcase of boys' underwear. She buried the pairs (Curious George; dinosaurs) under sweaters and socks. Then suddenly, she thought: *Does Finn wear underwear? If so, why were they using diapers?* She would have to ask James.

Ana looked around for a stuffed animal, anything she might remember Finn loving, but there were only block puzzles and flashlights, nothing huggable. As she turned out the light, Ana thought: *I'll buy him a teddy bear, something that James will approve of.*

She continued.

In the basement, Ana moved the laundry to the dryer, stepping over the detritus that ends up in basements, the remnants of Finn's babyhood: pieces of a crib, a high chair. Skates. Did Marcus play hockey? He'd never mentioned it.

When Ana emerged from the basement, darkness had

pulled up to the windows. She went to the empty fridge that she had already wiped clean and pulled out its one occupant, a half-drunk bottle of vodka. She poured a glass and drank it whole, a snake with a mouse, then turned up the music to hear it above the vacuum.

She remembered sitting in this living room with Sarah and Finn on several weekend afternoons in the wake of James's firing.

When it happened, she realized that she had been waiting for it. She was prepared always for the great bad thing, and when she reached the porch that evening, James's box of books on the porch confirmed exactly what had happened. Her heartbeat doubled. She assumed a neutral face.

She had opened the door and hung up her coat, and James's, which lay in a heap in the foyer. James was in the kitchen, but he wasn't cooking. He was drinking a beer, leaning on the island like he'd been looking for a place to rest. Ana laid the groceries on the counter.

"I got fired," he said. Then: "You might want to sit down."

"There's more?"

"What?"

"Why do you want me to sit down?"

James stared at her.

"Because I got fired. I thought you might want to brace yourself."

"Oh. But you told me first and *then* you told me to sit down."

James had drunk the beer from the bottle. Ana saw that she was making him furious, and she began to move around the kitchen quickly, trying to piece together a strategy. But there was still this twister touching down in her stomach. As if looking in from the window, she saw the two of them with all their sensible choices, and all of it vanishing like an invisible man in a movie, top to bottom, just fading out. A rush of noise erupted in her skull. She concentrated, braced herself to do the right thing.

"I'm so sorry," she said, and went to James, putting her arms around his body. He smelled her neck. He moved a hand down around her waist, grabbing for her ass, rubbing his groin against her. She broke away.

"You need to eat," she said, rooting in the fridge. Then she returned, ruffled his hair, and retreated again to look through cupboards.

Over her shoulder, she asked: "What happened? Was it Sly?"

James told her the details, sitting on a barstool while she lined up vegetables, began chopping onions and leeks into her glass bowls. She said: "What an asshole," and "Did you talk to HR about severance?" and "We can file for wrongful dismissal"—all the things James wanted her to say, each comment another application of balm until the wound was fairly covered, and James a little drunk.

"We should put the adoption thing on hold," said Ana, tossing the salad. She thought James would fight her, but he didn't say anything, his head down.

The two of them sat in front of their pasta at last, neither of them eating. Ana wondered if her husband was also feeling that they had lost their grasp. Something had been severed and set adrift; Ana was left feeling arid. But she suspected James's sensation of loss, radiating off his curved back as he picked at his food, was something entirely different, bound to a manhood she could scarcely bring herself to imagine.

In Sarah's living room, weeks later, Ana had told her friend: "James has a beard."

"Is it sexy?" asked Sarah. Ana had never considered this possibility, as the beard was so clearly linked to his firing, to the strange new arrangement in their house. It was the opposite of sexy. It was impotent.

"No. He looks like a fisherman."

"Fishermen can be sexy."

Ana shook her head from side to side and raised her eyebrows, as if considering this possibility.

Finn was sitting with his legs out in front of him, staring up at the TV, where a cartoon someone named Peep and a cartoon someone named Chirp were running through a stream. Finn had a large red ball in his lap, ignored.

Sarah sipped her coffee. She was barefoot, like Finn, both of them optimistic of the spring. Ana wore tall, slim boots over her jeans. In Sarah's house, she never felt the need to take off her shoes.

"Did Marcus ever have a beard?" asked Ana.

"Oh, God, yeah. He went through a whole proletarian thing in his mid-twenties. He was breaking from his parents for good. Bought a van and went west, worked in a national park."

"You're kidding." Ana couldn't see this, picturing Marcus in his plain black sweaters and wire-framed glasses that made her think of German architects. "Where were you during that time?"

Sarah stretched one arm over her head, groaned a little. "Probably backpacking, or screwing around or something. We weren't so serious then," she said. "Really, it was only a summer, when I think about it. I guess he hasn't had too many beards, actually."

The credits of the television show moved across the screen.

"Mommy, more TV. TV on," said Finn, not taking his eyes from the screen.

"Sure, tomorrow," said Sarah. "Can you press the Off button now?"

Finn stood up and pressed the button.

"Good job, Finny! Good job!" said Sarah, clapping. His jeans had little loops on the side, like he might be doing carpentry later. They were about an inch too short.

"I can't seem to get the sizes right," said Sarah as Ana glanced at the pants. She opened her arms for her son to run into. "Everything he owns is either way too big or way too small." The boy took a kiss on the head, then disentangled himself and ran toward a pile of blocks in the center of the room, beginning to stack only the blue ones. Ana wondered if Finn learned these things at daycare—stacking and sorting. She couldn't imagine him at daycare three mornings a week, away from Sarah, though apparently he went. She had never seen them apart.

"Did you notice how I didn't say n-o to him when he asked about the TV?" said Sarah in a low voice. Ana nodded. "I've been reading up. You say: Yes, later, or yes, tomorrow, instead of n-o-t now. It's a tactic. It confuses them, offsets the meltdown."

Ana felt a little sorry for Finn, unwitting citizen of a country of deferred pleasure. The block tower teetered.

"I think James might be depressed," said Ana. "He reminds me of my mother these days."

"What, is he drinking?"

"No, it's something else. He's just not"—Ana struggled—"alive to the world like he used to be. Does that make sense? James has never had any bad luck."

"Do you think it's only bad luck?"

"What do you mean?"

"Well, don't take this the wrong way, but James has a kind of... certainty that might be hard to work with," said Sarah carefully. "You know what I mean. I mean, we love James because we know him, but I wonder, in a workplace, if that could be..."

Ana felt a touch defensive on James's behalf, but she knew that Sarah was right, and the certainty she referred to was, in fact, arrogance. James had left the university when he became a hot young pundit, in high demand after a seminar he designed on the decline of masculinity made him an expert on men. He had a national newspaper column and a radio show by thirty, and then ten years on TV, hosting this and that, called upon to air his views on any subject. James always had an opinion: the return of debauchery, the need for a new waterfront, why hockey matters. Somewhere in there was the book about cultural identity. Oh, James had been so proud at that book launch, but there had only been two trays of cheese. The lack of cheese was the first sign that, as an author, James had arrived late to the party. Store shelves were already heaving with books on cultural identity. No one bought James's. He went back to television, a little stiffer, a little meaner.

"I worry about him," said Ana, but the reason went unsaid because, suddenly, Finn burst into tears. Sarah was on him instantly. Ana watched: Sarah identified the problem—the collapsed tower—and talked to him quietly through his screams, asking him questions: "What can you do to make this better? You don't like it when things you build break, do you?"

Out of habit, Ana imagined herself with a child that age. She stored away Sarah's wisdom and words, trying to picture herself applying them later. But the picture was fainter now than it had ever been. Any child to come would not be hers, in all likelihood. This hypothetical child might even be out there right now, floating in a woman's belly in a faraway country, being carried through a rice field, out of the hot sun. The image didn't excite Ana, or sadden her. It seemed absurd; the stuff of science fiction, of a future she hadn't arrived at yet.

She looked again at Finn being stroked in Sarah's arms and tried to envy it. She knew how James felt when Finn was nearby: She had seen his face, for once entirely drained of rage. After dinner with Sarah and Marcus, she watched her husband on the porch as Finn was wheeled away, sadly waving good-bye at the stroller. Ana rooted around for some feeling to match James's but came up with only a casual affection for this boy, for all boys, a mild curiosity that didn't demand investigation. Hadn't there been a time when the sight of a pregnant woman had caused her to look away, yearning? Hadn't she hidden in that hotel room after the final miscarriage and wept? A chill crept over her body: She needed to find that person again, or James would be lost to her.

When Finn calmed, scurrying toward a basket of clean laundry on the edge of the room, Sarah returned to the couch, rolled her eyes at Ana, and looked expectant, waiting for her to start the conversation where it had stopped. Ana admired Sarah's silences; they had a kind of presence, like rooms she was inviting Ana into.

"I feel like..." said Ana, groping for it. "I feel like I miss him. I miss something we were." She was remembering the previous night, how she had returned home and James was gone, as usual. He had made some kind of silent commitment to not being home when she got home, as if to sustain the scaffolding of the life before he got fired. Ana did not ask him where he went.

In the immediate wake of the firing, there had been meetings, interviews, and then a long late-night conversation about James taking "a break." Perhaps they could live off her salary while he tried his hand at fiction, maybe wrote a script on spec for a hard-hitting cop show about the politics of downtown living. Ana trod delicately while they spoke, knowing James did not want to hear anything but yes, yes, yes, that he saw everyone but her huddled together against him in a giant no. They could afford for James not to work, after all, because Ana had always made more money, and because, most of all, they didn't have children. Neither of them said this, but it was there, breathing between the lines of the conversation.

James had come in after Ana had changed from her dress into blue jeans and a T-shirt, was pouring herself a glass of white wine and standing at the back French doors, looking out at the churned-up garden, still unfinished. The landscapers had vanished around the time James lost his job.

James slammed the door, dropped his jacket on the floor, kicked off his shoes so they blocked the doorway. Ana was watching all of this from far away in the kitchen, across the first floor, seeing through the walls that used to be there. James had a drink in his hand within seconds. He had not said a word.

"Nice day, dear?" she asked in a June Cleaver voice.

"Not really," he said. "Do you know the only thing worse than having someone say to you: 'Do you work in television?' "

Ana didn't answer, recognizing a setup.

"It's: 'Didn't you *used to* work in television?' "

Something had happened at Starbucks.

James told this story while lightly pulling at his beard, like he might be trying to hurt himself. Then he said: "Good night," and went to bed without supper.

Ana didn't want to tell Sarah these details. They were humiliating and could be used against her. Ana was still selective with her new friend, still wondering if she was like the other girls Ana had known in her life, with their dizzying switches from kindness to spite. James had told Ana she would always have a problem with other women because she lacked sentimentality, and because she was beautiful. But Ana hated this idea of her sex and refuted it, looking always for that woman friend who would hold her fire and prove James wrong.

And so Ana kept coming here to Sarah's, watching Finn grow, carving something into the space when the men weren't around, listening to her friend talk about her own long days, her fears for her son, her hopes for her future. Ana genuinely liked this woman, this chaotic person who left a huge bag of cat food in her hall for weeks and weeks, just walked around it instead of moving it to the pantry. The house was filled with unfinished gestures, doors off their hinges propped against half-painted walls.

Her own home was a study in paucity. In the past couple of years, Ana had gotten rid of every little tchotchke: a pink velvet bobbleheaded rabbit she bought in Chinatown on a whim; a virgin pencil case, useless because it was too short for pens; an empty picture frame; little half pads of stickies. Over the course of one week, she moved from room to room, drawer to drawer, putting items in liquor store bags. Days later, when she heard the rattle of the garbage truck in the alley, Ana watched from the window, wondering if she should cry out: "Wait!" and save the bobblehead, or even the pencil case, save them not because they were attractive or useful but just because they were hers, and in that way, valuable, maybe.

And yet, Ana felt calmed at Sarah's. She didn't require her white space when Sarah was around.

She helped her clear the coffee dishes. Finn circled their feet like a shark.

"Sarah..." Ana began, moving the dishes around on the counter.

Sarah turned to her, open-faced.

"How did you know?"

"Know what?"

"Know you wanted a kid."

Sarah raised her brows a little. "Oh," she said. She puzzled a moment. "Well, I guess it's kind of like when you ask gay people, 'When did you know?' and they say, 'I always knew.'" Then she added: "What about you? When did you know?"

Ana moved the dishes side to side.

"I'm not sure," she said. Then she looked up. "Same, I guess."

Finn moved in, and Sarah leaned over to pick him up, distracted by his murmurs.

At the door, Ana kissed Sarah on the cheek, and Sarah tilted her head. "Everything okay?" It sounded so much like a statement that Ana could only nod her assent.

When she'd arrived home that night, James had dinner on the table, a glass of red wine poured and breathing for her. It was as if he had felt her pulling away, betraying him just a little over coffee, as if her lack of faith were casual and passing.

He was funny and light. Even the beard looked trimmer. They ate dinner in the breakfast nook, with the French doors open, looking at a huge hole in the yard. After months of delays, the contractors had showed up with shovels and begun digging again. James had simply found them there, as if it were the most normal thing in the world. He did not ask what they did with all the dirt they removed.

After dinner, as Ana cleared the dishes, James rubbed up against her, and to his surprise, she responded, pushing back, putting her hand down his pants. He had developed a nut brown tan from the sun where his face was unbearded. Ana wondered if he'd had a good day writing, and felt, maybe, that a corner had been turned.

James pulled the blinds in the living room and the kitchen, sealing the house from one end to the other. Ana appeared behind him naked. She unfolded a clean kitchen towel, carefully placing it over the sofa cushions before lying down, spreading herself open, and he stood above her, looking down, breathing heavily. It was the first time in a long time that they had been together without the presence of this third, shadow person, nudging them forward, giving them reason. The absence flickered as sadness in James, and then it snuffed itself out. He buried his face in his wife's neck, moving his tongue between her breasts. For Ana, she felt as if she had been fucking while swathed in a gauze for two years, trying to feel through the thing between her and her husband. But now, with her hands on his hips, her body was greedy, ferocious for him. They closed in on something like joy.

Only when she had tied the last garbage bag and closed the windows and drawn the curtains and folded the laundry and put it away—only then did Ana stop and take a different kind of tour of the house, touching surfaces with her fingers. In part, she was checking the thoroughness of her work, but also, she fingered Marcus's shirts hanging in the closet, ran her nails through a mound of necklaces in Sarah's jewelry box. She touched the walls of photos in their mismatched frames. The family was so young; no old or sepia shots of ancient relatives, nothing from a life before. It was as if when Finn arrived, he brought with him the present and erased everything behind him. The city was filled with these urban orphans. Ana had seen cases of erasure often in her Legal Aid work as a student; poverty and aloneness arrived together often. A few circumstances and they were in the system: an only child; a refugee claim; a parental estrangement; an accident.

But there were different kinds of connection now. Why hadn't she considered this?

Sarah and Marcus had one desktop computer, in a room that was part den, part office. A small spotted blanket with a stuffed cow's head curled on the office chair. Ana suddenly remembered Finn dragging it around by the head, holding it up to his mother, saying, "Moo." *That's something,* she thought, putting the cow blanket in the basket of things to take home. *I know something.*

The computer flickered and hummed, and Ana imagined the many Facebook friends who must be curious or devastated, saw the static hands stretching out from the screen—Password.

She tried a few: "Finn." "Finneas." "12345." Then she froze herself out; too many failed efforts. She was helpless against the electronic locks, truly disconnected.

Ana added to her mental list: password retrieval. She knew the law: There would have to be a death certificate. But Sarah wasn't dead. It could take weeks or months, then.

She turned off the computer.

Ana removed three frames from the wall: one of Finn as a baby in a bathtub; Finn as he looked now, but with shorter hair, wearing blue overalls, his chin covered in whipped cream, grinning. The third showed the three of them together, heads touching, Sarah's eyes squinting with laughter. The camera was close to their faces, as if held at arm's length, taken by Sarah or Marcus. The background was blue, unrecognizable. Ana studied the picture for clues and then placed it with the others in her briefcase.

Ana changed back into her skirt and blouse, folding Sarah's clothes into the suitcase. She would wash and return them before...what? *Where is this going?* Ana had never done well without a deadline. She still looked at every completed report at work as a potential A. She sometimes accidentally said: "Can I get an extension?"—the vernacular of a model student. This, in the end, was why she had chosen law. The organization, the binding of the fat books, the long, determined answers, and passes and fails. And to be paid! Ana still couldn't quite believe how well compensated she was simply for making sense out of chaos, which she would do for no money at all.

Ana pulled the duffel bag onto the front porch, placed the garbage in the bins at the side of the house. She put a laundry basket of toys in the trunk. A small brown rabbit smiled up at her. She turned it on its side.

When she was safely in the car, with all the doors locked, she let out a long, soft whimper, a sound she was getting used to hearing.

On the way home from daycare, Finn had stories to tell, about bananas and a soccer ball that went missing and Elijah and Kai and Ella B. and Ella P. They walked side by side, Finn stopping every few steps to pick up a broken straw or a leaf, past the eyes of the old Portuguese men on their porches, their compressed bodies upright, hands on knees.

James pulled a narrative out of the streaming chatter, repeated it back to Finn: "You told Ella B. not to take your Jingo block?" Finn nodded, continuing the story.

They stopped in the park. Finn climbed the jungle gym while James stood below him like a human mattress.

It was dark already by the time they reached the sandwich store on the corner surrounded by houses with wrought iron fences and birdbaths.

"Should we get some sandwiches for dinner?" asked James.

"For Ana?" James was surprised. Had Finn said her name out loud before? He nodded.

The boy ran ahead, pulling the heavy door of the sandwich store open with determination. He instantly homed in on a dusty jellybean machine in the corner and stood twisting the dial.

"Do you want a sandwich?" James asked Finn.

"Girl cheese."

"We can get that at our house. These are veal sandwiches."

A girl a little older than Finn came in with her mother and installed herself at the jellybean machine, too, hitting the top of it with her fist. Her mother glanced at James, smiled distantly.

"I called...," she said to the man behind the counter. He went to retrieve her food, leaving the woman and James side by side, each regarding a child.

"Lilly, no banging. Don't bang. That little boy was here first." The girl scampered to the pinball machine and began hitting the glass instead. Finn followed, staring at her.

"Lilly, don't bang!"

"Give me a quarter!" yelled Lilly.

"No, not now. Dinnertime," said the mother, tucking her bag of sandwiches under her arm.

"No! I want to play pinball!" screamed the girl.

The mother glanced at James woefully.

"He looks like you," she said.

James wanted specifics on this comment. "Really? You think so? How do you see that?"

But there was a flurry of activity at the counter, paper bags crumpling and a loud cash register churning, and when James had finished paying, the woman and the girl were gone. Finn stood at the pinball machine, tapping it lightly.

James felt smug that they had made it through the ordering, the waiting, and the paying, without incident. He followed Finn, the bag of sandwiches in his hand, the little boy running ahead then turning back to check on James every few moments, just in case.

The sun was setting, and the fall light stained the rooftops of the houses caramel. At the top of James's street, the curtains in the brothel house fluttered as they walked past, as if someone had just backed away from the window. James knew Ana's theories but had never seen anyone come or go from there. He glanced at the recycling bin on the curb, bottles of vodka and Diet Coke. Nothing edible.

Finn ran from the sidewalk into the brothel's muddy front yard, pocked with cigarette butts.

"Come on, Finn. You can't be up there," James said, trying to sound casual. Finn kept going, up the stairs, as if he lived there, as if he might reach up and turn the knob, step inside to some other life awaiting him there.

From the sidewalk, James yelled: "Finn, get down! That's

not your house!" Finn ignored him, focused on his repetitious ascent and descent of the stone staircase. Again, the flutter and shadow in the front window. James stormed the walk.

"Finn! I'm talking to you!" He grabbed the boy's wrist—So light! A wishbone!—and pulled him. Finn's body buckled. He yelped, making himself liquid. James was forced to drop the sandwiches and grab Finn, who kept slipping from his hands. He finally located two solid parts and hauled his smallness over his shoulder, trying to squat down and grab the sandwiches, all the while half running away from the brothel house.

Finn squawked like an injured bird. James glanced back to see the door to the brothel open and a woman's shape appear. She was transparent, the tops of her bare legs covered by a long T-shirt. She held a cigarette by her hip. James moved quickly away.

They approached their house like this, with Finn wailing, a slab of snot and tears across James's body, his legs kicking. Ana opened the door to them.

"I heard you coming," she said, glancing up the street toward the other houses, their insides lit up in the dusk. Noise traveled between the houses and got trapped, like a tunnel.

James dropped Finn on the couch. The boy lay on his back, still screaming and kicking. Electrocution. Drowning. Ana hovered in the doorway.

"Is this normal?" She had to shout to be heard.

"I don't fucking know!" screamed James.

"What are you going to do?"

He glanced at her. She was shivering; she looked barely born.

James went to Finn, squatting down, trying to pin him like a wrestler.

"It's okay! Finny! It's okay!"

Finn's arms flailed, and his small right fist jutted upward, clocking James in the eye. James reeled back; Ana screamed, and at that sound, Finn went still and silent at last, shocked to hear Ana scream, shocked to see James, his hand over his eye, staggering backward in a stream of fuckfuckfuck.

Finn sat, bewildered, his face streaked.

Ana was upon James, pulling back his hand, looking at his eye, a small trickle of blood.

"Oh my God," she said.

"His fingernails are too long," said James.

"His fingernails!" gasped Ana, reaching for the blood. Finn watched from wide eyes as Ana quickly stroked James's hair, then hurried to the bathroom for supplies.

James watched her leave the room and felt the familiarity of Ana in charge. Something fluttered nearby, in the corner of his bloodied eye. Finn, terrified on the couch, quivering.

"Hey," said James, opening his arms. "It's okay. It was an accident."

"Sorry," said Finn, flinging himself into James's embrace. James wondered if he could hear the man's heart up against his child's ear.

"Me, too."

Ana came upon them like this, a tube of medicine in her hand. Her first impulse was to turn around and give them the privacy they looked like they deserved.

James knew how to reclaim Finn. He whispered to him until he began laughing, rocked him gently.

"Kleenex," said James with his hand out. She frowned, but found him a Kleenex in her purse.

"Blow," said James, and Finn did.

Finn's breathing slowed to something human. James sang quietly: "'Rockin' rockin' leprechauns . . .'" Finn smiled.

Ana blurted out: "Look, Finn, I picked up some of your things."

James glanced at her.

"I left work early," she said. Finn was off James's lap, toward a stack of books on the dining room table. Ana had lined up his toys as if they were for sale: a puzzle, a small Thomas the Tank Engine, a flashlight.

"Scaredy Squirrel!" he crowed, flipping pages.

In this way, the evening was rescued.

There was a pattern now, after only a week. The script was foreign to Ana, but James recognized in it shades of his own childhood. In James's earliest memories, he was older than Finn, in kindergarten. James and his brother walked home from school together past rows of identical stucco houses differentiated only by the garages: single or double, left or right. Lawns were square. Trees were thin and young. James's mother waited in the kitchen with a tray of Yugoslavian cookies. James and Michael sat cross-legged in front of the television. James licked the frosting off the cookies, leaving the soggy wet breadstick. No one else had these cookies in the unmarked plastic bags from the market downtown.

With his mother's nudging and prodding, the family moved from wake-up to breakfast, from breakfast to school, school to sports, and on through the steps until bedtime, when James leaned between her knees as she combed his wet hair. The entire day's effort designed to push the clock toward sleep beneath *Star Wars* sheets.

If James's father ever brushed James's hair, he tugged and pulled. He had a job like Ana's that bored James to the point of cruelty. He came home late and got up early, always catching the train into the city or back from the city. *Where is he?* "He's on the train," said his mom. So when James pictured his father, he was astride a train: a superhero with legs dangling past the tiny windows, hurtling down the tracks, briefcase under his arm.

The year James entered high school, his mother got her own job, at the library. It turned out that she had been going to school, too, while he was in school. Where was the evidence of this? The studying, the exams? In the house, her talk was only expended on two boys and a man. Their mother vacuumed, shooing them from the room. And they would go, the three of them moving into the next empty space, still talking baseball and hockey statistics, a triangle that kept relocating as she approached with her machine.

James was the handsome one and got a little leeway for it, space to grow his hair and start smoking pot. He hung out with older kids who were into Bauhaus and New Order. When he didn't sign up for any sports teams in eleventh grade, he and his father had nothing left to talk about. (Years later, James started playing hockey again and following the NHL like he had as a kid, memorizing statistics over the evening paper. Hockey returned as the animating force of holiday conversations with his father.)

With his mother at work, his father stayed in the city later, and the house was empty more and more, so James kept out of it. He began taking the train himself, hopping off downtown for concerts, hovering until closing in record stores and bookstores, absorbing Aldous Huxley and Tom Wolfe and Bob Dylan. Meanwhile, Mike got his hands on a computer and began programming. Tapes gave way to floppy discs until finally, at twenty-six, he built a software company and designed a font called Tamarind. Then, a decade later, he sold both for an amount that was never made clear. Millions. Mike was still around, living in a northeast pocket of the city where people had driveways and no sidewalks.

James hadn't called his parents in weeks. When he spoke to them last, he hadn't told them he'd lost his job. That they hadn't called to ask him why he was no longer on TV was confirmation of what he'd suspected for years: They weren't watching. It's not that they disapproved of what he did, but it had never occurred to them that it mattered.

James went over this story. He didn't think about it often, but it had been rising up in him lately, especially as he held Finn between his knees after the bath, combing his hair. What had happened between Marcus and his parents? How did Sarah's parents die? Only vaguely, James remembered a tale of a car crash. Maybe.

Though James had a gift for the narratives of strangers, he had never been good at keeping straight the most dramatic events of his friends' lives. He'd had a girlfriend for two years in university who told him in the first week of their relationship about having childhood cancer, and it left his mind almost before she'd finished speaking. Then, a decade later, James had run into her on a crowded street, thin and wasted, a toque pulled down over her forehead. "It's back," she said hoarsely, and for days, he had no idea what she was talking about until the memory slithered up, its head poking through the potholes in his memory while he was alone on the southbound University line: leukemia.

If Sarah's parents had been killed in a car accident, she probably felt inured to that particular disaster; she had been struck once, it could not happen again. What are the odds? He once interviewed a woman who gave birth to a child the size of a pop can, a preemie born at twenty-six weeks. She told him: "As soon as you're on the wrong side of statistics, statistics don't mean anything."

James saw Finn before the boy noticed him in the doorway. Finn sat in the middle of James and Ana's bed, surrounded by stuffed animals. Past him, through an open bathroom door, Ana's back was bent, yellow gloves pushing, scrubbing out the tub.

James snuck up behind him, then leaned down and kissed Finn's warm neck. Finn squealed a little, as if he'd been tickled. As he clipped Finn's fingernails with his large nail clippers—he could fit two of Finn's fingers between the blades—James was filled with a sensation of pure joy. He had escaped so much. Loss was all around, but it had never really landed on him. This realization gripped him and shook him into something like dizziness. He looked at the small pile of fingernail clippings on the tissue, and thought: *Oh, happiness, happiness, happiness.*

James read Finn the book about the squirrel and tucked him under his new sheets, beneath a swirling mobile of a bald eagle. "Sing light," said Finn.

"Can you sing it?"

Finn shook his head. "You."

"'You light up my life'?" sang James in a silly voice. Finn laughed and was distracted enough to let James lead him away from this unmet wish. He turned out the lamp.

"Door open," said Finn. James opened it a crack. "More." And that was fine.

James had one leg in his sweatpants when Ana appeared in the bedroom doorway.

"Where are you going?"

"Wednesday. Hockey," he said, pulling his Maple Leafs jersey over his shirt.

"You're leaving me alone with him?"

"Yes, but I snuck a pound of horse tranquilizers into his sippy cup so I don't think you'll have any problems." He gave Ana his cute face.

"Seriously, James. Do you really think it's good for him? He's attached to you. If he wakes up..."

Fully dressed now, James moved past Ana in the doorway and into the hall. She followed him downstairs.

"It could it be traumatic for him," she continued. "More traumatic?"

"Wait a second," said James, again brushing by Ana to the basement. She waited in the hall, chewing the meat from her thumbnail. James returned with his hockey bag.

"Are you listening to me?" asked Ana. James squatted at her feet, tying his running shoe.

"Yes, but you're being crazy. He's not going to wake up, and if he does, so what? He knows you. Give him a hug, change his diaper."

"Don't talk to me like I'm an idiot," Ana snapped. "That's not what I mean."

James let out a long, slow sigh, eyes raised to the ceiling. "What do you mean, then, Ana?"

"Don't talk to me in your TV voice."

"Come on—"

"You know what I'm trying to say." She sounded panicked, invoking a tone that should be reserved for fires and accidents. "I think it might be bad to leave him so soon. How important is hockey tonight? Is it an important game?" Ana's understanding of sports was so limited that she believed James was working toward something, a cup or a pennant.

"If I don't play, the numbers aren't even." His bag began to pull uncomfortably on his shoulder. James opened the door. A gust of cool air came upon them, but Ana was still hot with anger.

"I hate it when you tell me I'm crazy," she said, and James recognized his mistake.

"I didn't say you were crazy. I said you were *being* crazy." He leaned in and kissed the top of her head. "You'll be fine. He never wakes up. And he likes you, Ana."

"That's not what I mean," she said, pulling away. But even as she watched James walk down the street toward the rink, his stick bobbing above his shoulder, she could not exactly figure out what she meant. She was trying to get him to recognize some new kind of failure that was waiting for them. She closed the door.

She wanted him to feel it the way she did, the certainty that every interaction with Finn was changing the boy, altering his being in ways that could not be undone. She wanted her husband to recognize the impossible weight of that and return to shield her.

She felt that James was leaving her there as a test, that she was forever under scrutiny now, since Finn's arrival. The expectations were smothering. For so many years, she had tried to join James in his unspoken resolution that a child would be the release of something in her. She knew that he believed she needed saving, from her drifting parents and sharp-edged youth. He was the first part of that rescue plan; the baby would be the second part. He had said it in the beginning of their life together, often stroking her hair: "My poor girl," he said. "Let me take care of you." That was the great unspoken switch of their relationship: Everyone thought she saved James from his slovenliness, his intellectual chaos, but in fact, up close, it was Ana who was in need of salvation. The birth of a baby, then, the small hand that would pull her over to grace.

But up rose the black and wild doubt: *What if I can't do it?* She had felt uneven since Finn's arrival, staring at walls and windows, barely able to put on her boots that morning, staring at the zipper pull in her fingers.

How is motherhood supposed to feel? Because she wasn't sure that it should feel like this, so much like terror. And her husband was leaving her alone with that feeling, while he went to play hockey.

That was what she had meant to say.

The game was particularly cruel, and James wasn't up for it. Doug, especially, had his elbows out and some kind of rabies bubbling up in him. James couldn't get the puck, and after one ferocious futile burst down the ice, he lost his breath and had to stop, leaning over with his hands on his knees.

There were two women playing: Alice Mitchell, who ran a small catering company, and a tall woman James hadn't seen before. Her blond hair sprayed like a skirt from the bottom of her helmet.

Alice skated up to him and gave him a gentle whap on the butt with her stick.

"Doug's an asshole tonight," she shouted.

James nodded, touched and embarrassed by the sympathy. He skated away fast but only got to the puck a few times, once on a generous pass from Alice. Doug plucked it from him within moments.

After, they went for beer. James checked his cell phone for messages from Ana, but there were none. Six of them sat in the small bar, a converted diner with Dixie music on Sunday mornings. James had been going there for years, but this time he was acutely aware that Ana could not be with him. Someone had to be at home. He felt her out there, tethered to their house, to Finn's sleeping body.

Doug leaned in, separating him and James from the rest of the group.

"Where the hell have you been? Lee's all: 'Where's Ana? We never see you guys,'" he said. Doug was an old friend, but possibly not a good one. They had worked together years ago. When Doug left for a cable station, that might have been it. But somehow Doug had kept up the momentum, phone calls and birthdays and hockey. In the moments when Doug was at his crassest, James suspected he kept in touch only on the off chance that James would prove useful to him at some point. For all his hard drinking and cultivated blue-collar vulgarity, he was a ruthless independent producer with a constantly rotating staff, usually quitting because of his tantrums. In the burning desert in Jordan, working on a documentary, Doug had stayed in a broken, overheated truck while an unpaid assistant pushed it. This incident had made him famous in TV circles. His name caused fear in the twentysomethings who did his grunt work. He won an International Emmy for the Jordan documentary, which was about relics.

"I've been busy. The book's coming along," said James, quickly burying his face in the pint of beer.

"Who's your publisher?" asked Doug.

"It's early stages. Not sure yet." James raised the glass again.

Doug recognized that pause and changed direction.

"We're having a small dinner thing. You know Rachel Garland, right? She did that figure skating miniseries?" James knew them all and all of their accomplishments and failures, those who made weekly commutes to Los Angeles, taking meetings, selling themselves. James had been excused from that particular footrace. He had designed his life to be above it, in fact, by staying at the public station for fifteen years. But it gnawed at him, the mystery of the commercial world. He tried to imagine being inserted into a life where he had to buff and box and sell himself like Doug did every day. Making pitches at boardroom tables in Los Angeles; throwing out a hundred ideas and having one stick. James recoiled from such odds.

He couldn't bear what he knew was coming: a litany of other people's successes. Doug did this under the guise of catching up.

Off Doug went. Rachel was running a big international coproduction cop show. Lee had a new gig adapting a children's series involving turtles. Rachel's second husband, Bill Waters, would be at the dinner. He was back from being director of photography on a feature in New York. Many of these people had passed through James's show at one time or another, and then moved on. James had the sensation of being a high school teacher watching his most promising students in cap and gown turn around year after year, waving good-bye or giving him the finger. And now he wasn't even the teacher. He was the janitor.

Did any of them have children? He looked around the table, which had filled up with empty beer bottles. Alice had kids, from a first marriage. There was a period when all the women they knew were pregnant, and then, at parties, babies appeared early and disappeared later. But these babies lacked specificity; James hadn't connected with any of them. Now those babies had become children, large and staring. James found them at the same parties when he was looking for the bathroom. They sprawled on couches in rooms with the television on, or were tucked far away, sleeping. Suddenly he felt acutely aware of all he had not been privy to; the conversations he had been excused from in his life, just by being male and having a barren wife.

"We'd have to get a sitter," he said.

"What? Are you joking? Did you guys adopt or something?" Doug laughed then, as if such a thing were entirely improbable. "Did you get a dog?"

"We're looking after a little boy. His parents died," said James. "Well, his father died. We don't know if the mother's going to be okay or not." (James didn't mention that the daily call to the hospital was always the same: "Stable." Ana had visited twice, while James looked after Finn. With her coat on, she reported: "Stable," pouring a glass of wine so quickly that it splashed.)

"What the fuck? Who? Are you serious?" said Doug.

"You don't know them."

"Maybe I do."

"Marcus Lamb and Sarah Weiss."

"Don't know them." Doug's voice contained a hint of disappointment, as if he'd been unfairly excluded from a party.

"How old's the kid?"

"Two. A boy. Finn."

"Todd Banks and his wife, you know them? They've been trying to adopt from China, but it's totally fucking impossible right now."

"I guess we're lucky," said James, and Doug didn't notice the sarcasm in his voice, or let it be. (But a gnawing thought now: What about China? What about the baby in China, separated from them by only a few signatures and uncut checks?)

"That is fucking crazy, man. How's Ana?"

"She's okay. Good."

Mark Pullen, sitting on James's other side, leaned in. "Did you hear that? Alice sold her screenplay."

James turned to her.

"I didn't even know you wrote," he said, trying to add a smile to the observation.

"I don't really. It's a comedy about catering for the rich and famous. I wrote it in three weeks." She beamed. Mark, her husband, put an arm around her. He directed commercials, and in all the years that James had known him, he'd never heard him aspire to anything else.

Alice Mitchell had only ever been kind to James, and her peanut brittle was a phenomenon. But he hated her a little in that moment.

"She's being modest. She's a great writer," said Mark. "We just got back from L.A., and the producer said she had a voice like Nora Ephron."

"'Like Nora Ephron before she got boring.' It was more of

an insult to Nora Ephron than a compliment to me." Alice kept smiling, so wide and bright that James could hardly look upon it.

He stood up suddenly, searching his pockets for cash.

"Alice, I'm thrilled for you," said James, leaning down and giving her a kiss on the cheek.

"See you Friday?" shouted Doug as James walked off, waving over his shoulder. James didn't answer.

At home, he dropped his gear in the hall and walked quickly up the stairs to Finn's room. He went in and put his hand on Finn's chest, which rose and fell confidently. This touch drained him of his anger.

After he'd showered and crawled into bed next to Ana, sleeping soundly, James had a thought: *This might be temporary.* Finn might be only a houseguest. Marcus's parents could appear, with their blood ties ready to tighten around the boy. Or Sarah—Sarah could wake up. She could wake up and Finn would be reabsorbed into her, never to be seen again.

James turned over these scenarios in the dark, still feeling Finn's chest under his hand. These futures burned behind his open eyes, waiting for an answer.

"Should we wait out here?" James always looked for a reason not to go into the nursing home. Usually he would arrive after Ana, with coffees purchased in slow motion, or drop her off to circle the block several times under the guise of looking for parking. This time, of course, with Finn in the car, he had a good reason to be absent. Still, Ana was irritated; he had begun to throw Finn in front of her to block motion—conversations and fights ceased because the boy was there, indicated by James with a flick of his head, a finger to the lips.

But he was right, of course, that no child would want to come into this place, especially when there was a playground across the street. A few patients had been wheeled there, and they sat with their wheelchairs pointed toward the jungle gym like it was a television. Knit blankets sausaged their legs. Their faces ranged from glazed to sleeping. A nurse, jacket over her green uniform, huddled and smoked, ashing behind her back.

"Come in and say hi. She'd like it," said Ana. James nodded.

It had taken forty-five minutes to reach the home. Ana had carefully chosen this old age home, in a quiet, unvisited patch of the city. It had a good reputation, but that wasn't why Ana selected it: Placing her mother in a home closer to their house was unthinkable. Ana couldn't imagine being out on one of her night jogs and running past a building that contained her mother or turning a corner to see it on her way home from an evening out. Her mother being groomed and fed in the daylight was an image of some comfort, but to think of her locked in at night, her favorite time of the day, forced into her room like a cat in a cage—this wasn't something she could bear to stumble upon accidentally.

She had been feeling responsible for her mother most of her life. That responsibility trailed faintly after her, a tissue on her heel, slightly shameful. Even as a child tucked away in her room where the window looked at a brick wall, and on that wall she could see India, where her father always talked about going. She pictured cows and cinnamon and swarms of silk-swathed bodies in crayon colors, a *National Geographic* spread. She thought about India when they moved again, lying in her room with the window that looked at another window, or the next time, when there was no bedroom for her at all but a bed in the hallway. By then, her father had his wish. He went away, transforming from flesh and blood into a series of Christmas cards and occasional phone calls. Examining the stamp (Nepal) and opening the worn, translucent envelope one year, a photograph fell out—a young woman clutching a baby. "You have a sibling!" he wrote. It took another year before Ana found out the sibling was a boy.

Her father moved to Costa Rica, and the letters never again mentioned this boy, or his mother. Ana got older and stopped opening them. And as if her father knew the audience had left the theater, they stopped coming. Silence, now, for eight years.

So Ana and her mother became a pair. Ana went with her mother to the courthouse and, in front of the judge, erased her father's name, took her mother's. There was love, but also the bottle. Once her father left, Ana's mother navigated them toward the smallest apartments in "better neighborhoods," a phrase peeled from the walls of her own childhood in a riverside university town. Her mother had been a child in a house that could properly be called a mansion, with a small circular swimming pool and a brainless Doberman pinscher that barked at the bushes. Ana spent weeks there in the summer heat. She saw her grandmother's long, teenage fingernails on her curved hand, shot through with purple veins; her grandfather's high-waisted pants, his box of war medals.

They wept when Ana waved good-bye in the driveway, days before September. Her mother sat sober and stared straight ahead, shaking hands clenching the wheel.

"You don't know what they're really like," she said, when Ana began to echo their wails, dramatically reaching a hand through the open window as her mother revved and reversed. "You'll never know, thank God."

Before entering the nursing home, there was the unbuckling and the gathering of gear that had spread across the car during the drive—water bottle, diaper bag, book, octopus toy. Finn himself came last, the final object.

Finn ran whooping up the wheelchair ramp, then hopped in and out of the electric sliding doors. James did the same, leaning his body outside: "In!" he called when the doors began to shut and then opened again as he kicked a leg over the invisible line. "Check it out, Finny! Out! In! Out! In!"

Ana signed her name in the reception book. "Hi, Lana," she said.

"Hi, Ms. Laframboise," said the nurse loudly. Lana spoke to the patients the way she, Ana, spoke to Finn: masking her discomfort with volume. It was Lana who put up the flimsy photographs of pumpkins and elves around the holidays, cut from women's magazines. Now, in September, with nothing to celebrate, little circles of cellophane tape peeled off the walls.

Ana scanned the offices behind Lana for her favorite person in this place, the young man who James jokingly called Charlie the Chaplain. Charlie had been a tree planter in British Columbia in his early twenties, which was only a few years ago. Now he crouched and spoke kindly to the men and women who punctuated the corridors and dining area. Ana had seen him walking from room to room, turning off televisions where patients had fallen asleep. Ana could talk to him about neural pathways and reasons, and he always had an unsentimental, interesting bit of science on hand to soothe her with. There was nothing evangelical in him—no condescension, no appetite for cuteness in a space abundant with both. Ana wondered if she could talk to him about Finn, and the uncertainty that was swelling in her. But she felt too shy to ask for him, picturing his lean body, his alert eyes.

"Harry Glick died. Do you remember him?" said Lana.

"No, I don't think so."

"He and your mother used to eat together quite often. You might want to speak to her about the loss."

Ana tried to imagine that conversation and suppressed a laugh.

In his knit hat with frog eyes on the top, Finn was a rock star in the nursing home. The halls cleared for him. Spotting the boy, an old woman with a walker, spine like a C, stopped and, with the exertion of a bodybuilder, raised one fist in a small cheer. Wheelchairs ceased their slow crawl and murmured. Ana had never seen so many smiling faces. They erased the smell of antiseptic and dish soap.

What a horror movie for Finn, thought James. The half-living inmates roused from their coffins. He kept the boy close, their hands locked together. James glanced at him and was surprised to find that he did not look frightened. He looked curious, which was his most common look: a mouth like an O.

James watched Ana gain her rigidity; she could not know how angry she looked, how frightened. It was an expression she wore only in this place, breaking it slightly to smile at the occasional patient as if cued to do so.

"Good afternoon, Mr. Wainwright," said Ana. Mr. Wainwright, a former civic politician of some prominence (he developed the city's waterfront in the fifties—a factoid that popped into James's head as if in a cartoon bubble) sat in front of the television. He waved, smiled slowly, like his mouth was breaking through an icy surface.

Her mother's door was closed. *Lise Laframboise* in calligraphy, a French name that haunted her in government offices and lineups, two generations out of Quebec, and not knowing a word of French.

Ana knocked. "Mom, it's Ana, Mom." No response. She opened the door a little, wondering what she might see. Only once had the fear been fully realized: That day, her mother had been naked, pinballing between the walls, looking for her money. The panic, when it came, was often about money or jewelry she had hidden, or that had been stolen, things lost or taken from her.

This time, her mother was in bed with the lights out, covered up to her chin, her short gray hair a puff atop her head. *Who knits all these wool afghans?* Ana imagined a sweatshop somewhere.

Ana was followed by James and Finn, who stood at the foot of the bed. Ana opened the curtains, and her mother winced in a finger of dusty light. She was not actually asleep, then.

"Mom, do you want to sleep some more?" asked Ana, praying for a "no" so she wouldn't have to return later.

Lise shifted and rumbled, rubbing her eyes. She smiled.

"Ana," she said, a relief for Ana that they could start from this point—her name, Ana—that she didn't have to go back to the beginning today: *You're my mother. I'm your daughter.*

"Hi, Lise, how are you feeling?" asked James, leaning in to kiss her cheek. She brightened falsely.

"Hello," she sang. "I'm fine. It's so lovely today. Warm, isn't it?"

Lise had adored James, his rowdiness, his good looks. She

had never said it, but Ana knew she thought her daughter wasn't quite enough of a spitfire for this man; not enough like Lise herself.

Finn was batting at the bar on the bed, trying to hoist himself up.

"Mom, I want you to meet someone," said Ana, lifting her mother's hand and offering it to Finn. He looked at her, surprised, and James skipped a breath, wondering what Finn would do. He took the old woman's hand, its dead weight, and looked at it against his own small fleshy hand, curious. James realized something: Finn was optimistic.

Ana lifted him up, placed him on the bed, his legs dangling. He turned at an awkward angle to see Lise's face.

"Hello. It's so lovely to meet you," said Lise. Ana almost laughed: Her mother, to whom sobriety was once a special occasion, used to swear like a sailor and had never used the word "lovely" in her life. But these days, she sounded regal when she spoke. In her old age, she was becoming the daughter her own parents had prayed she would become. She had recited a psalm the other day, something Ana had no idea was inside her.

"He's staying with us. There was an accident, and some friends of ours, uh, bequeathed him to us," said Ana.

"Bequeathed?" James laughed.

"Well, how do you explain it?"

"We're looking after him until his mother gets better," said James, feeling an anxious twinge over the possible truth in that sentence.

Lise wasn't going to make sense of the scenario. She stared out the window, frowning.

"Before you leave, can you ask the lady, the tall lady, if

she's finished with my camisoles? I give her my camisoles, and only the white ones come back, but I know there's a black one."

Ana pulled open the top drawer of the bureau to find the white camisoles, and several pairs of underpants, in a gigantic ball, as if her mother had been searching. "Mom, if you can't find something, you have to ask for help."

"I'm quite cold. I'd like my black camisole."

"Well, let's find it." Ana dug down.

"God, maybe she's right. That expensive one I bought her, the silk one, isn't in here. Do you think someone would steal it?" Ana asked James.

"I doubt it. It's probably just in the wash." He hoped Ana wouldn't find it and need to dress Lise. He dreaded his mother-in-law unclothed, her sunken chest and lazy belly, and Ana's rough daughterly care.

"I think I have to ask."

"Don't. You'll seem crazy and then, you know, that could make it hard for your mom."

"What? You think they'll punish her? Is that how this place works?"

Finn slid off the bed and stood between Ana's legs, opening and closing drawers himself, imitating her slamming.

"Lise, would you like me to read to you?" asked James. It was the one task he enjoyed. It gave him something to do and broke the tension of Ana's hovering. He used to bring Lise the kind of literature he believed women liked: *The Age of Innocence, Beloved, The Color Purple.* But his voice always sounded strange around women's words, and soon he turned to Lise's own stack of books, mostly self-help. They circulated on a library cart every couple of weeks.

"Do you have a preference? Eckhart Tolle? *The Secret*?"

"You can read her a banana sticker, it doesn't really matter," murmured Ana, opening the closet, stepping around Finn, who stayed close to her.

"Oh, I like that one," said her mother.

James settled into the lounge chair. The print was enormous. " 'The world can only change from within,' " read James.

Ana didn't bother to stifle a laugh. Finn had found Lise's purple hairbrush and was brushing his hair slowly, in the center of the room.

Lana walked by the open door, quickly, as if hoping not to be caught.

"Excuse me," said Ana, rushing toward the door. "Is it possible that my mother is missing some clothing? I bought her a very nice camisole and I can't find it."

Lana stood opposite Ana, eye to eye. "We do ask our clients' families to label everything very carefully," she said loudly. "But I can check. What color is it?"

"Black, and her name is sewn inside, just like you said." As Lana walked away, Ana shouted after her: "It's an Elle Macpherson!"

She turned to James. "Was that hostile? Am I imagining things?"

"Definitely hostile," said James, turning back to the book: " 'When you are present in this moment, you break the continuity of your story, of past and future.' "

"James, are you even hearing what you're saying?" Ana interrupted. "Really, do you think someone with dementia needs to be reminded to live in the present? The present isn't the problem."

Ana spread a throw over her mother's upper half, and in return, Lise smiled a new, grotesque parody of a smile that she'd been trying out lately.

Ana leaned in to straighten her mother's cardigan and saw, poking out of the back, the Elle Macpherson tag.

"Mom, you're wearing the camisole," said Ana, snapping the blanket in place.

"Ana, you can't get mad at her," said James.

Finn had dumped Ana's purse into the middle of the room—keys, Kleenex, her phone, beeping with texts. He raised his arm in the air, a tube of lipstick northward, its red tip poking through the black casing.

Ana moved toward the lipstick. "Finn, no!" she snapped.

"Ana—don't yell—" said James as Finn opened his mouth and smeared red over his lips.

"Jesus, Finn, that's mine!" said Ana, grabbing the lipstick from his hands, trying to corral her objects of vanity, grasping for a rolling bottle of foundation.

"Oh," said Ana's mother. "What a pretty little girl!"

"Am I interrupting?" Charlie stood at the door, one hand on either side of the frame leaning in, as if stretching after a basketball game. James always thought of basketball when he saw Charlie. He always made sure not to stand too close to him.

"You've got a suit on today, huh?" said James, putting down the book.

Charlie pulled his tie up sideways, sticking his tongue out and bugging his eyes. Then he blushed a little. Ana was always surprised by his boyishness—the shaggy, rock star hair, the West Coast drawl. She had always thought of the church as a kind of elaborate hiding place, tunnels and spaces dug underground, with priests like little black ants moving and scheming far below the real world.

"How are you today, Lise?" he asked, moving into the room, standing near her, without raising his voice.

"Oh, I'm wonderful. My family's here. My camisole is here!" she laughed.

"This is Finn. He's staying with us for a while," said James. Finn hid behind Ana's legs.

"Ah. He has great taste in lipstick, I see. Nice to meet you, Finn." Charlie turned: "Ana, I wonder if I could have a word with you in my office before you leave? Do you have time? Is that cool?"

"Go, go," said James. Charlie's use of the word "cool" irritated James. If some guy under thirty was saying "cool," then clearly James shouldn't be. "We'll meet you in the lobby."

Ana leaned over and kissed her mother on the cheek while the men looked away. Finn returned to Lise's drawers, pulling out pantyhose and twisting them up around his arms.

As they walked down the hall together, Ana noticed the top of a small notebook jutting from Charlie's back pocket.

"Sit down. But don't look around too closely," he said. The room was small and windowless, a desk and a bookshelf filled with stacks of science and philosophy, some spines in Hebrew. A guitar case leaned against the shelf. The desk was a puddle of papers ringed by a pair of mugs and a stack of cardboard coffee cuffs.

Charlie saw her looking at the cuffs and said: "I know. I keep thinking I'll reuse them, but I never have. Not once." He suddenly picked up the entire stack, opened a drawer, and with a dramatic flourish, dropped them in. Ana smiled.

"I can't throw them out," said Charlie. He shut the drawer.

"Is everything okay with my mom?" asked Ana.

"Oh, yeah, yeah. She's doing fine." He riffled through papers, searching. "The reason I wanted to talk to you—I've been writing these songs, and I'm actually going to be performing."

"Oh, I didn't know you did that," said Ana, surprised. "I know you sometimes sing with the patients...."

"I used to be in a band, a long time ago. This is just an open mic night, it's not a big deal."

Ana remembered all the songs that James had played for her over the years, the ecstasy in him, her own feeble efforts to match it. "I wish I were more musical. My mother was. She was always singing under her breath."

"She still does," said Charlie.

"Really?" Ana said, surprised. "I never hear that." She looked at Charlie. "It's primal, isn't it? Some need to express oneself, to be heard."

"Researchers have actually found that listening to music activates empathy in the brain. It gets you out of yourself," said Charlie. "It's almost the only way of communicating with some of the people here." Ana knew those women, the advanced cases, who had lost language entirely. It had begun that way with her mother, searching for a word, an image, a name.

"It must be difficult to work here," said Ana.

Charlie shook his head. "No, it's not," he said. "The managers can be assholes, but the people who live here—that part of it is easy."

Finally, he found the paper he'd been seeking and handed it to Ana. A flyer for his show. "Anyway, I have these songs. I think they're pretty good, some of them. Trying to spread the word."

Ana attempted to imagine Charlie's songs. She pictured holy rollers and heard hymns. "Are they—Christian songs?"

Charlie laughed. "Not in any way that's creepy."

"No, no," said Ana. "When you say 'songs,' I think of love songs, and it's interesting to me, you know, a priest—"

"I'm not a Catholic priest. I'm a chaplain." He leaned in faux-conspiratorially: "I have girlfriends. I don't right now, but you know, I hope to again. At some point." The tops of his cheeks grew pink, reminding Ana of a time when handsome men became unstuck in her presence.

She glanced at the flyer. "I'll try to make it. Thanks, Charlie."

"Tell James, too," he said. Ana stood to leave, and Charlie did the same. "I wondered..." he said. "Have you thought about what we were talking about last time I saw you?"

Ana cast around in her memory.

"Wait—what was it?"

"About your mother, about coming to terms with death."

Now Ana remembered. The conversation had taken place in the lounge, during teatime. Lise had fallen asleep suddenly, and Ana was leaving when she ran into Charlie in the hall. They had sat for an hour or so among the old women in their wheelchairs, against the hot glass windows in the last days of summer. They talked as the kitchen staff cleared plates until only one woman was left, playing solitaire on her tray.

"Oh, yes. Epicurus, right? You were reading him—"

Charlie spoke in a comic, booming voice, as if auditioning: "'Where death is, I am no longer,'" he said, "'and where I am, death is not.'" The hamminess didn't suit him, and quickly, the humor dropped from his face. He spoke quietly. "Did you want to borrow the book? Maybe you'd find it useful."

Ana was ashamed to admit that she had left the conversation with a list of errands at the foreground of her mind. By the time she had made it through the organic market, her cloth bags overflowing with basil and farmer's milk, Epicurus had evaporated. Even now, though Charlie had just spoken, Ana could feel the words' meaning entering her and then immediately exiting. It angered her, this sensation that she could not contain anything of substance anymore. It explained, perhaps, this floating, this inability to come down, for what was there to land on? What did she really know?

"After I saw you, only a few days after, my friend died in a car accident. Finn's father," said Ana.

"Oh, Ana," said Charlie. "I'm sorry."

"It's strange. Until you brought it up right now, I had completely forgotten our conversation. Why were we talking about death?"

Charlie raised an eyebrow, pointed out the open door of his office. A woman in a wheelchair inched past with an electronic whir.

Ana smiled. "Yes, but something specific. What was it?"

"Your mother. We had talked about her degeneration, and you said you were afraid for her."

Ana started. "I did? I said that?" She closed her eyes for a moment. "I've been so tired lately." With her eyes shut, she could sense that Charlie was looking at her face fully, maybe mapping the lines around her eyes, the groove of worry between her brows.

Ana opened her eyes. Charlie glanced away. She remembered the conversation. "And you talked about heaven."

"I couldn't sell you on it, so I tried Epicurus."

"Tell the line to me again."

Without irony this time, Charlie said: "'Where death is, I am no longer, and where I am, death is not.'"

"Right," said Ana, hearing it. "The ending of life can't be

feared, because there's no there there. The cessation of suffering." She paused. "But you—you think of bliss. Angels."

Charlie laughed. "Not really. I think more about grace, being finally in God's grace."

Ana considered this and then said: "You have to die for that?"

They looked at each other, for a held moment.

"I should—James is—"

"Of course," said Charlie.

She clicked the information into her BlackBerry, then placed the flyer in her purse.

"I keep meaning to get one of those," said Charlie. He pulled the small spiral pad of paper out of his back pocket and waved it in the air like a flag.

The visit with her mother had drained Ana, which meant she curled up inside herself like one of those red paper Japanese fortune fish that fold into a tube from the heat of a palm. James saw it, her insides recoiling while the skin of her continued on from task to task.

This faded Ana was next to him and Finn as they walked through the grocery store, as she stood inside the gas station at the cashier waiting for him to fill the car, staring straight ahead, a British beefeater in a cashmere coat. There she was again, barely speaking in Ikea, picking a quilt for Finn, standing back behind the other parents. (*Other* parents? He stopped here: *Real* parents?)

Finn ran in the children's area, sat himself inside a shell-shaped chair, and pulled a vinyl top down so that only his feet stuck out. James tickled his ankles, threw him onto a beanbag hedgehog, tied a stuffed snake around his neck. *Ana, Ana, Ana, a faint outline wavering on the hot desert horizon—where have you gone? Come back to me.*

Ana, staring at the quilt covers blurring together, was thinking: *If you act like a mother, you will feel like a mother.* She chose one that felt soft in her hand.

Then she finds herself back in the basement apartment, her bedroom just large enough for a twin bed and a dresser, the window an air slot up high. She is eleven or twelve, blowing between groups of girls at school, back and forth, following the dictates of the girl who rules them all, Tracy with the large breasts and pink sweaters and thick lips like a wrung-out tea towel.

Ana has consented to bring home Tracy and another girl, named Siobhan. Siobhan is dark—black Irish, she likes to say, an image that conjures up African American leprechauns to other children—and bewildered, except that there is a clot of meanness at her center. She will forever be known as the girl who didn't mind putting her hands on the dead pigeon and flinging it furiously into the bushes.

For this, Siobhan has become Tracy's second. *How did they get here?* Ana can't imagine she invited them, but there they are, they who only tolerate Ana because when she arrived at the school in the middle of the year, near Christmas—her fourth transfer in seven years—a boy named Matthew, a boy who mattered, told another boy that "the new girl is cute." Cute is the most desired currency, and Ana was allowed in. But maybe she is too cute, or not cruel enough or funny enough, because there is no small amount of irritation circling her presence in the group. Still, the girls persist in pursuing her for now, overlooking her oddness in favor of the cute, and she does what is required to keep the scales tipped her way. She fulfills their tasks.

Tracy tells her to walk up to another girl—a girl with a sweaty forehead and sweaters that cradle the fat rolls on her back—and say: "You should tell Jason Cowie you want to kiss him. He really likes you." Ana does this thing, with a grim stomach, but for a few days, she does not have to worry. She is tolerated again.

And then, on a bright spring day, Tracy and Siobhan are behind Ana, two steps belowground at the front of the house, at the door of the basement apartment. She has never taken anyone here before, has not even unpacked her second suitcase. But she has succeeded in humiliating the fat girl, and this visit is her reward. A wave of worry washes over her as she takes the rainbow-striped shoelace around her neck and puts the key in the lock. The door gives, unlocked after all.

Inside, an empty ashtray on the coffee table sits next to two glasses, wet streaked with melting ice. Everything else is sparse. It's not that they haven't unpacked yet, it's that they don't have much to unpack. There's a television on a wheeled stand and a beige corduroy couch, both belonging to the landlord. Empty walls. But her mother's African violets line the windowsill. Any new apartment must have one sunny window where they can sit, rotated a quarter turn every other day. Her mother plucks the dead outer leaves, and uses a toothbrush to remove grains of soil from the fresh foliage. Once a week, Ana and her mother carry the pots into the bathroom where the hot shower is running and the mirror lined from steam. "How are my babies?" murmurs her mother, and now Ana does this, too, when her mother is off teaching her ESL night classes, and she hears the feet of the landlord's family overhead. "How are my babies?" Ana murmurs.

"Who lives upstairs?" demands Tracy.

"I don't know," says Ana, high-pitched. She is looking at her mother's closed door, wondering if she's awake, if she'll come out and see her. The place is so small that if Ana turns her body here in the living room, she can see all of the little kitchen, and the time on the stove: 3:45.

"I gotta whiz," says Siobhan.

"I'll show you my room," says Ana, but they only have to walk a few steps from the living room to the bedroom, banging into one another.

"Nice poster," says Tracy, and Ana combs the comment for sarcasm. She looks at the poster with Tracy's eyes: a pink satin toe shoe balancing on an egg. Ana has never taken ballet in her life. Her mother had a boyfriend last year who gave it to her for Christmas. He was a dancer once.

They are in her room long enough to complete this exchange before Ana notices the bundle under the blankets on her bed. She sees it heaving, face covered. Ana breathes quickly, spins on her axis, tries to lead Tracy out of the room. At that moment, a scream from down the hall, and Siobhan appears, jumping up and down, her arms flapping, a yell that sets off a yell in Tracy, and there they are, the three of them in the tiny hallway, two screaming and one frozen in anticipation.

"Your dad's in the bathroom! He's in the tub! He's totally naked!" Siobhan's eyes like planets.

Her dad? It can't be; he's gone, gone away. But a small part of Ana thinks Siobhan knows something she doesn't, thinks: *Maybe today, maybe*—and shoves the girls to get past in the dollhouse dimensions of the basement apartment.

"Watch it!" shouts Siobhan, and Ana, for once, ignores a command, flinging her body through the open door to the bathroom. There is a man in the bathtub, but the bathtub is empty of water, and the man is not her father. He is older, with a thatch of gray pubic hair, a flaccid penis hanging to the side, an afterthought. His hand flops over the edge of the tub. *He's dead,* thinks Ana, matter-of-factly, and she wonders if she should draw the shower curtain, like in police procedurals on TV.

"He's dead," she says out loud.

Behind her, their bodies against hers in the little room, Tracy has her hand over her mouth, moaning softly. Siobhan is alert, electrified.

"Don't be stupid. He's breathing," says Siobhan, and she is right: The spilling stomach, lined with hair, rises and falls. The natural order of things.

It is this, the breathing, that infuriates Ana, that shifts her mood from terror to rage.

"Go outside. I'll meet you," she says—growls, really, and the girls halt their flapping, surprised to hear Ana, pretty Ana, issue a feral order. They obey, stumbling over each other, and Ana hears their footsteps running, the slamming of the door.

The man's legs are folded, his feet under the taps. Ana gags as she reaches past his toenails and quickly turns on the water, cold, pulls the lever so it comes pouring out of the shower. She pulls the curtain shut, a sound like a train whistling past that covers just a little the scream of the man, the "FUUUUUUUCK" that shakes the thin walls of the bathroom. Ana slams the door behind her.

In her room, she pulls back the quilt on her bed. Her mother has pink underwear on, a thin white T-shirt. Bruises are spaced up and down her legs like piano keys. Her helplessness repulses Ana; the incongruity of her mother's size in her little bed.

Ana leans over her. Quietly, she says: "Mom, Mommy, Mom," and her mother murmurs, rolls, and goes still again. Down the hall, she hears the man stumbling, falling against the little corridor, cursing to himself. Ana imagines the girls outside constructing their story, waiting to pass it along the corridors of the school, to use it to maneuver Ana into a corner where she has nothing, where she will grovel not to be lonely.

And in this moment, Ana—who has wept for dead caterpillars in jars, who has nodded and agreed and packed and unpacked and arrived in new classrooms again and again, genial, amicable, okay with it, the most remarkable, adaptable, malleable daughter!—that Ana exits her body, and a new one settles in. This new one arrives in the split second where she lifts up her open palm and brings it down, down, a cartoon anvil from the sky dropped upon her mother's face, a cheek that jiggles pathetically beneath the weight of Ana's fury. Good. She wants it red, wants it bleeding, down to the bone.

Her mother's eyes flash open, confused. "What—?" She stares at Ana with the blankness that will define her later, in her dementia, right up until her death. "Ana—" But Ana can't look at her, and she is moving down the hall, past the naked hulk of a man in the living room searching on his hands and knees, a glimpsed shadow that Ana refuses to focus on. She grabs her backpack off the kitchen chair and the rainbow shoelace that holds her key. She opens the door to the bright day, the smell of lavender and gasoline.

Tracy and Siobhan are still there, staring at her, wondering how far this transition will go. The new Ana, coarse and livid, stays with them the entire afternoon, as the three girls walk the neighborhood, buying fried chicken and potato salad and Coke at a fast-food place. They carry all of this to the park, eating atop the jungle gym, scaring away the little kids.

When they are finished, Ana says: "I'm staying up here. Show me something funny." She is trying it on. The girls glance at each other; they are unnerved enough that they are willing to obey, for a while longer anyway.

They climb down, and from the top of the jungle gym, Ana watches as Tracy throws her legs over a bar on the swing set and turns upside down, hanging from her knees, back and forth, her arms folded across her chest. Siobhan finds a patch of grass, juts one leg in front of her, throws her hands to the ground and begins flipping her body up into the sky, then back down again; a perfect handspring. One into the next, as if she could go all the way home like this, as if she could start a new human race where everyone walked on their hands, spun with joy from moment to moment.

When she stops, finally, she makes an exaggerated Y shape with her body, like an Olympian, facing Ana in the role of judge. Ana gives her nothing, nods, knowing that boredom is the only right response with these girls.

But she is reeling. The heat of her sore hand spreads through her whole body, up the top of her head, where it pours down over her forehead, into her eyes. The heat combines with the sensation that she has become totally disconnected, as if she is dangling with one hand from the sun. She wants Siobhan to keep flipping, out into traffic, hands first, into a car. She realizes suddenly that she has been bracing herself, living her whole life in anticipation of the bloodiest, most gruesome disaster. Maybe it has happened today.

The sun sets, and the two girls go off, walking west, backpacks bobbing. Ana walks in the dark, past shops that are closing, through the courtyard of a small church. Cars are parking; fathers emerging; teenagers with hockey bags over their shoulders and ballet slippers in their hands. This is when Ana sees the woman get out of her Audi, high heels over black stockings, a gray pencil skirt. This is a businesswoman.

Ana stops, and sees herself in the woman's eyes: a girl in a pink ski jacket, blond hair and bangs. She knows already that if she didn't look like this, it is unlikely that she could stop and stare without being chased away. If she had gray teeth; if she were ugly—then what?

The woman gives her a small, puzzled smile and opens the backseat door. She leans in and backs up with a baby in her hands. Over her other shoulder, the woman has an overstuffed purse, and she balances these two things in the smeared beige early evening, striding toward her home with its porch light on. Its plain redbrick facade is almost identical to the house that Ana and her mother have just moved into. She imagines it might have an identical basement apartment. Who might be down there?

James was searching for a place to park.

"Look at that bastard," he said. "He's taking up two spaces! It's so contemptuous! Where's his humanity?"

Ana nodded, not certain to what he was referring.

"Car!" cried Finn.

"You guys get out here, and I'll circle around," said James.

Ana did what she was told, unclipping Finn and letting him go ahead of her up the walkway. James, glancing from the car, thought: *Take his hand, Ana, take his hand.*

Inside the house, Finn lobbed himself onto the living room couch and sat, legs straight out in front of him. Ana dropped the shopping bags of Finn things: the plastic-wrapped blue sheets; the owl-printed quilt cover. She sat opposite Finn on a white club chair, divided from him by a glass coffee table. Suddenly, Ana was exhausted. She gave in to that pulling, that dark, stuffed feeling in her gut. *Sarah,* she thought, *Sarah.* She felt without gravity.

Finn was picking at the beads on a throw pillow, puzzling over Ana's expression across from him. This was how James found them when he entered. He stopped at the strange configuration of Finn's concerned expression and Ana, head in her hands.

He went to her and placed a hand on her shoulder. She grabbed it hard, and looked up, a slash of sadness across her face.

"I'll make dinner," said James. Ana nodded.

"I come," said Finn, sliding off the chair. He held out his hand and James dropped Ana's to grab it, pulling up Finn to his chest like a monkey plucking a baby from a tree branch.

"That's quite a move," said Ana, trying to bring some lightness. But James and Finn were already in the kitchen, too far away to hear her.

After leaving Finn at daycare, James began walking. He realized that he had not returned to the scene of his firing in weeks and felt a little burst of pride.

James walked past a bleak stretch of tile stores and boarded-up facades. Then, the changes. Two coffee shops side by side: One, a chain with COFFEE written in a yellow-and-maroon font on a grimy awning. A few dry doughnuts on a shelf were enough to draw the old men, thought James. They all sat alone. One worked the belly of a doughnut with his fingers, gazing into space.

And then, a new place—James felt instantly slighted that he had not seen it before, considering that since he'd been fired, he was on these streets all day, every day—filled with people who looked like younger versions of himself, men with beards and laptops, women in black sweaters. These patrons sipped from garage sale mismatched coffee cups, caught in the glow of computer screens. Their feet rested on thick pine planks meant to remind urban people of barns, of something purposeful and only accidentally beautiful.

James caught a glimpse of himself in the large mirror over the bar. The angle caught its own reflection in another mirror across the room, so that James could exactly see the back of his head, right there, floating like a balloon above the gleaming Italian espresso machine. This always ruined his day. His hand rose to the spot, and then dropped quickly, embarrassed by the possibility of being caught. It would have been different, he thought, if he hadn't looked the way he had when he was young. He had always considered himself exempt, and now—this thickening of everything below the neck, this thinning of everything above.

His concern was the most revolting part. He wasn't that kind of guy, was he? The kind of guy who cared about losing his hair? What was he, a woman? He knew better. He'd interviewed a blind woman who climbed Mount Everest! He'd been to the Gaza Strip (or on a helicopter that flew above it, at least)! He had perspective! And yet, and yet—oh, how it used to be: those girls in university, the plain ones who unbuttoned their pastel polo shirts to reveal the bodies of strippers. All that, just for him, because he was kind, or kind enough, and asked one or two questions, and paid for a beer—and then all that body, all the consent to enter and be risen—oh, it was easy.

Until Ana, who was tightly buttoned at first, the friend of a friend of a friend, connections all lost to him now.

Then James set to work: James in the hallway of the law school. James on the doorstep of her apartment. James finally cast as listener, and meeting her mother—her mother, for Chrissake—he had never met a girl's mother before. Ana's was drunk. On the subway ride home, Ana burned with anger and James wanted to put his hand down her pants and push through her, bring her moaning back to him, but he put a protective arm around her shoulder instead.

But what he liked most, maybe, was that once he had Ana, once he could lean close to her and watch other men's eyes flutter in defeat—what he liked most was that he meant it. That he did actually love her. She was strong, but she could be very still, and he craved that. She was never desperate for anyone's approval, and casually comfortable in the demimonde she'd grown up in. They attended parties with her mother's friends, artists and poets, in the kinds of book-lined downtown houses that James had dreamed about from the distance of his suburban childhood. Ana's mother could make her daughter laugh just like James could, teasing her for being the sell-out daughter, beloved and feared for her efficiency.

And when he wasn't with her, he still got the glances, still pushed at the edges of his manner to see if he could get the woman to bend her head back, a throaty laugh, the slight spreading of the fingers around a glass, or the knees in a skirt. James knew: *If I wanted it*... He fed on that *If*, even now that the women he saw most often were the wives of his friends or the aging producers at his old office. A line from a poet he'd interviewed: "A naked woman my age is just a total nightmare."

The women he considered his peers were changing; he had noticed a shift in silhouette, a meatiness between the ass and the knee that didn't exist before, the shape of a traffic cone. Soon they would revert to their ethnic stereotypes, these once exotic Italian and Portuguese women. In a decade or so, they would look like snow women, circles on circles. His mother, once petite, now sported the body of an old Yugoslavian woman in the hills. But not Ana, with her hollows. Not Ana.

It didn't matter how gorgeous his wife was, because he needed, still, the collective giggle of the young women whose lives were just beginning and who let him in under the mistaken assumption that he had some grown-up wisdom to impart about what came next. He needed it through the wedding, and the rise and fall of Ana's attachment to him, the wane of their sex life, the renovations of the house. He needed that small, cooing possibility.

So how had he missed the moment when it stopped? He couldn't pinpoint precisely when his presence in a room began to generate boredom, or when the women got even younger, and the Jessicas became Emmas. At the staff party last Christmas, the handful of pretty young girls were text messaging the whole time, heads bowed. They couldn't keep eye contact. In the months before he was let go, one of them, Ariel, had begun doing segments for his show. She pitched gauzy academic takes on lowbrow subjects: Is Hip-Hop Dead? Teens and Sexting. Why We Need Cute Animals on the Internet. She had a Tumblr, Sly told him. She "repurposed content."

During interviews, she seemed to be always laughing or on

the cusp of laughing. She was furiously short and wore an array of colored scarves, shooting her own work on a handheld camera, writing and producing herself. James remembered when he was surrounded by a cadre of writers and producers and directors and cameramen, a different person for every job. They were all expected to be one-man bands now. What had happened to those guys? Technology had shrunk the world. He made a mental list of all the things that had vanished because of the Internet: newspaper boys; breathless first meetings; the slips of paper he used as a teenager to withdraw money from the bank. These were all things Finn would never know, and that these girls had already forgotten.

At the party, the young women's eyes had skimmed his body with tolerance, stopping on Sly—Those ties! Those tasseled loafers!—with flat-out revulsion. They all had long straight hair, as if there had been a conference to decide, a hairstyle colloquium. James, wearing an Arcade Fire T-shirt under his blazer, had caught a glimpse of himself in a window and found he had no idea what he had been trying to achieve. He'd left the party early to watch the Leafs on TV.

In the café, James positioned himself so that none of the mirrors caught his bald spot. He had his laptop open, the cursor on the blank space blinking. *If terrorism exists, what does it look like?* Delete. *The earliest known terrorists were the Zealots of Judea. Faced with the prospect of the erosion of their Jewish belief in the hands of an idolatrous Roman—*

Faced and hands? Would anyone care about this? Maybe fiction. Maybe a screenplay, about police corruption. He remembered hearing about a local police captain who used to dangle criminals from windows by their ankles. Serpico-ish. Could that be something?

"Wow, you look really serious," said a figure from above, and James began at the feet, eyes moving up the black boots, tights, the long leather jacket with the coffee in hand. Short, unpainted fingernails curved around its sides.

"Emma," he said, and she smiled her red-lipped smile. Her hair was in a ponytail, which had the effect of making her look even younger. She didn't ask to sit but was suddenly next to him. He shut his laptop.

"I read that book you gave me," she said, taking off her jacket.

"You did?" He shifted his features into something meaningful, hoping to hide the fact that he couldn't remember what it was.

"What's going on with you? Everybody said you vanished."

James decided to ignore the question. "Did you like the book?"

Emma nodded. "I think so. It seemed a little"—she paused—"outdated. 'The meaning of television.' I mean, really—television? Does anyone even watch television?"

"I couldn't agree more," said James, sipping his Americano. "Wait, you work in television."

"I'm in digital, remember?"

James nodded and recalled Emma badgering him to blog about his interviews. She had called his footage "content."

"So what's up?" she asked again.

He answered like an echoing cave: "What's up with you?"

"I'm down to part-time. I got a grant to complete my art."

"What kind of art do you do?" asked James, instantly imagining sculpture involving silicone vaginas or a performance piece where Emma sat atop a pile of rotting meat for days at a time.

"Photography. Okay, third time: What the hell are you up to?" Emma shifted her body closer to him, leaned forward a little. James recognized this as flirtation and flushed accordingly.

Emma smelled like food, mangos or cinnamon, a perfume from an oily antique bottle found at a flea market.

James smiled. "I'm playing dad to a friend's kid."

"Single dad?"

James's smile retreated.

"What? No, I'm married." There. He'd said it.

"You said, 'I'm playing dad,' like it was just about you," said Emma, sipping coffee through a take-out lid.

"Well, my wife doesn't play dad. She's, you know, she's the mom." This sounded even worse in tandem with Emma's remote, blank expression in front of him. "That's all I meant. Don't look for subtext, you denizen of the post-post-modern generation." She laughed, even threw back her head. Bull's-eye.

"Where's your friend at, the kid's real dad?" Why the slightly ghetto vernacular among this generation? James was fairly certain that Emma had gone to a liberal arts college somewhere in the Northeast. Swarthmore?

He considered the question, answered slowly. "The boy, Finn, his father died. His mom's in the hospital. There was... this accident," he said, surprised to find the words catch in his throat, surprised because the catch was totally sincere, but also surprised by how well it worked (the old James recognized the panty-loosening effect of this confession, while the present one was proud of himself for being honest with a pretty woman). Emma blinked, put down her coffee, and shook her head: "I'm so, so sorry."

"Yeah, thanks," he said. She looked at him closely, as if anticipating something more. "His daycare's right over there, so I'm going to pick him up later. I came here to write."

"How old is he?"

"He's two. Almost two and a half." And then James couldn't stop himself: "He's a really gentle kid, but I don't know when it's going to back up on him. He seems okay, and his teacher said he's doing well. He knows the alphabet and can count to fifteen, which I looked up online and the number thing, that's advanced, actually. His dad was an engineer, so maybe that's why. I didn't really know Marcus that well, that's the strangest part of this. I knew Finn's mom, a long time ago. She dated my roommate, but I barely remember her. She remembered me—"

Emma nodded, frowning. *What am I saying?* wondered James. *What is this?*

"Anyhoo," he said.

Emma looked at her watch, started to put on her coat.

"I live just over there," she said, pointing across the street to a Portuguese bakery.

"Among the flans?" asked James, with immediate regret. Not funny, not sharp. Emma ignored the awkwardness.

"Above, actually, in the apartment with the green door," she said, rising, tightening her scarf. "Come by sometime and I'll show you my pictures. You might like them." James felt certain that was not true, though he thrilled at the invitation. He tried to imagine Emma's apartment. Would she have milk crates for furniture, like he did at that age? A futon? Somehow he doubted that kids in their twenties lived like that anymore. He couldn't smell poverty on them. Their teeth were very white. Emma's jacket looked as expensive as Ana's.

She leaned in and gave him a double kiss. He sat very still

as she did this, aware that if he so much as moved his head, all bets were off, lips would brush lips, and then what else might touch? He was hungry enough, tired enough of Ana's trail of gentle pushes and rejections, so tired that he might throw a little tongue in there. And then a whorl moving toward the green door above the flans.

He waved at her through the plate glass window of the café, watching as she was absorbed into the accepting crowd.

Ann Silvan moved slowly through the house, as if she might buy it. Ana and James trailed her, up-selling: "I tightened this railing," said James. "Just to be safe." Finn waited at the top of the stairs. "Hellooooo!" he called. Ana noticed that he was barefoot. It felt too cold in the house for barefoot. Would this be marked down on the social worker's notepad?

Ann Silvan walked slowly around the room that Ana had made for Finn. She glanced out the window at the half-finished yard. She asked how he was sleeping, eating, how much he cried.

"You should probably get a safety rail for the bed," she said.

"What's that?" asked James.

"A plastic rail, to prevent tumbling. Any toy store will have one. You just tuck it between the mattress and the frame."

"I put cushions down at night, in case he rolls out," said Ana.

"A rail is better," said Ann Silvan.

Finn jumped up and down on the bed. Ana stared at his bare feet; should she immediately go and fetch socks?

Then Ann Silvan asked: "What time do you get home from work, Ana?"

"Oh, it depends," said Ana. (When had she felt this naked,

this tiny? A job interview? An oral exam? Oh, yes—wheeled into the operating room, looking at the panels on the ceiling. The silence of the nurses with their burka eyes peering over their masks, holding the plastic cap of gas over Ana's mouth. And what they said they did to her: sliced her stomach open like an envelope and put a tiny camera in there, dropped it down like a periscope to peer around at all the bad news. Yes, thought Ana, this felt a little like that.)

Said Ana: "Right before arbitration, or, you know, a closing, then I stay a bit later." Ann Silvan looked confused. "But usually six. Earlier if I can." She was shaving hours off her day the way her mother had shaved years off her age. James cleared his throat.

"I'm here, though. I'm with him all the time," said James.

"When he's not at daycare," Ann Silvan corrected him. Then she smiled. "May I spend a little time with Finn alone? Just a few minutes."

Ana and James nodded.

"We'll be downstairs, Finny. Ann's going to play with you for a little bit," said James. Ana was already on the stairs.

"Did you hear that dig about my job?" whispered Ana.

"At least you have a job," said James.

They sat on the couch. The coffee Ana had prepared grew cold on the table in front of them. Ann Silvan had left a tiny bite mark in a Leibniz cookie.

"I really hope she's not sexually abusing him up there," whispered James.

"Don't. I'll start laughing," said Ana.

"She could be nasty. What do we know about her? We should go to her house with a little pad of paper and fucking—"

The door upstairs opened, and Finn came hopping down the

stairs, both feet on each step. James leaped up to monitor his descent. Ann Silvan followed.

"Everything seems good," she said, moving toward the coatrack in the hall. Ana rose from the couch, surprised.

"I'll write up my report. I know you're seeing the lawyer in a couple of days, correct?" Her black coat had a massive fur collar. Ana looked for eyes in it as Ann and James exchanged information and schedules. Finn sat on the bottom stair folding a plastic robot, trying to turn it back into a truck.

"Can I ask you a question?" said Ann, with her hand on the door.

"Of course," said James, fear rising up to his shoulders. *This is when they take him.*

"Are prices dropping in this neighborhood, since the crash? Where we are, things have really fallen." James exhaled.

"Where are you?"

"Out in the east end. Downtown was the way to go, wasn't it? We should have stayed downtown."

James felt embarrassed now. His home suddenly seemed designed solely to humiliate this social worker.

"Well, Ana's the one in charge of the money. She knew it was a good investment. We're, you know, lucky," said James.

"Yes, you are," said Ann Silvan. Ana searched the comment for a sneer, to no avail. Ann crouched down to Finn's level. "I'll see you soon, Finn. Be happy."

James had the telephone tucked under his chin.

Ana, on the other end of the line, spun around slowly in her office chair, picturing the house where James stood. She knew that the housekeeper had left two hours ago and that by the time she got home, one basket of folded laundry and shiny floors would be the only signs of her efforts. It was constant, the garbage bags and diaper bins full, then empty, then full. What went into the body came out of the body, into Finn's pants, onto towels and cloths. The small, environmentally friendly washing machine for two, tucked behind a door in the corner of the kitchen, was suddenly ridiculous, barely able to contain all the secretions he generated. Then they migrated to James, handprints on his T-shirts and stained-cheek imprints on his sweaters.

"I have to go to the lawyer's," said James, crunching Cheerios under his stocking feet. Finn was picking up the ones that didn't get crunched and stacking them, placing the occasional Cheerio in his mouth. "You need to take Finn in the afternoon—"

"James, I'm working. I need to get my hours up this week. I took the afternoon off last week. Can't he go to daycare?"

"It's not his day. You can't just drop them when you want. It's not a kennel."

"Can we get a babysitter? I can't miss any more work—"

"It's one afternoon. Tell them you have another doctor's—"

"I've missed drinks twice—"

"Jesus, really? Drinks?"

"It's marketing. It's part of the job."

James pictured Ana in that chair in front of her computer, spinning and spinning.

"You have to be back here by two."

Ana paused. "I have another call."

In the afternoon, James waited for her, circling near the living room window, checking his watch. Finn babbled and hummed, pulling books off shelves and flipping through them, then chucking each opened book over his shoulder.

At 1:45 in her office, Ana tried to look like she was going to be returning later. She put her jacket over her arm in a casual way, as if she might be picking up a coffee. On the elevator, she thought of the women who had come back from maternity leaves and requested flexible schedules, part-time. It was a vocabulary Ana didn't exercise, though theoretically, she sided with that litigator who had brought up on-site child care (but thought the gym they ultimately put in was better). That litigator was long gone now.

When Ana's cab pulled up, James was waiting at the door. He shot her an angry look: "I'm going to be late," he said.

Ana shut the door, removed her coat. Then she noticed Finn, leaning against the credenza, looking up at her.

"Oh, hi," said Ana.

"Park?" he asked.

"Sure. That sounds fine. Let me just check my e-mail."

Finn said again: "Park?" His request seemed utterly democratic, as if it would go out to anyone he met. Ana nodded.

She clicked her BlackBerry as they walked.

What Ana noticed first at the playground was that the parents outnumbered the children. She had brought along an ethics committee report on soybean seeds, picturing herself getting a little reading in while Finn played. If Emcor had patented these seeds, which were living things, what did it mean for other kinds of seeds? "Higher life-forms"—she had been investigating this phrase for days. There were issues of cloning and sperm banks. Could people be manufactured and trademarked, too? Ana was sure that one day the law would kick a hole in the government's feeble protections. She was sure that if she assembled the information correctly, Emcor could do whatever it liked.

It immediately became clear, as Ana and Finn opened the park's iron gate and set forth, that reading did not happen here. The mothers shadowed their children, digging bigger ditches in the sand next to the children's smaller ditches, boosting them onto the slides, scooping them up from the bottom of the slides. Where the kids went, the mothers were already there, their invisible sensors beeping, rushing ahead to intervene.

The first blow of winter was upon them, and a few kids had on hats. One Chinese girl wore a scarf, winter boots, gloves. Ana looked at Finn, who walked a little ahead of her. He wore a fleece jacket, sneakers. Ana wondered if he was cold, but what if? What could she do about it? She decided not to ask him.

"Want to go swing," said Finn in his caveman dialect. Ana nodded, feeling a knot of anxiety as they approached the swings. They were all filled, but a mother was extracting a child—a baby, really; *a baby on a swing!* thought Ana—from one little bucket seat. Ana walked toward it quickly, with Finn in tow. She was lifting him up, always surprised by his weight, when a frizzy-haired woman appeared beside her.

"Excuse me, we were waiting for that," she said. "There's a line, actually." She punctuated this sentence with a smile as insincere as a mime's. Ana looked around, and sure enough, there were two other mothers lined up a few feet away, gazing into the distance, pretending not to notice the confrontation.

"Sorry, I really didn't know," said Ana, lifting out Finn. He started to scream. "Swing! Swing!" She held him in space, and his running shoes kicked at Ana's thighs. "My turn! My turn!" Snot. Tears.

"Finn, no, I'm sorry. I didn't know, I didn't know," said Ana, trying to put him on the ground. He threw his arms around her neck and his legs around her torso, refusing to let go, his wet face gumming to her neck.

Where Finn had tried to sit, the other kid swung cheerfully, pushed by her blank-faced mother.

Ana found a bench, sitting them down, lightly patting Finn's heaving back as he whimpered.

A woman next to her lit up a cigarette. She was a little heavier than the other moms, and older, with a battered quality in the ridges of her face. There was no makeup on her eyes, but they were bright.

"I know Finn," she said. "He goes to daycare with Etta." She gestured at the Chinese girl in the hat, digging in the sand with her mittens.

Finn heard this, peeked out from Ana's chest, his breathing slowing.

"Where Etta?" He spied the girl sitting in the sandbox and slid off, ambling toward her. Because Etta's mother was sitting, Ana decided it would be okay to sit, too, wiping Finn's wet marks from her neck with a Kleenex.

"How's he doing?" asked the woman. Ana appreciated the directness of the question.

"He's good, I think," said Ana.

A father appeared, bracketed on either side by toddler boys. The littler one licked sand from his palm like sugar.

"You're not allowed to smoke here," he said. "And is that your dog?" A dog tied to the fence near the gate offered a bark for emphasis. The woman squinted up at him.

"First of all, I'm hardly blowing smoke in your kid's face, and secondly, the dog's tied up," she said with that same matter-of-fact voice. "Call the fucking parks board if you have a problem."

The man paled. "You're very rude," he said.

"Your kid's eating sand." She took a long, dramatic drag on her cigarette and blew the smoke straight out in front of her like a finger.

The man gathered his children, and they tottered away. Etta's mother butted the cigarette with her foot, then picked it up and peeled off the paper. She sprinkled the last tobacco into the garden behind her, and placed the filter and paper in her pocket. "And how are you doing? Are you his aunt?" she asked.

"No, no, we're just... friends of Sarah's," said Ana.

"Kids of your own?"

"No," said Ana, wondering when this question would stop making her feel as if someone had just torn off the shower curtain while she was midscrub.

"Well, then, you're probably really enjoying the park," said Etta's mother, with a grim smile.

"It definitely feels like a scene," said Ana.

"Don't talk to anyone about vaccinations or breastfeeding."

"Good to know. Thank you."

Ana noticed that Etta had made her way to the jungle gym, where she stood banging her head against a post over and over, laughing.

"We don't know what it was like for her before..." said the woman, standing up.

"Before?"

The girl stopped her banging and returned to digging next to Finn.

"In China. They showed us the orphanage, and it was pretty

nice, but now we're hearing that's not where they lived at all. They really kept them in a shed or something," she said, and then looked at Ana and smiled darkly, shrugging.

"That must be—" said Ana. "You must worry."

"What can you do?" she said, lighting another cigarette, offering one to Ana, who shook her head no.

"There are these cases now, where it turns out the kids weren't actually given up in the first place. You know that whole 'foundling by the side of the road' idea?"

Ana nodded.

"Seems that might be a little exaggerated. Maybe some guy drives up on a moped, while the mother's cooking or cleaning, and he just snatches the baby off the porch, sells her to an orphanage for a thousand bucks, which is a lot of money over there."

"Jesus," said Ana. "How do you know?" She pictured the adoption forms, unsigned, waiting in her desk at their house. Then she saw James in a long winding line marked RETURNS AND EXCHANGES, the last of hundreds of white people clutching Chinese babies, taking them back like defective sweaters.

Finn and Etta were pulling each other's hair now. Ana didn't know if the squeals meant pain or delight. She was about to say something—but what?—when the mother yelled: "Etta! No!"

Ana tried again: "So how do you know? What will people do?"

"Eh," said the woman. "We love her. There's very little to do but that."

She picked up a courier bag from the bench. At this gesture toward leaving, Ana was filled with desperation.

"My name's Ana," she said suddenly, surprising herself.

It was the kind of awkward introduction she suspected little children were enacting every few minutes on this exact playground—a proclamation, mired in need. But this woman had loosened a stream of loneliness that Ana hadn't realized was hidden beneath all the events of the past few weeks. What she felt now, in this park, as Finn dug in the sand, was that she missed Sarah. She was aware of how selfish it was, but she missed Sarah's friendship for herself. She missed her kindness. And if Sarah were back, if Sarah woke up, then Finn would be secure again, and Ana would be released. Sarah.

"Nice to meet you," said the woman. "I'm sure we'll see you here again." She began to walk off, and Ana, stung by rejection, looked away, up at the trees, considering all the hurt feelings circling a playground. Out of the corner of her eye, she saw the woman stop after a few steps, perhaps confronted by her own embarrassment, wondering how much sympathy to give, what shape she should lend to this tragedy. Ana saw her waver and root around for her better instincts. She left Etta to the sand a moment longer and returned to Ana's side.

"I'm Jane," she said. "I don't think I said that. And, uh, you know—good luck with this. I'm sure it's tough."

Ana nodded, blinking back her gratitude.

With his friend gone, Finn came to Ana and stood close to her legs, fingers in his mouth. He seemed to be scanning the playground for the next distraction.

"What should we do, Finn?" asked Ana.

He pointed outside the iron fence, in the general direction of the open park, toward trees and far-off tennis courts. As they walked, he held out his hand, and Ana took it. She gripped the warm palm tightly.

Finn led her to a large tree and pointed up at the squirrels. There were two chasing each other around the trunk, first the brown one after the black one, then, with no warning, an unspoken shift, and the black one began chasing the brown one, furiously fast, their tails bobbing, ducking, and weaving. Finn was laughing and pointing, and Ana laughed, too, brought up by his lightness.

"Silly!" cried Finn.

"They are silly," said Ana. "Ridiculous."

Finn was laughing so hard he dropped her hand and placed his palms on his stomach like a small Santa Claus, shaking with giggles. Suddenly, Ana leaned down and hugged him. The gesture was a surprise to her but not to Finn, who separated from her embrace and then came in for another hug immediately, as if love was entirely expected.

October

ANA ROSE AT 6 A.M. in the darkness. She changed into her running gear in the bathroom so the light wouldn't wake James. But also, she was hiding her body a little bit, not out of shame but fatigue, knowing that if he saw her naked leg, her toe extended en route to a sweat sock, he would rise sleepily and grab her, try to knead her flesh until it gave way to his. She would acquiesce, usually, and then the order of the morning would be flung apart, the pieces falling in the wrong place. This was James unemployed, always grabbing at her, rubbing up against her in the kitchen, in the foyer, winking when Finn appeared to quell things. Ana found it distasteful, drawing the child into some adult fantasy, the turn-on of the forbidden. If she indulged James so early in the morning, she would live with a tilted feeling all day.

The door to Finn's room was open. Ana peered in at him, so small on the double bed. In the light from the hall, she saw that he had kicked off the quilt and lay sprawled on his stomach like a starfish, his back rising and falling. Ana shut the door, but after walking down the staircase, she questioned this gesture, wondered what fears he might have in him that only light could slay. She returned, opened it slightly. The boy had flipped onto his back, his arms still sprawled.

Outside, Ana felt the crack of the day opening wide as she ran. The streets were cold; she should have worn gloves, a hat warmer than the baseball cap on her head. She ran north, up the slight hill, past the houses that were beginning to rattle and stir. A light on here, a light there. She saw an old gray woman at a window, sipping from a mug. This woman lived only three houses from Ana, but Ana had never seen her on the street, did not know her name. She ran a little faster.

By the brothel house, a bag of garbage sat inside a recycling bin. It was always the dirtiest house on the block, the darkest. She could imagine, though, that when it went up for sale, it would go for near a million, just for the property itself, which had a huge parking pad at the side and a long elegant oak. The house would be razed. Something new would rise in its place, probably a modern echo of the houses around here, a gray concrete and glass structure with a winking Victorian sloped roof. A yard surrounded by imported grasses, sustainable and expensive. Ana could see in her mind's eye exactly this oncoming glass house and thought: Fingerprints. All those fingerprints.

As she crossed Harbord, she saw the lights flicker on in a coffee shop. Her heart was beating fast now, and her fingers weren't cold anymore. She never ran with music because she wanted to hear the city, really hear it, and she did. A dog barking, the whir of the streetcar. She thought of her work, of all the patent violations waiting for her. She passed an older couple, their arms linked cautiously, galoshes on their feet in anticipation of some weather Ana did not know was coming. They walked slowly. Ana tried to imagine herself and James as old as this, as entwined and frail.

What she had not imagined when she married was that love would turn out to be in constant movement, that it crept alongside most of the time but sometimes dove down, down into depths that Ana did not fear, but found repulsive, black, unwelcome. She knew that what they had was substantial, that it would rise again, break the surface to the light, but she was still angered by how often it left her. She had not known that she would have this in common with her own parents, who finally missed it too much, who could not bear its absence, and so split apart. But Ana did not want that. She did not want to be too weak to keep up with love. She needed to be stronger, to call it back to her. But she was so afraid, afraid of what it had become while it was away from her, afraid of what had gathered along its spine in the murk below, afraid she would not recognize its shape when it returned.

She thought of Finn, sleeping, and was relieved not to be there when he awoke. What was it in her? She wanted Finn safe, she wanted him clean, she wanted him fed, happy. She wanted all the things you want for any other person, known or unknown, simply because you are both human, and alive together at this shared moment. But that was not the same as mothering. She knew it was not. She thought of Sarah with him, and she could not match her. She could not match her sonar, the way her eye was always on him even as she spoke, that every gesture was infused with Finn, for Finn, about Finn, in spite of Finn. Then she realized that James was like this now, too. James had developed the same animal instinct. Yesterday, James had handed the boy his sippy cup before Finn asked for it. He changed him fast and exactly when it needed to be done. Finn stood in front of James in the morning, waiting for James to zip his jacket. Why could she not feel his needs in the same way? When would it come?

Ana sprinted around the park, passing the same homeless woman in her sleeping bag twice. Another runner overtook her, striding on great long legs like a spider. Ana didn't want to trail him and turned away from the park, taking an eastern street, past houses more expensive and older than her own, with beveled glass windows and huge stoops. The streetlights were old-fashioned, fake gas lamps. The sun was high now, the frost melted. Everything around her caught in an autumn gleam.

And then she had an image of her mother with her reading glasses on. The two of them, mother and daughter, toe to toe on the couch in the rental apartment with books on their laps. The images came at her like a deck of cards being shuffled: Her mother stroking her hair when her father left, whispering—but what? What did she say? Ana remembered only the stroking and the dimming of the roar when she was resting against her mother, looking up at the African violets.

And then: Her mother taking her to a party where she met Mordecai Richler, and in the cab home, her mother said, "Something to tell your children about."

She had been loved. She had known a mother's love, its touch and glance. And so, then, she could now recognize its absence.

What had she expected, exactly? Why had she endured all those gynecological appointments at 7:30 in the morning, on her way to her work, day after day? James would talk about what would come after, when the appointments bore out: peewee baseball games, and summers out of the city, and the kind of idyllic childhood his brother could never pull off for his own kids even with all that money. And Ana had thought: *Yes, if I do it, if I build it, then I will live in it, and it will become a home, a life. It will. It will.* She ran. But now they had Finn and she thought: *It is possible to fail at this. It is possible to fail at loving a child. Why doesn't anyone tell you that?*

At the house, James was cooing into Finn's ear, then leading his sleepy body to the bathroom, changing his wet Pull-Up, wiping him down. James had decided to move him from diapers to Pull-Ups. He had been accumulating information on toilet training from the Internet and had bought a potty. He felt ready to usher Finn to the next stage. For now, the potty sat unused in the corner of the bathroom with a rubber duck on it.

It was a good morning: no fussing, no anger. They hummed along, eating cereal together at the kitchen island, Finn's legs swinging. Ana barreled into this, covered in sweat, panting.

"Ana!" said Finn. James could sense something fierce in her this morning. She let off a hum of agitation. She waved before heading upstairs. When Ana returned, quickly, she was dressed and made up. James and Finn were now on the ground surrounded by plastic dinosaurs. Finn wore pajamas, and James his equivalent: boxers and a thin, shapeless Nick Cave T-shirt.

"He goes, yeah, kill! Kill! He goes nooooo!" said Finn.

Ana ate her yogurt.

"We have to go to Mike's tonight," said James, grunting as he rolled onto his back.

"Oh, God. What time?"

Ana picked up the empty cereal dishes from the counter, wondering what would happen if she didn't. Would they be sitting there at the end of the day when she returned from work? How much would get done if she didn't do it? She could never bring herself to attempt this experiment, knowing her own fury when James failed her.

After putting away the dishes and wiping the counter, Ana moved through the room, putting drawings in a drawer, making a stack out of the loose books. A broken crayon stopped her; she got a broom, a dustbin.

"I'll do it," James murmured, lying on his back. "Go to work."

Ana rattled the garbage can loudly.

"Have a good day," she said. Finn looked up as the door slammed shut.

"You never replied to our Thanksgiving video!" Jennifer spoke with her back to James and Ana. As she rooted in the refrigerator, her behind, round and denim-clad, appeared like a separate comic act: the talking behind. She emerged upright, a little flushed, holding an armload of juice boxes. James leaned in and shut the refrigerator door, which was covered in the same white recessed paneling as the cabinets. The kitchen held two refrigerators—one for cans of soda and beer, the other for food; wine was in its own separate climate-controlled refrigerator—but stealthily. All the appliances were hidden away. The kitchen had reached a point where mess was self-eviscerating.

"There," said Jennifer, and just the slightest hint of Newfoundland leaked out: "Dhere." The children gathered around, the two girls and Finn, who was wearing fairy wings. The three heads bobbed and sucked the juice, then scattered. "We made it on this website. I can't remember what it's called. Didn't you get it? Sophie's head was on the turkey? Olivia's this big tree..." James and Ana shook their heads, murmuring shared obliviousness. "Oh, darn it. I'll see if Mike can find it before you go. It was hilarious. I really thought I put you on the list..."

As if summoned, Mike appeared beside his wife. Ana was always struck by their physical similarity, except in opposite sizes. Both had a kind of ruddy plainness, with wide unblinking eyes and a smattering of freckles across the bridges of their noses. Mike was taller than James, though years at the computer had caused him to fold at the neck, collapsing his upper half. Jennifer was the kind of small that made Ana feel gargantuan; she had a little-boy body except for her large breasts, breasts that had been feeding babies for years, it seemed. Their eldest, Jake, was sleeping at a friend's house, a reward for completing a tournament of some kind.

It had been silently agreed, years ago, that James was a bad uncle, not only for lack of trying, but because he couldn't stay on top of the volume of accomplishment that rushed out of the large brick house. Everyone was gifted. Everyone was a genius. What happened to such people in adulthood? No one ever said: *Meet my friend, Dave. He won an award for Best Handwriting.* The future pointlessness of all these accolades made it hard for James to respond in the present. Driving home from evenings at Mike and Jennifer's, fuming, he delivered the same anecdote: "Studies have proven it's the B students who run the world." But that morning, when he saw Finn scribble on a piece of cardboard and hold it up for offer, he understood, just a little, the full force of parental pride, the greed for a child's future. He understood, for the first time, why his brother and his wife bored others so relentlessly.

"Can we help?" Ana asked, nodding toward the woman at the sink, her apron tied tight around her waist, dividing her body like the twisted end of a wrapped candy. The plates from dinner formed a tall pile, tilted at an angle from all the uneaten food between them. The carcass of a large chicken spilled its bones greasily over the edge of a white serving plate.

"Oh God no. That's what we pay her for. Right, Julie?" said Jennifer. The young, dark-skinned woman looked over and smiled, holding up her yellow washing gloves as evidence.

The four began to walk out of the kitchen, which took a while, passing the large marble island, the rack of gleaming pots and pans raining down from the ceiling.

"Did you get a new countertop? Something's different," said Ana, stopping in her tracks.

"You notice everything, Ana," said Mike, leading her back to the island. "We couldn't take the granite anymore. It seemed really dated. Maybe it was an indulgence, but we thought, *Let's go marble. Now or never.*"

"Now or never" was one of Mike's favorite expressions. James could never figure out what the hurry was. Mike's life seemed entirely ungoverned by clocks. He had worked at home for the past few years, since the sale of his company. Once, after an occasionless bottle of four-hundred-dollar wine, James had asked his brother to describe, in detail, a week in his life. It was worse than James had imagined, involving early-morning online trades, sailing lessons, an Italian tutor, a trainer. The children were shuttled to and fro by a squadron of nannies and housekeepers. A couple of times a week, Mike did this job himself, to stay "connected." James thought of him in his luxury minivan with the TV screens blaring, idling as the girls jumped out and ran up the steps to the private French school. He pictured Jake wending his way across the grassy concourse of his Eton-like campus while Mike waved at him at the end of the day, cranking up his $10,000 sound system, listening to music he'd downloaded not because he liked it, but because it appeared on lists as Most Downloaded. Beyoncé. Jack Johnson. Mike had always been without taste, and in James's eyes, this made him wispy and unsubstantial, despite his height. James was held together by his preferences, his books and movies, his loud opinions on politics and art.

Jennifer existed to provide shape, to ground this dangling way of living. She had always worked, and always would, she said, even when there was no need. The need, as she saw it, was on the other side, from the severely handicapped adults to whom she administered physical therapy at a rehab center. James had never asked her to describe her week. Rarely did anyone inquire about those men and women (swollen tongued, pants wet—James turned away from the image), but they loomed somehow, shadowy in the vastness of the house. The knowledge of Jennifer's hands on their gnarled bodies every day, morning to night, was a relief to all who visited there, pleased to know that some sense of purpose still propelled this couple through their days.

Right after the accident, Jennifer had sent James links to papers on the importance of physical rehabilitation during "coma vigil," a new phrase for Sarah's unroused sleep. James had been grateful and was reassured by a nurse that yes, every day, they were moving Sarah's limp arms and legs as often as they should be. But it was "coma vigil" that stayed with him. His vigil was for Finn. James was keeping watch over Finn while Sarah lay in her darkness, enduring other women's hands rearranging her scarecrow limbs, while her son was someone else's devotional object.

Mike and Jennifer sat on the couch, and Jennifer stretched her legs into Mike's lap. Ana, James noticed, was far from him, the only one who had not taken a seat on the wide curved couch. She sat across from them in a stiff-backed brocade-covered chair, each arm at right angles on the armrests, her fingers curled over the edges.

"How's work, Jennifer?" asked Ana. "How are the cutbacks?"

She continued that way, pulling information from the two of them with her concise questions, murmuring support. It looked like warmth, or inquisitiveness, but James recognized it as a sort of vacancy, too, a way of passing the substance of the interaction to someone else.

Ana was feeling massive, as if the chair could barely contain her. Jennifer had this effect on her. She was trying not to glance at her sister-in-law's tiny feet in their childlike gray-striped socks, now being massaged casually by Mike's hands. He pushed and pulled as he told them about their Christmas plans in Mexico, a beach house that they should come visit. These kinds of holiday invitations were always extended only once, and never accepted nor rejected nor brought up again by anyone.

"And you, Jimmy, how's the book?" asked Mike. Whenever he called him Jimmy, James was reminded that he was the younger brother and always would be. James had wanted a brother who would put him in headlocks and throw him to the floor and kick his ass, someone with badness to worship. But Mike shrugged at James's schemes of revenge against the asshole down the street; he was too old to join a united front, and he preferred the computer. He sat. In James's recollection of their youth, his brother is always seated in his desk chair, in front of the computer. Only the changed color of his T-shirt indicates that he does, in fact, rise on occasion and mark the passing of the days.

James was beginning to regret the way he had framed his firing. He had done too good a job of blocking the horror by inserting this distracting fantasy of a book. There was not enough sympathy for him, he felt, not enough commiseration over the shortness of his stick.

"It's okay. Tough times in publishing, with the economy. Not a lot of new contracts," he said.

"You don't have a contract?" Mike raised his thick eyebrows. "I didn't know that." He looked then at Ana, as if seeing her as something new: imperative to his brother's survival.

"Let's not talk about work!" said Jennifer. "How is parenthood? At long last! Do you absolutely love it?" She lowered her voice: "Come on, can I ask that?"

"Jenn—" said Mike, flicking her toe with his finger.

"What? Come on. We know you guys were trying. The circumstances aren't ideal, of course, but now you get to be a mom and dad! You get to parent!" Ana noted the verb: "to parent." Something to do, not to be.

"I know this is going to sound weird, but Ana, he really looks like you! It's crazy! You have exactly the same eyes."

"Really?" said Ana. "Well, they're brown, I guess—"

A chorus of screams burst forth into the living room, followed by three bodies.

"Finn's a fairy! He's a fairy, Mommy! And we're the queens who are taking him to our kingdom to do our bidding!" Sophie, at six, was the eldest. On her head she wore a crown of toilet paper. In her hand, she waved an elaborate wand dangling beads and stuffed hearts. She was followed by Olivia, age four, who also wore a toilet paper crown, wielding a Barbie in each hand.

"These are the elves!" she cried. Finn looked pleased, toddling to James and leaning on his legs.

A look passed between the two girls—as if a switch had been hit—and Sophie began chasing Olivia, who responded by screaming happily, which made Finn scream, too, joining the chase. "Attack! The fairy is attacking!" bellowed Sophie as the three raced in figure eights around the couch. Then James noticed that Finn had a juice box in his hand; he reached to grab it just as Finn slipped out of the line and wrapped himself in the curtains. The curtains were so shining and sumptuous that Ana imagined tearing them from the wall and lying down in their silky arms.

"Get the fairy! Get the fairy!" screamed Olivia.

"Girls! Girls!" cried Jennifer.

"Finn! Don't pull the curtains!" cried James, alarmed at the sausage shape in the golden fabric, straining at the top of the rod. He jumped up to try and undo him, to rescue the juice box before the inevitable stain.

"My elf!" wailed Olivia, stopping suddenly, holding in her hand the head of one Barbie, grasping its naked torso around the stomach. The adults breathed in, anticipating. Olivia screwed up her eyebrows, her jaw dropped to her chest, and a sound escaped, like a pig with an ax at its neck. Rivulets of snot and tears sprayed through the air. Ana leaned backward.

Jennifer and James went into the fray, untangled and soothed, calmed and hugged. Ana took a drink of her wine. Midsip, she recognized that her isolation might appear unsavory, and she reached for a coffee table book on an "Edvard Munch and the Uncanny" exhibit, as if to appear preoccupied.

"We saw that show in Vienna," said Mike, leaning across, shouting over the diminishing din. "A bit dark for me. I bet James would like it." Ana flipped to the back of the book, stopping on an etching by a German artist she had never heard of named Max Klinger. She recognized one of the German words in the title, *Kind,* and her body stiffened. A woman in a full garden, carpeted with grass and rimmed with furry bushes and tall trees, lay resting on a bench, her eyes closed. Beside her, a hooded baby carriage. But the carriage was empty, the blankets had tumbled onto the ground. A path from the blankets, trampled by feet, revealed a figure in the distance, walking away from the mother. In his arms was an unfurling bundle, too small to be deciphered, white and unseen. Ana put her finger on the path, traced its line. She felt, again, that strange flutter, a feeling of ascension.

James and Jennifer had been successful. When the screams had slowed to whimpers, and the whimpers to whines, the two girls curled up on either side of their mother like cats. Jennifer stroked the head of each: "There, there. Silly queens."

Ana put the book down on the table. She wondered if the girls had seen it. It seemed to her now as inappropriate as pornography. She drank her wine quickly.

"Uncle James, how come we never see you on TV anymore?" said Sophie.

James pulled Finn a little closer.

"I got fired," said James.

"On fire?" asked Finn, and everybody except James laughed.

"Why?" asked Sophie.

"That's a complicated question...." interjected Jennifer, but Mike tilted his head, as if equally curious. Ana felt her body reassembling into something normal, the effect of the picture beginning to cease.

"It's okay, Jennifer," said James. Addressing Sophie, he said: "I'm too old for TV. It's a job for young people. You should be on TV." He leaned over and tickled her. She laughed. Ana had never seen him so engaged with his nieces.

"I know. I could be on TV," said Sophie.

"Sophie was amazing in the Thanksgiving play. I know all parents think their kids are great on stage, but it was really striking. The teacher said she has a natural aptitude for theater," said Jennifer.

"Now we're adding acting lessons to the roster," said Mike, in the part of exasperated father.

"I played an aboriginal person," said Sophie. Ana laughed.

Sophie snatched a remote control from the coffee table. She hit a button and a large, wood-framed abstract painting—red and blue swirls on red and blue swirls—moved to the side with a gentle whoosh. A large flat panel TV appeared.

"Jesus, Mike, how James Bond," said James.

"I know. It's extravagant. But now or never, right?"

"Sophie, we don't need the TV on," said Jennifer. "You can watch upstairs if you want."

But Sophie clicked, and the TV came to life. There, across the screen, was James's former colleague, Ariel, each strand of her long straight hair clearly outlined with the perfectionist brush of high-definition television.

"I worked with her—" said James.

"What? Is this your show?" asked Jennifer.

Mike said, "Sophie—turn it off—"

"No! Let's see Uncle James!"

Ariel was sitting in a hotel room across from a famous singer, a block-headed young man with one raised eyebrow.

"Who's that?" asked Ana.

"The new Frank Sinatra," said James.

"Really?"

"He thinks he is," snapped James.

Ariel was breathless. "Just tell me, seriously—is this song about any particular girl? Or is it about girls in general?"

"This is news?" James shouted. "This is documentary?"

The singer chortled, winking and shifting in his seat, his

nonanswer running atop the video clip: the singer in the rain, embracing a tall blonde. "What can I say? When love hits you, it hits you!"

"This is a fucking national news program," said James.

"James, watch the language—" James turned from Mike's pious face.

"Soph, turn it off—" said Jennifer.

Ana placed her wine carefully on the table. On the screen, Ariel threw back her head and giggled. Jennifer grabbed the remote out of Sophie's hand and clicked the TV to silence.

"You can't be surprised, James. TV's always been this way. You were just this unusual little exception," said Ana. She gestured to the blank screen. "This is what people want."

"People don't know what they want. Give them shit and they'll eat it," said James. Olivia giggled into her hands.

"Jimmy! Language!" said Mike. The painting moved slowly and smoothly, until finally it had covered the entire TV with red blur.

At the door, Finn kicked at the stoop outside. As Ana buttoned her jacket, Jennifer appeared with a paper Whole Foods bag.

"Olivia's too old for these," she said. The bag rattled with puzzle pieces and Legos. Something made a few electronic grunts, then silenced.

This was how people did it, then—an ongoing exchange.

Mike appeared, put his arm around Jennifer's shoulder. The girls had joined Finn on the porch. They, too, kicked at the leaves and squealed.

"Not in your socks," said Jennifer, then rolled her eyes at the adults.

"Hey, Jimmy," said Mike, clearing his throat, alerting James to the fact that a speech had been prepared. "Listen, if you need any—you know. If we can do anything for you guys. With Finn, I mean. It's a big change. We have a little experience with this stuff." Jennifer laughed loudly, nodding.

"Thank you," said James. "It's going all right, but thank you." His brother was never good with tenderness. It didn't suit him. James wanted to point out that they lived only a half hour from each other but got together maybe three times a year, so how much, really, could they help? But alongside that first thought, James found himself moved by his brother's awkward gesture. He tried to picture a future of commonality, devoid of the decades-long strangeness.

He rode on this idea as they gathered and moved toward the car at the top of the circular driveway. James knew that Mike and Jennifer's three-car garage was filled. A fourth vehicle—a Lexus SUV—sat outside. The surfeit of parking spaces seemed like mockery. It was the first puncture in James's warm mood, but he refrained from commenting.

Jennifer called something from the stoop. All three were buckled in. Ana rolled down her window, cupped her hand to her ear.

"I'll resend you the video card!" called Jennifer.

"Great!" Ana called back.

Finn repeatedly pressed buttons on the electronic toy, a counting game, with red and blue lights, and a robot voice: *1! 2! 3!* They moved through the empty, wide streets, past the sylvan glade gardens, under the ancient trees. When they hit Bloor, the traffic thickened. Cranes and bulldozers sat unmoving by construction sites cordoned off with plastic, warning of disaster. Cars blew their horns at a taxi doing a U-turn.

"Did you get that video?" asked James.

"Yeah, I did," said Ana.

"Me, too."

Now was the time where they would usually dismember the evening for a solid hour or two. James would go first, noting how Jennifer referred to the girls as "Princess Sophie" and "Diva Olivia." Then Ana would talk about the marble countertops, Mike's crippling boringness. James might revel, once again, in the way that Jennifer had very specific opinions about very small things—the right temperature for drinking water; why Jay Leno is hilarious—but at the mere mention of politics, she left the room to fuss about in the kitchen. The kitchen. The excess.

But not that night. The venting had been neutered by the unavoidable, continuous kindness the family had shown them, by the way Jennifer had crouched down and whispered in Finn's ear, ending the night with him in an embrace. Had that always been there? Had they just never seen it, never needed to call upon it until that moment?

"Did you have fun tonight, Finny?" James asked.

"Go see Mama," said Finn. The beeping of the toys stopped.

Ana straightened; it was Jennifer, with her abundance of maternal warmth, who had triggered this yearning in Finn. It was seeing a real family in its chaos that made him miss Sarah.

"Go see Daddy," said Finn.

"We can't see them right now, honey," said James. "I'm sorry."

Ana looked behind her, expecting Finn to erupt, and why not? He must know he was at the center of a terrible injustice. He must be furious.

But he was simply staring out the window.

"Should we put on some music, Finny?" asked James, turning on the radio.

The three were quiet for the rest of the ride. James found a parking space right in front of their house but didn't comment on it.

He carried Finn upstairs, leaving Ana to her work. She took the laptop to the breakfast nook. The sound of Finn in the bath moved through the floor above Ana's head. Squealing and thumping, laughter.

Dim light from the inside of the house caught the yard, and something looked different to Ana's glance. She leaned closer to the French doors. The men had been coming. James had not mentioned it, and with her late nights, she had been returning in the darkness and had not noticed. Day after day, while she worked in her tower, they had been transforming the yard. The limestone was laid, a gray skating rink in the center of the garden. A large red Japanese maple stood in a bucket, waiting to be planted. The perimeter was empty of plants but covered with rich, churned soil. These invisible men were determined to bring life into the place, even though winter was coming. They had been so late that James had negotiated a discount. No one used landscapers in this infertile season.

Something in the limestone unsettled Ana. She felt a tug of certainty that the hole was still beneath it, that a toe on a stone could break through the surface, pull her down into a muddy pit. This reminded her of Sarah, in her hospital bed, perched on the edge of the depths. The last visit had been the same: no change. Decisions were waiting for them, Ana knew. Decisions about Sarah, who had decided everything for them.

She pulled her face from the glass and turned to her e-mails.

Soon, there would be plants in the ground, or at least seeds. She should think about that instead. She reminded herself to look again tomorrow.

Ana didn't want her personal life stuffed into files at her firm, so years ago, James had found a lawyer downtown whose two-room office was over a fish shop.

He went there first, to sign papers delivered from Sarah's lawyer, whom he had visited the day before. That office had been fancier, in an office building, with a receptionist. Despite Sarah's pigpen cloud of mess, and Marcus's Zen-like quiet, it turned out they were affairs-in-order types. And now he, James, whose affairs had never been in order, had power of attorney over their family. He could see their bank account, which was healthy, and their credit card bills (Sarah charged $3.76 at Starbucks four or five times a week, which made James laugh). One day, he would be able to access that money. The insurance company moved along at its arthritic pace, but there had been a decent policy. If Sarah died, Finn would be rich, or richer than James.

All of these revelations were intimate and unwanted (Marcus was a careful, clever investor; their portfolio was almost as impressive as the one Ana had put together). As he met with each official and signed each document, James remembered the feeling of having sex with someone he didn't love; a little part of him kept repeating: "I can't bear this. I can't do it. I'm the wrong guy."

But as he was informed many times, Sarah was not dead. So this was just the preliminary hacking of the weeds of Sarah and Marcus's life. The deep digging would come later, if and when. For now: temporary guardians. Although the will clearly stated that Finn was to go to Ana and James, James couldn't find an argument against the lawyer's suggestion that they place notices in newspapers in major cities, and online, just in case there were complications later. He pictured Marcus's father sitting at the table with his morning paper to find an ad: "Seeking grandparents for orphan child." James tried to imagine the most monstrous things parents could do, and then he imagined those things happening to Marcus, calm and gentle Marcus. What was it? Prodded in basements, cigarettes burned out on his forearms. Something caused that little scar on Marcus's face. He thought of Finn, all softness, and was struck by a future in which an older Finn would have questions. He would have to anticipate those questions and be ready. He would have to work, gather the stories of Finn's life and have them waiting.

Unless Sarah woke up, of course. If Sarah woke up, then what? He tried to want this, because it was the right thing to want, and because of Finn, looking out the car window for his parents. But when he thought of Finn leaving, and the room becoming a guest room once again, he ached.

On the streetcar, watching the city take shape in the cooling gray light, he knew Ana would be anxious for him to return, still uncomfortable alone with Finn. This was how he saw her these days: waiting for him, hovering around windows and doorframes, needing him, something he always thought he wanted. That aloofness he had tried for years to break through had been replaced by some kind of anxiety he couldn't placate. She was angry, too, at the mess in the house, the toys, the overflowing Diaper Genie. But he left the mess to her because only she could calm herself. He fucked things up, stacked the dishwasher wrong, didn't put the laundry in the bureau quickly enough. That was the conversation. He was tired of it. He was speaking less.

James stepped from the streetcar, moving with the crowd toward the hospital. At the second door, a security guard pointed at a dispenser of antibacterial soap. James's first instinct was to refuse, as was his wont in the presence of a direct order, but the security guard issuing the order was bull-bodied and redheaded with a slack jaw and the bored arrogance of a bouncer. Then James spotted a withered old woman sitting on a bench, coughing into her curled waxed hand, sport socks pulled up to her green-veined knees. Eagerly, James hit the soap dispenser, slathered, and rubbed.

Up the elevator, along the painted footsteps on the floor. But he was following the wrong painted feet and suddenly they ran out. James found himself up against a pair of doors with ship's portholes at the top; half of one of the painted feet was lost on the other side of the door. Only the heel remained. James pushed at the doors. They were locked.

He turned around and kept walking, following green feet this time and trying to make sense of the signs overheads. GR4–T76. The numbers and letters seemed random, something Finn would produce banging away on the computer.

Then he found the door, but inside, the bed was empty. He shut the door quickly. A machine on wheels, knobs and buttons, came crashing through the opposite doorway, and attached to it, a woman in scrubs.

"My friend was in here last week—"

"We're repairing this part of the hospital." She moved around him, pushing the cart. "Check at the nurses' station."

It seemed strange to him that certain ventricles in a hospital could be closed when all he ever heard about was overcrowding and waiting rooms leaking unattended illnesses. He decided to take that as a good sign, then; some kind of lessening of the amount of suffering as a whole contained in the city. Of course, the other reading, he realized as he walked, was that there was the same amount of suffering, but nowhere to put it.

A nurse confirmed that Sarah had been moved to a ward. She no longer needed a private room because there was no private self, nothing that could be infringed upon, thought James.

Outside the correct door at last, he stopped a moment, took a breath, and then regretted it, the cold black coating of hospital chemicals settling over his lungs.

The curtain around Sarah's bed was undrawn, and she lay on her back. Of the three other beds in the room, only one contained a person he could see, a middle-aged woman with dark hair, sitting up and watching television with headphones on. Another had the curtain drawn, but a murmur came from the slit, and feet passed below. An orderly gathered food trays. Because of this normal pulse of movement, Sarah looked a little out of place, entirely still in a room of movement, the last little house on a city street of skyscrapers.

Flowers sat on her bedside table. James picked up the card, both sides of the interior covered in the signatures of her colleagues in neat, teacher handwriting: "We are thinking of you." "We'll see you soon, Sarah!" The water in the vase was murky gray, the stems covered in slime.

James had been to visit three times, and each time, he left his coat on. He stood above Sarah, careful not to bump into the churning machines. The bruising had cleared, and she looked more like herself, except for the long black lines of stitches crisscrossing her face. Today, her head was flung back, mouth open, crusted with white. She might have been a woman talking, frozen in midsentence. The tracheal tube running from the moist, gauze-covered hole in her throat was held in place by a white plastic collar (*Like something worn by a priest, or a cat,* thought James). Her hair was slightly matted, the roots grown out. James had never thought about Sarah's hair, about the number of small decisions she made that led her to dye it so black. What was coming in, forming a slab along the side part, was gray, wiry.

"Finn's doing great," James said quietly, glancing back at the woman watching television. He crouched down and spoke directly into her ear. "We're taking care of him. I don't want you to worry." He saw her hand, bonded to tubes and tape, and placed his own hand on it. Her fingers were warm, soft. It had been years since he had held another woman's hand. He had become used to Ana's poor circulation, her corpse fingers yellow-tipped from November to April.

"What would you like to know?" he said. On his last visit, the nurse had told him to talk to her, that it might fire up her brain, shake her to life. Online he had read of a teenage boy who woke up after months in a coma and said: "I hate that doctor. He called me a vegetable."

"Finn's funny. I bought him Pull-Ups, and we're working on that. He has this dance he's doing, pretty hilarious. He's all—" James waved his free arm. The breathing machine whirred. "Bruce at the daycare says he's doing really well. They went on a neighborhood walk and picked up fall leaves. They made these elaborate collages. You should see Finn's. It's clearly the best one. He's a master gluer."

James straightened the card on the bedside table.

"The Leafs suck, as usual. The economy—it's not good. You

picked a good time to check out," he said, laughed, then cleared his throat. "Sorry."

He thought a moment. "We took Finn to my brother's. He seemed to really like it there. They have an entire floor devoted to toys, so you can guess why he likes it. They also have four cars. Four!" James shook his head. "The parking downtown is still bullshit. There's a systemic bias on Sundays, when the church people take up all the spaces on the block and the cops never ticket them. So last week I parked across the street, which is always no parking, right? And the parking guy was coming along and was about to write me a ticket. I couldn't believe it. I ran outside—and hey, don't worry, Ana was with Finn in the house, we wouldn't leave him alone in the house—and I said: 'Look, those church people don't have permits, they park here for hours on Sunday, taking up all the permit spaces. Why don't you ticket *them*?' And you know what he said?" James dropped Sarah's hand, which landed hard. He was pointing and poking the air. "He said: 'We make exceptions for religious observation.' What the fuck? Is this Iran or something? Aren't we a secular state? I wanted to kill the guy, just smash him—" The woman with the headphones cleared her throat loudly. James turned and saw that she'd taken off her headphones and was exaggeratedly flipping through a magazine.

He lowered his voice. "Anyway, that's not so interesting." He glanced at the woman's bedside table, which looked as if it might buckle under the weight of photographs: two little girls dressed up like Easter bunnies; two little girls in matching red dresses. James realized there was no photo of Finn by Sarah's bed. He would have to bring one in.

"I saw your lawyer today, and he said you guys had very clear directives around guardianship. You were protecting him from Marcus's parents, I guess. I wish I knew more about that. I wish I could..." Could what? As the possibility burst at the seams of this sentence, James croaked a little, then silenced himself.

"You're a good mother, Sarah," he said, again touching her hand. "You and Marcus were such good parents. You have this beautiful child...." He didn't continue, embarrassed that he'd immediately transformed a thought about her to one about himself, and all he hadn't made.

James stopped talking and stood again in his coat, looking at Sarah's affectless face, listening to the machines.

"Are you family?" asked a nurse, one he hadn't met before, a small black woman in cornrows punctuated with glass beads. Her hair clicked as she checked numbers on a screen by Sarah's bed, jotting them down on a chart.

"We're guardians to her son. We have power of attorney." James used "we" even when Ana wasn't with him.

"Have you spoken to the doctor lately?"

"No. Why?"

"She's stable, and we're continuing with therapy. But you need to talk to Dr. Nasir about your plans for her."

James heard a different kind of question. How could there be plans when she hadn't come back yet? Or died? James couldn't imagine any movement between those two possibilities. "What do you mean? Plans for what?" And as he spoke, it came to him: He worked on a documentary about this once, a woman who had been in a coma for a decade; her husband's wish to divorce her; her family's outrage. Would they move Sarah into their home, would James wash her body with a sea sponge, change feeding tubes, bedpans? Would Ana pluck stray hairs from Sarah's chin? He remembered the mother of this woman, her mouth tight from worry, insisting that the strapping young brother wheel her bed into the living room for Christmas. And there she was, year after year, a wedge of person growing older at the side of the room while the tree lights twinkled and grandchildren scattered the trash of their opened gifts.

"Long-term care is one option," said the nurse, her pen scratching: *kstch, kstch, kstch. Such music in this woman,* thought James, listening to her hair clicking, her pen. "You have to talk to the doctor about a DNR. Emergency measures. We have counselors here—"

The size of his circumstances came upon James suddenly, an encyclopedia dropped from a top bunk.

"This is fucked," he said out loud, rubbing his hands through his hair until it stood in a forest of tufts at different furious angles. The woman reading her magazine froze. "We didn't even know them that well."

The nurse ceased her scratching and looked at him firmly. "Well, this must be very difficult for you, then."

James deflated a little. It wasn't compassion, really; there was a tinge of mockery in it, as if this nurse had seen much worse than James ever could. He nodded.

"I'll see you soon, Sarah," he said. He leaned down and gave her a kiss on the top of her head. In her ear, he whispered: "He asks about you."

Then he stood and, at the door, turned and waved at Sarah.

In the hallway, the nurse appeared again by James's side.

"It's not that uncommon," she said. James looked at her for the first time. She was about his age.

"These days, not everyone has a family. If something happens to me, my kids are going to my doorman. He's the best person I know."

James smiled at this. "Did you give him any warning?"

"No need for that," said the nurse, handing James a photocopied list of phone numbers, counselors' names. "People rise to the occasion."

When James opened the door to the house, the scent of cold and streetcar on his jacket, Finn was alone in front of the television watching a small animated hamster singing about summer. He didn't so much watch TV as sit prostrate before it, concentrating entirely, as if he were a medical student observing an operation. The Moo blanket that Ana had brought from his house was clasped between his fingers. He rubbed and rubbed, frowning. The joylessness around TV concerned James. Ana was letting him watch too much.

"Hey, Finny," said James. "How was daycare today?"

Finn broke his concentration and grinned upward. "Hi, James! Hamster!" Then he turned back to the TV and vanished again.

Ana was in the kitchen. A small pink plastic plate of spaghetti sat on the island. Ana placed a blue plastic fork beside it.

"How did it go?" she asked.

"It's done. We're in charge. It's official," said James, and he beat his chest for emphasis. In one hand, he had a Ziploc bag that he placed before Ana. Plastic parts of a cell phone, the silver of a broken chip.

"This is all they found?"

"The police have a few other things. They'll be released when the investigation is settled."

Ana put her hand on the bag of phone parts. "Was it awful today?"

James considered this. "Neutral. It was like opening a bank account. Lawyers." He was trying for a joke, but Ana didn't respond.

"The body's been cremated," said James. "I guess I arranged that." It occurred to James that Marcus's dying was becoming his new job.

"Oh—will we get the ashes?" asked Ana. "What will we do with them?"

"Save the box for Finn, I guess. When he's older."

Ana pictured a grown man with Finn's little boy face tossing ashes into a roiling sea.

"I know you don't want to talk about it, but the funeral…" said James.

"I think we should wait."

"What about closure?"

Ana raised her eyebrows. "You don't actually believe that exists, do you?"

James sighed. "You're right. It's bullshit."

"It's her husband's funeral. Sarah should be the one to—" said Ana. "She could still wake up."

"I don't think she's waking up."

He moved a glass of water over an inch on the table. They were quiet for a moment.

"We should still wait," said Ana. She took James's glass of water, dumped it in the sink, and put it in the dishwasher.

"I have to go to work," she said.

"Now? It's five o'clock."

"Yes. I missed the afternoon, and we're busy. I told you. It's Emcor. Discovery is coming up "

The legal profession's use of the word "discovery" had always struck James as abuse. "Discovery" was a magic word, one that should only refer to new planets or sexual pleasures. But in law, it meant a bunch of suits interviewing another bunch of suits to drag out enough information to ballast their theories in court.

Finn appeared. "'Getti!" he cried, climbing onto the stool. James steadied him, snapping a bib around his neck.

Ana put her laptop in her briefcase, which was filled with days of notes from combing over the definition of "life": *If soybeans could be patented, then what next? What other living things would they see bought and sold in their lifetime?* She wanted to tell James about how the case made her heart race. The possibilities were terrifying, exhilarating. But Finn was singing as he ate, filling the room.

James had an urge to tell Ana about visiting Sarah, but something stopped him. Before the accident, his afternoons with Finn had seemed like a judgment on Ana, and he hadn't told her. Now, these visits to Sarah had come to feel the same. It would be humiliating for Ana to know that her husband was at the bed of another woman over and over while she stayed in her office tower, only blocks away. He told himself this anxiety was ridiculous, and Ana would be happy to have Sarah looked after. But still, he didn't want to speak until he knew what he needed to say.

Ana leaned in and pecked a kiss on his cheek. From afar, she called: "Good-bye, Finn!" before shutting the door.

At ten o'clock, Ana was not the last to leave the office. The law students stayed, surrounded by their empty Styrofoam food containers. They circled the boardroom table, clicking on their computers. Ana was not sure why they didn't separate and use their cubicles, but something compelled them to come together at night. She suspected part of the evening was spent updating their Facebook profiles or texting people they sat across from all day. On these late nights, laughter sometimes came out of the room.

When Ana said good night, the comic mood broke. "Good night," they chorused, soberly.

The night was warm. Ana decided to walk home. When she arrived in front of the bar, she didn't bother to feign surprise at herself. She had known all along, then, where she was going.

It was a place she had first gone to when she was still a kid. Her mother had dragged her to poetry readings there. Ana had been too short to see through the crowds. She'd sipped ginger ale and kept her head below the adult currents, eyes watering from the smoke. Her mother had looked so happy, cigarette in one hand, white wine in the other, her uncut hair moving in all directions as she laughed. Men watched her and listened to her. She talked and talked and cheered at the dirty words. Ana leaned against her, warm and smiling. It was, Ana decided, a happy memory. She cut it off at the drunken edges.

Inside, the room was half full. A young woman in cowboy boots and a dress stood on stage with a guitar, tuning it. When she turned to the side, fiddling with an amplifier, Ana saw that her guitar was resting on a pregnant stomach.

A clatter of glasses and low conversation filled the space. One table was flanked by beer-drinking guys in plaid shirts, murmuring to one another through their facial hair, art students assuming the look of lumberjacks. Another table held an older couple: a man with electrocuted thin gray hair; a woman in granny glasses.

Ana found a small table near the back. She kept her jacket on until her beer arrived. She sipped and warmed herself. She no longer felt nervous alone in public; it was an advantage of reaching forty-one and becoming less visible. She reveled in the peace, anticipating the singer.

The singer leaned into her microphone and tapped away a blast of feedback. She adjusted it to the right height and strummed. "This one's about what's going to happen to me in about three months," she said, pointing at her stomach. A few laughs.

The song was silly to Ana's ears, filled with wishes and half-lullabies. But the woman had a strong voice. It climbed around the words with confidence, put them in their place. Ana stared at her. Her eyes closed, then closed harder, as if she were squinting her way to the high notes. One leg buckled and straightened at the knee.

"Hey," said a voice. Charlie crouched down next to her. Ana was startled, she had almost forgotten about him.

"You came," he said. "Can I sit?"

He did, pulling the chair close to Ana, speaking in a low voice, something James always did in bars, too, out of respect for the musician.

"Guess what?" he said. "You missed me. I already went on." She saw now that his black T-shirt was wet with sweat around the collar. Part of her was relieved; she did not feel like playing the fan tonight.

"I'm sorry to hear that. How did it go?"

Charlie grinned, put his hands together in prayer, and looked up at the ceiling. "Terrible," he said, laughing. "But it doesn't matter. I lived through it."

A beer arrived. Charlie thanked the waitress with familiarity. She squeezed his shoulder as she left. Ana was surprised to see him drinking, the foam caught on his upper lip. She could not associate religion and pleasure; they were back to back in her mind, walking away from each other, like dueling gunfighters.

Why had she come here? The smell of the place, years of watery beer and old smoke, seemed to be rising up from between the spaces in the wood floors, seeping out of the old, cracked chairs.

"This is a cover," said the woman on stage. She strummed a few chords, and Charlie exclaimed: "Oh, this is a great song. She does this—yeah, it's—she does this beautifully."

The woman on stage closed her eyes and began:

"You are the light in my dark world. You are the fire that will always burn...."

Ana watched her. The woman strummed, her voice swelling: *"When I can't stand on my own..."*

Ana wanted to turn away from the woman, the guitar on her absurd belly. She was rocking, her eyes closed, in what could only be described as rapture. But Ana felt a kind of heat, and sadness, too. She glanced at Charlie. If he was moved, he didn't show it.

The singer repeated the line, and dove down inside it: *"You are the light"*—until she came back around the other side quietly—*"in my dark world."* And then she opened her eyes. Shook her hair. Exhaled. It struck Ana as obscene all of a sudden, that they should be all together for this moment. It would be better to experience it alone, with the blinds drawn. People clapped. Ana felt her cheeks redden.

"I should go," said Ana.

"Really?" said Charlie. But Ana had her coat on already.

"Okay, I'll walk you."

"No, no. You don't have to—"

"I know."

They walked past the bars, the restaurants, through the bodies going in all directions. Charlie was carrying his guitar in a padded case on his back, turning at an angle to avoid hitting people with it. Ana was aware of how tall he was next to her compared to James.

When they turned south, onto a residential street, Charlie said: "I always liked these windows." He pointed to an old mansion, a huge house with colored glass leaves curling in a vine around the doors. It had been divided into apartments; a row of ugly silver mailboxes, things found in a skyscraper, stacked up by the doorframe.

Ana tried to imagine going home right now, tried to picture herself in the living room, surrounded by toys and sippy cups. "Where do you live?" she asked.

"Not far," said Charlie.

"Can I see it?" He glanced at her quickly, flickering, and nodded.

They had to turn around, retrace their steps.

"I like those windows, too," said Ana as they went past the house again.

Charlie's house was only two doors down from College. The noise of the street spilled over onto his lawn. Two front seats of a car were on his porch in the place where a nice café set should go.

Seeing Ana's glance lingering upon the seats, he said: "That's not mine." Charlie unlocked the door. "Those guys have the front apartment. We have the top."

"We"? thought Ana.

Half of the hallway, large and smelling of rotten food, was taken up by a pile of men's sneakers and boots.

Ana walked up the creaky stairs. The banister wobbled.

As soon as the apartment door opened, Ana saw the "we." A man played a video game on a couch, connected by a long wire to a console in the center of the room. The TV blared gunshots and "Incoming! Incoming!"

"Hey, dude," he said, his voice coated in gumminess.

When Ana could separate the hallway and the sticky little gamer from the space, she saw that the apartment was actually warm and clean. The furniture was cheap but minimalist, and shelves of books tidily arranged lined the walls. Art books. Philosophy. Several different editions of the Bible.

"Ana, this is Russell. Russell, Ana," said Charlie.

Russell nodded. "I'd get up. I'm not usually this bad, but I'm killing here...," he said.

"Don't bother, really," said Ana. "Nice to meet you."

Charlie led her into the kitchen. He shut the door behind them, muffling the sound of missiles.

"Ambush!" screamed Russell. "Die! Die!"

Charlie said loudly: "Tea? Wine?"

Ana found a place for herself at the kitchen table. It was white and empty but for a stack of newspapers and a bowl of oranges.

"Wine, if you have it," she said.

"Russell lost his job," said Charlie in a low voice, uncorking a bottle of red. Suddenly, he looked at the label: "I don't know too much about wine. Does this seem okay?" Ana glanced at it. It was from a winery in Prince Edward County that she had visited once with James, years ago.

"It's fine. What was his job?"

"He worked at the university bookstore." Charlie passed her the glass. "Cheers," he said. "Wait—it sounds like we're celebrating the fact that Russell lost his job. Let's think of something better."

"Okay. To music," said Ana. She felt like James, like she was doing an impression of James, his impulsiveness, his ability to be touched by things.

"To music." They clinked. The wine was good.

"Do you worry he won't be able to handle the rent?" asked Ana.

Charlie shook his head. "Nah," he said. "He's an old friend. I'll carry him. He'll be back on his feet."

"That's a nice idea, but you probably make very little money, if you don't mind my saying that," said Ana.

Charlie laughed. "This is true. My father points out this fact to me from time to time."

The word "father" peeled ten years from his face.

"Charlie, how old are you?"

"Wow, first my salary, now my age!" Ana was struck by how much he laughed. It filled his spaces like breathing.

"I'm twenty-eight," he said. "I'll be twenty-nine next month. Then thirty. Aah!" He raised his hands like he was going down a roller coaster. "It's weird to think my mom had three kids by thirty."

"My mom had me at thirty," said Ana. She finished her glass of wine.

"How much did she drink, your mom?"

Ana paused. "You know about that?" Files. Everything in files.

"She's pretty young, and alcohol-related dementia is common. And when she first came, I don't think she ever told me a story that didn't take place at a party." Now Ana laughed.

"God, is that true? She's declined a lot in two years, hasn't she? I haven't heard her tell a story in a long time."

Charlie nodded. "What are you thinking these days? How are you doing?"

"Oh, well, you know, mostly I'm not thinking at all," said Ana.

"What do you mean?" His head was turned, close to hers.

"I don't know. I think I have dementia, too. There are things I can't remember...."

"What kind of things?"

"About my life. About what I was trying to achieve."

"Wow," said Charlie, and he laughed. "That sounds awful."

Ana laughed, too. "It does, doesn't it? I don't know what I'm talking about, really. I guess you're around that all day, nobody making sense. "

"Well, sometimes. Mostly they make sense to me, though." Ana noticed that he drank slowly. "When I started doing this work, I thought I was prepared for it. But I had times when I would see things—I'd see this, you know, decay—and I'd think: What's the value in this? What's left here? But you see them every day and..." He stopped.

"And what?"

"You don't feel so scared. You think you stop living because you fragment, because the mind gets less reliable, but you don't. There is something primal in there. There's something that eclipses the damage. There's this instinct for life. It's, you know..." He paused again.

"Holy," said Ana.

"Yeah, that's better. I was going to say 'awesome,'" said Charlie, laughing.

The conversation moved to small details, films recently

seen, Ana's work and how Charlie had arrived in the city (on a bus from Victoria, with a scholarship in his pocket). These ordinary things seemed intimate now, because of that one true moment that had come before. They finished the bottle and looked at each other.

"Well," she said. She saw that Charlie was blushing. "I should go."

He nodded.

They made their way through the war zone in the living room.

"Private Miller, noooooo! Charlie—the Emperor is totally giving the signal!"

Charlie didn't answer.

At the door, Ana wondered if she should lean in and give him the two-cheek kiss that had become fashionable among her friends. But she wasn't sure she could put her face so close to his without wanting to add her body, so she moved fast, waving as she went down the rattling staircase.

Ana walked light-headed, uncertain. She headed back along College. The bar where she'd seen the woman sing was now closed.

When she got home, the lights were off. She flicked them on and saw the living room strewn with toys, plastic bits and Lego and animals. She began to move through the room, tossing objects into Sarah's wicker basket, which sat now in the hearth. Occasionally, things beeped and whirred. But halfway through her tidying, Ana felt exhausted, weighted. Without finishing, she turned out the lights. Upstairs, she passed the door to Finn's room, slightly ajar. She glanced inside at him. He had kicked off the cover and was lying on his side, his legs scissored. He was covered from neck to toe in new fleece footie pajamas that James had bought for the cooler weather. His chest rose and fell.

Ana undressed in the bathroom and slipped into bed next to James, who was half snoring on his back. She nudged him to roll onto his side and he mistook it for sex, coming at her hips with his hands, throwing a leg her way.

She pushed him away gently, rolling him like an overturned car until he was facing the wall, away from her.

The next day James made lunch for himself and Finn. Hot dogs. A tin of beans. Finn played on the floor, moving a wooden train through a forest of pots while James cleaned the dishes.

The doorbell rang. Finn ran ahead.

"Wait!" called James, wanting to stop Finn from discovering if the person on the other side would be wielding an ax or a clipboard.

Finn scurried around James's ankles as the door opened.

"Sign here, sir." The invoice read: Kingston Engineering. Though young, the man had a military demeanor, chest puffed. Maybe it was just the courier uniform.

"Box!" cried Finn. James signed, and the courier nodded, turned on one toe, and marched away.

James tore off the tape strip: CD-ROMs, memory sticks, file folders labeled with various projects: ROBERTSON CREEK, GARRISON PARK.

"Look," said Finn. He had removed a piece of white paper covered in a crayon scrawl. At the bottom, in an adult's handwriting: *The Windy Day by Finn Lamb*. Along the top, holes from a pushpin, as if the picture had been moved around a lot.

James pulled out a stack of business cards: MARCUS LAMB,

Civil Engineer, Trenchless Technology Specialist. There were so many of them, the box was brick heavy.

"Put the picture back in, Finny," said James. Finn shook his head.

What was he preserving it for? For Sarah's great awakening? What movie did he think this was?

"You want it?"

Finn nodded.

James pressed the curled tape back along the box's spine and carried it to the basement, Finn trailing behind. The walls were cement, stacked with boxes and bicycles. Ana had imposed order even down here, in what was little more than a cave.

One of them, in black marker, read: THE BOOK. James stopped and pulled it down. Finn immediately tore at the tape, and James let him, watching as he worked open the flaps.

"What this?" Finn asked, pulling out the hardcover book. *Identity Crisis,* and James on the back, with a short-lived goatee and a blazer. James picked up a copy, too; there were at least a dozen in there, both the hardcover and the softcover. Every year his agent sent him the statement of earnings, and it was always negative. It seemed there were so many books out there unsold that they'd be flooding back forever, salmon spawning in reverse. He flipped its pages, realizing that if he ever wrote anything again, people would probably read it on their telephones. The edges of the paper were yellowing. Cheap. Disposable. The shame of it was overwhelming. He took the book from Finn's hand, threw it in, and was sealing the box when the doorbell rang again.

Finn charged up the stairs first, skidding down the hall in his socks. On his tiptoes, he opened the door.

"Wait for me, Finn! Did you forget something?" said James,

confronted again with the young man in the yellow courier suit.

"No," he said quickly, reddening. "I have another package, that's all."

As James signed, the courier muttered: "Our computers were down. I just got flagged."

He handed James another box, smaller, the size of a paint tin.

BASIC CREMATION SERVICES, said the invoice.

James shut the door.

"I see box?" asked Finn.

"Not now," said James. He tried to walk past Finn.

"Box?"

James thought of the $1,600 charge on his credit card and reminded himself to invoice Marcus's insurer quickly.

James knew that he was focusing on his credit card because he could not think about what would befall this little boy were he to learn that the box contained the answer to every question he would ever have, and that the box would never speak of these things, and the box was filled with dust, and the dust was the father he would never know. *This is his childhood. It's happening right now,* thought James. *And he has no father to take him through.*

Finn looked up at James, holding the drawing. He had his mouth in the O shape, puzzling over the world again.

James rubbed at his eyes and managed a smile. He walked back down to the basement, to the shelf containing Marcus's business detritus. He put the box on top of the larger one so it resembled the world's brownest, most depressing wedding cake. He gave the small box a gentle pat.

Finn, who had crushed the picture to the size of a walnut, was now kicking it across the basement floor.

"Hey, wait a second," said James, rescuing the balled-up picture. He smoothed it out against the wall. "Now, this is a really good picture. I think it should have a place of honor, don't you agree, Sir Finn?"

In the kitchen, James put it on the fridge. It was a blank stainless steel canvas. They didn't even have a magnet, and James had to root around for tape.

"Fantastico," he told Finn, who pointed at the picture. "Mine," he said cheerfully.

Hours later, James put Finn down for a late afternoon nap. Finn crawled in like it was his duty, holding his cow blanket and squeezing his eyes shut. James kissed his soft hair.

The door to James's office was closed. He hesitated, then went inside.

He hadn't been in there since Finn had arrived a month ago.

James felt instantly soothed by the chaos of the room, the papers and teetering books. He removed the hockey helmet from his guitar and plugged in the amp. He turned it high and began to play. How long had it been? His fingers on the strings were too silky, uncallused, but the pain felt good. He went back and forth through the chords, closing his eyes, trying not to see Marcus when he did. He breathed hard, letting the sound get bigger and bigger.

When he opened his eyes, Ana and Finn were in front of him.

"Finn try!" cried Finn, jumping up and down.

"You smell good," said James. Ana was wearing a fitted black dress, her breasts flattened in a way that was incongruously boyish and sexy at once. Her eyes were painted gray, her lips red.

"Where are you going?"

"Me? We. We're going out, remember? This is the great sitter experiment."

James had forgotten. He could see instantly in his mind's eye the firm party, the new restaurant at the top of an office building overlooking the harbor, the grim black lighting and reflective surfaces that ensured you could never escape anyone's face. The room would be filled with Ana's colleagues, men growing fatter and louder in their pressed suits; the women thinner and meaner, denying themselves hors d'oeuvres.

"Let me shower," he said.

"Finn try!"

"We need to get going," said Ana.

"I can't not let him try it." James squatted and held the guitar across his knees. Finn made a few swipes and laughed.

"Don't be Paul McCartney," said James. "Be Mick Jagger. People will tell you to be Paul McCartney, but don't."

In the shower, James looked at his hands and his buttery belly. He had put on weight; he was becoming immovable.

James's dress shirts hung in a dry-cleaned bundle, twist-tied at the neck of the hangers, bagged in plastic. Ana must have taken them in for him. He had not worn one in months, not since his final meeting with HR.

As he slid his torso into a blue shirt, the crease along his elbow like a margin, he remembered a party a decade ago in a different bar in a different tower. Ana was a new associate, and James showed up wearing a concert T-shirt—Jesus Lizard—under a black blazer. He was lighter then. He walked fast and everywhere, never taking buses or taxis or driving, held to the ground only by army boots under his black jeans. It was only when he set foot in the bar, glanced around at the feet of the guests, all high heels and dad shoes, buffed and barely worn, that he realized how badly he had misjudged. It was one of the first times his youth had been revealed to him as crass, rather than a badge of honor. In the cool, crisp spaces between people, placed in elegant groups of two and three, James recognized new worlds that required other currencies, worlds in which his father moved back and forth with ease. He thought of his father, standing outside James's bedroom door, his diagonally striped, navy blue tie in a full Windsor, his overcoat on, glancing bewildered at the posters on the wall, the guitar amp humming. And James in his white underwear on the carpet, having fallen asleep, deeply stoned and sixteen.

Finn appeared, holding Moo.

"Where you go?" he asked.

James scooped him up, pulled him close on the bed, breathing in his limbs, his small pumping chest, the worn comfort of the blanket.

"We're going to a party. There's a babysitter coming. She's really nice. You guys will play and you'll go to sleep, and when you're asleep, we'll come home and kiss you on the cheek," said James. Finn looked unconvinced.

"Ana!" called James. She appeared quickly, as though she had been lingering in the hall.

"We better get going. Ethel's here," she said.

"Ethel?" said James, incredulous, and then, to Finn: "The babysitter's name is Ethel."

"She's from the Philippines."

"Oh, God. This is someone's nanny?" He spoke in a hushed voice.

"Elspeth, from work. I told you that," said Ana. "She's her night nanny."

"Her night nanny? How many are there? Is there a dusk nanny? A dawn nanny? A midafternoon snack nanny?"

It was quite likely true that Ana did tell him about the evening, and he couldn't remember or hadn't found it worth noting. But now, suddenly, the thought of this Ethel alone with Finn—

"What do we know about her? Did you check her references?" Again, his career backed up on him: He recalled interviews with police officers, macho men of the law who appeared before him red-eyed and destroyed, choking out stories about child slavery rings; pedophiles masquerading as caregivers. All the experts he had sat across from, dumbly and humbled, and now all James could remember from those conversations was: *Don't trust anyone.*

"I just told you. She lives with Elspeth and her family. She's been here for almost two years. She has a whole family back there. It's quite sad."

James took Finn by the hand and walked toward the living room. Unexpectedly, Ethel turned out to be a boyish young woman with short hair. James wondered if the hair was a nod to her new modern life, if such a cut would fly back home.

Sensing a nervousness in her—she seemed to be shaking giggles out of her mouth like a swimmer shaking off water—James began to be James, spilling over with curiosity. Within a moment, she had a glass of juice in her hand, and Finn was sitting next to her playing with the clasp on her purse, and James had learned that she had two daughters in the Philippines, in a town he had never heard of. Still, he nodded with an insider's understanding when she said the name: "Oh, yes, of course." And Ana, putting on her coat in the hallway, heard her husband and recognized in his response the smallest lie.

At the door, waving good-bye, both Ana and James were flung backward into their childhoods, each separately watching a marching band of babysitters who had walked through their parents' doors over the years: the gum chewer, the sour old woman, the preadolescent with the babysitter course card. For James, the doorways were always the same, and his parents' assurances the same, and his excitement the same. For Ana, the memories arrived in an aureole of confusion. Everyone was faceless, and the doors led to apartments and houses she'd lived in for only months at a time, some of which she wouldn't recognize if she walked by them today.

"We'll see you soon, buddy," said James, preening a little for Ethel. He crouched down to give Finn a hug.

Ana made rustling noises, noting that James had never called Finn "buddy" in his life. Finn laid out Ethel's makeup kit on the coffee table. Ethel seemed unfazed.

"Good-bye," said Ana, who bent down and delivered an awkward kiss atop Finn's head. She felt a million eyeballs rolling over her as she did it.

They left him like that, lining up lipstick next to ChapStick next to hair clips. James wondered lightly if Finn lifted his head or felt any kind of sadness when they shut the door, if the boy's unease in any way echoed his. He pictured Marcus's ashes in the basement and felt a panicky certainty that Finn needed more comfort. For a moment, he thought of turning to Ana and saying: "This is insane. We have to go back." And pushing through the door to scoop up the boy and bury his face in his honey hair, feel his small cat paw hands around his neck. Ana would send Ethel home and lock the door behind her, keeping the three of them in and the cold October evening at bay.

He stopped walking.

"What is it?" asked Ana. She looked grave, as if anticipating exactly what he was thinking, but terrified to hear it said out loud. *He won't be able to leave him.* His wife, bundled and moving slightly to keep warm, her hands in her leather gloves anxiously swinging by her side.

"Nothing," he said. And then he lunged at her, grabbed her from the waist, and pulled her to his mouth, lips smashing.

"James..." She pulled away, ran her fingers through her hair.

"Let's go in an alley and fuck."

"Jesus." He reached for her again, tried to get his hand through the buttons of her jacket, but there wasn't enough space. "You're going to rip it—" said Ana before he closed his mouth over hers.

"Let's get ugly," whispered James. "Let's get a hotel room." He was panting now, shaking her lightly from the shoulders.

Ana shoved him back. "James. It's not like that," she said.

"Like what?"

"I don't know. It's not— We're not—"

"Animals?" he said, and he let out a dog bark. Ana stared, and James felt all the lust draining from him as his wife frantically pushed down her short hair, which was perfect, entirely in place.

He breathed in the cold and made a declaration: "Let's take a cab."

Rick Saliman had spent thousands of dollars bonding his teeth, and the result, when he pulled back the curtains of his lips, was a strange erasure of the lines between each tooth. Something smooth and terrifying, resembling a long, narrow bar of soap, sat where his smile should have been.

"James," he said, and gripped James's hand like they were jumping from a cliff together. This was Rick's greeting: No hello, just the loud singular recitation of a name. On the strength of this fantastic memory, and three decades of practice, the Saliman name was second on the firm's stationery, right after the dead McGruger.

"Rick," said James. Ana swooped over the waitress walking by and grabbed a glass of white for her, red for James.

"She does everything for you, is that right, James? Even gets the drinks these days?"

Ana tried a laugh.

"Only the things that matter," said James, raising his glass for emphasis.

Ana left his side, beckoned by a wave from Elspeth, who stood with two young associates, new hires. One was blond, breakably thin beneath feathery hair; she reminded Ana of Woodstock, Snoopy's friend. The other was tall, taller even than Ana, and less pretty, but she exuded a kind of burned anger—her eyes narrowed when offered Ana's hand.

"Jeanine is working with Steven's group," said Elspeth, and the tall one gave an exhausted sigh topped by a world-weary smile that Ana found falsely mature for her face.

The blond one gazed sleepily around the room as if looking for a place to nap.

Ana felt a pull in the back of her head, an interior whisper—*How's Finn? Who's in my home?*—and she wondered if it was like that for Elspeth all day every day. Elspeth had three children, boy-girl twins and a boy. Ana discovered these children only after the two women had worked together for a year, when she saw Elspeth waiting for a descending elevator at 9:30 in the morning, her eyes teary, her jacket on, clearly hovering in the shadows hoping to be unseen.

"What's wrong?" asked Ana, who hadn't sought out this moment but was merely on her way to the bathroom.

"My son's sick," said Elspeth.

Taken aback, Ana said: "You have a son?" And the son was sick, which could mean a cancer boy, bald in a ward somewhere being entertained by a volunteer clown. "Is he all right? What do you mean, sick?"

"Oh, he'll be fine. But the school sent him home, and my day nanny is having day surgery, and of course Tom can't take a morning off. I tried to get our night nanny to come early, but she sees our number on the phone and doesn't pick up. And I have a conference call at eleven...." And off she went in a gnarled, furious voice entirely unlike her calm, measured self at meetings. Ana stepped back a foot or so, overwhelmed by a mixture of sympathy and disgust. Ana had taken to heart the two tenets she learned early on from a female professor in law school: "Never cry, and always take credit." And at the same time, Ana was mortified to recognize in front of her exactly the situation she, who considered herself a feminist (Right? Didn't she? Had it really been that long?), knew was disastrous, unfair, a shivering, pathetic creature of inequality flushed out into the light.

She put her hand on Elspeth's arm and offered a Kleenex from her pocket. She rode down in the elevator with her and put her in a cab. The look of sheer gratitude on Elspeth's face when she glanced back through the glass filled Ana with self-loathing. Why was there so little altruism in her? She thought about those workplace surveys that get published in national magazines and newspapers once or twice a year: *Is this a good place for women to work?* In truth, the firm was not, but Ana liked the idea of working in a place that was and decided this was a moment in which to pretend otherwise.

Since that day, Elspeth had confided in Ana from time to time. Shutting Ana's door behind her, she gingerly showed her photographs of the kids. Ana nodded and murmured, and Elspeth relaxed into it eventually, growing more familiar, bitching about this and that family matter, presenting Ana with a picture of a life that was torturous in many ways, all drop-offs and pickups and nanny extortions and infected mosquito bites and exorbitant hockey fees. But sometimes, once in a while, great pride over somebody's triumph at school. A picture painted. A report of a surprise cuddle from the eldest late one night.

One time, she forwarded Ana a family photo from a weekend vacation to an amusement park. The kids tumbling off Elspeth's lap in front of a fiendish cartoon mascot, and Tom, Elspeth's husband, at the edge of the picture with half his body sliced away. This was the image Ana saw in her mind's eye whenever Elspeth spoke of her family, whom Ana had never actually met.

No one else at work spoke of Elspeth's outside life. She was sober and efficient, stayed until nine or ten at least two nights a week, took the bare minimum holidays, and moved up fast. And Ana would be next, everyone said, the next woman to make partner. Soon.

Ana heard the low laughing of the men growing more boisterous; drink three had been drunk, the volume was increasing. She grabbed a second glass of wine from the tray, dropping down her empty glass and taking a long, deep sip. Ana looked across at James, nodding as Rick gesticulated. These parties were one of the few places in the world where Ana saw James being deferential. She took this for love.

Ana recalled that Rick's desk contained a photograph of two children, sunburned on a boat, but he hadn't spoken of them in years, or not to Ana. Perhaps only Elspeth dared confide in the hollow crone. She thought of the word "childless," spreading like a fungus across her, infecting everyone: *She is less a child, so don't dangle yours in front of her or she might snatch it away.*

Ana was overcome with the sensation that she needed to speak. "Where are your kids tonight?" she asked Elspeth. The young women glanced about, surprised.

"Tom—my husband," said Elspeth, for the benefit of the juniors. "He has them, of course. He would never come to one of these things."

"One of your nannies is at my house," said Ana, finishing her second glass of wine, feeling it rise to the top of her head.

Elspeth smiled. "That's right. How strange."

The blond one inquired politely of Ana: "How many children do you have?"

"Oh, none. I just borrowed one from a sick friend." The three women shifted. Elspeth tried to intervene.

"Ana's a godmother to a little boy whose mother is in the hospital. He's staying with her."

"Godmother? Oh, Elspeth. That makes it sound so profound. Fabulous. Can I start using that phrase?"

Ana knew that this bitchy streak was awakened only with alcohol, yet she replaced her empty wineglass with a full one as the young waitress walked by. She took another sip.

The blond one took a swallow of her drink, as if steeling herself for what she was dying to ask.

"So it's possible, then, to have children and work here? I never hear anyone talk about that. The statistics about women lawyers..." Ana noticed a huge ring on her finger, an eyeball-sized diamond. *She won't be working in a year,* thought Ana.

"Of course it's possible. You don't have to sacrifice every feminine experience to be successful," said Elspeth in a hectoring voice. Ana dwelled on the word "feminine," picturing her childless self mustachioed, wearing a hard hat. "I'm surprised someone from your generation would subscribe to such a retrograde notion."

The blond woman colored pink.

"Well, Elspeth, I wouldn't say that's entirely true," said Ana. "Suppression is a significant aspect of the working world. What do people say? 'It's business, it's not personal.'"

The blond woman, buoyed by what she perceived as Ana's defense of her, piped in: "I read in some magazine that if someone at work ever says that to you, like because you were crying or something? That what you should say is: 'It might be business, but I'm a person, so it's personal.'"

Ana took this in then laughed bitterly for a moment until halted by the girl's crestfallen face. She had meant this anecdote seriously.

"I only have one piece of advice for your generation," said Ana. The two women leaned in. "Get off Facebook. It will expose you."

Ana excused herself, gliding through the room on rails, making stops here and there to shake hands, dole out praise, make mention of her most recent settlements and victories.

She was looking for James, because James was her way of

differentiating herself from this. Even now, he remained her rock 'n' roll connection, some vestige of her childhood in the demimonde. Whenever she drank this much, she longed to believe she had just been dropped into her work, temporarily, like someone in a witness protection program. This part of the job was tolerated for the sake of the hours it allowed her in the office. If she could suffer through these nights (and she did, adored by all), then she could retreat tomorrow to the sprawling problems waiting to be clipped and contained on her computer.

He was in the shadows, back to her, arms moving, beer sloshing out of his glass. When he pulled back, he revealed Ruth, looking less wan than usual in a black dress of indeterminate taste. Her feet, however, were in thick-heeled laced booties that made Ana think of war nurses. But her face was ecstatic, flushed, her eyes alight, and James, when he turned to Ana, was panting as if he'd sprinted through a door, his forehead shiny, his hair on end.

"Ana!" he said, too loudly. He leaned in for a nuzzle.

"James was telling me about when he went to Liberia," said Ruth, revealing the piled teeth. "I'm really into Afro beat." Ana nodded. She had almost forgotten about James's trips, how many years he'd spent traveling with a film crew and how he would return with stacks of photos and anecdotes and some unwearable beaded garment as a gift. What struck her about those trips was how similar they were, how every country suffered exactly the same poverty and the same corruption. Back and forth between those two poles, with James vacuuming stories from the inside of the countries, all that heartbreak residue to collect.

"You used to spend so much time on the road," said Ana,

reaching a hand out as a server walked by, plucking another glass of white wine.

"Do you guys want to go dancing?" asked Ruth. And if he were a cowboy, James would have taken off his hat, flung it in the air, and hooted: "Hell, yeah!" Ana considered the alternatives and nodded her assent.

The club was on a street between a Portuguese grocer—salted cod suspended in the window; a strange chemical soap smell as they walked past—and an auto garage. Ana rubbed her hands together to get warm while Ruth stood to the side, texting invisible friends about guest lists and entry.

James said: "We should call Ethel."

"Should we?"

He dialed, his fingers growing colder. Ana couldn't hear what he said, standing between two people on their cell phones in the nothing streetlight, watching the babies, babies going in and coming out, their unlined faces under knitted caps and curtains of long hair. This season, Ana noted, beards were back. Almost every guy entering had a grizzly backwoods coating. Was that where James had gotten the idea for his?

But around their eyes, only youth, flat and nervous and boyish, like they couldn't believe they were out on a school night.

"Everything's good," James said, putting his phone in his pocket. Ana looked at him blankly.

"With Finn. Everything's good."

"Oh," said Ana. "Good, good."

"He went right to sleep," said James, covering a little pull of disappointment over the fact that Finn didn't require him at bedtime.

Inside the club, the band, too, was bearded, all except the female singer, who had bangs that covered half her face. There were so many of them, Ana felt like she was looking at a Dr. Seuss picture of alike creatures populating a village: This one has an accordion, this one has a saw, this one has a tuba. But when they turned it up, it sounded good, cacophonous, pure.

"It's not a band, it's a collective," shouted James at Ana, delivering a new piece of information.

Ana laughed. "How Stalinesque!"

Ana sipped her beer, far from the band, near the bar, while James and Ruth attempted to talk over the noise, their heads tilted together, nearly touching at the top. They gave up and James separated, stood upright, and stared, fighting the impulse to go to the front, to climb up on stage. *I could have done that,* he thought. *I could have been that!* This exact thought was already snaking through the room, especially in and out of the heads of the few guys older than thirty. For the younger ones, there was no sense of regret yet; still a possibility, still a chance.

James bought two beers, knowing that the severance money was going to run out in six weeks and wondering what that would look like: Would he get an allowance from his wife? He shut up the thought, taking in the stink of old bar cloths and the deodorant of strangers. He saw his wife moving away from him, cut off from her by young men who looked like James used to look, and women in lipstick who seemed black in the dark.

"Do you want to smoke?" asked Ruth. James couldn't see Ana, and he nodded, feeling bundled in bandages. He handed Ruth a beer.

He went outside with her, under the streetlamp. He lit a cigarette and offered her one. She raised an eyebrow, led him to an alleyway, and pulled a joint out of her wallet. James laughed at himself: "*That* kind of smoke," he said. How long had it been since anyone had invited him to smoke pot?

He studied her face as she lit up: slight lantern jaw keeping her from prettiness, and a kind of a put-upon sadness that was unappealing. But she was sympathetic, too, because she was trying so hard. He took a long, deep drag, and another.

Nearby, a small crowd of people were doing the same thing, two guys and a girl. A pretty girl with black hair, smiling at him as she exhaled, lifted her fingers in a wave. Emma.

She walked with her hips forward. Her jacket was tight around her breasts and came out from her waist like a bell. As she moved, she was backed by the muffled sound of the band, frantic and ominous. (An organ? Did they bring out a goddamn organ, too?)

"My God. How weird is this." She said it like it was a good weird. "I see you everywhere."

Ruth, if James wasn't mistaken, looked a little annoyed. Her hand was extended into space, waiting for James to take a drag.

"I don't—this is Ruth."

"I think I know you. Were you at Yoshi's book launch?" asked Emma, peering at her.

Ruth shook her head no, suddenly a bumpkin, and the difference between the two women glared like a lantern in the darkness.

"Do you want—" Ruth thrust the joint at Emma, who plucked it from her fingers and inhaled.

"Where's your wife?" Emma said, as if she knew Ana. She was bolder tonight, perhaps buoyed by the frisson from the club, the pot. She passed the joint to James, who was feeling the widening of his sensations but inhaled deeply anyway.

James gave Emma a backstory: A few hours earlier, she had come from her father's place in an Edwardian in the north end of the city. There, in one of her two childhood homes, she had sat through a long meaty dinner, enduring a simpering lecture from her stepmother, whose face was so chemically altered that she resembled a bank robber with a stocking over her head. On her way out, she'd stolen a handful of Xanax from the master bathroom, chewing them up on the subway platform. So probably she was afloat right now, even higher than he was. James watched her burning electric, like a neon-colored cartoon character outlined in black ink.

James didn't know how he got separated from Ruth. Later, he pictured her forlorn expression, her stubbed-out half-joint gingerly placed in her wallet for later, her trudge inside the club to the tune of a slow morbid song, the organ and the saw. He was certain that she had reentered the bar, searching the crowd for Ana, nowhere to be found.

But James hadn't tried to find her. He stayed in the alley, crushed against the body of a woman eighteen years younger, the scent of gutter urine absorbed by his ankles. He pushed her to the wall, and it all came back to him, what to say, the slow constant patter—*You're so beautiful, you're so, so, so*—and his hand, and then his fingers, all this with her coat on but opened and the feel of her soft bra, black, he thought, but even with his eyes open, he couldn't see much, just shadows. But he had mapped the body in his mind so often that he knew where to go, and found her wet beneath her clothing, moving until she shuddered in his hand. Then she had her hand on his buckle and he thought of his belly hanging over the edge of his jeans, but it wasn't repulsive enough to stop her sliding down the wall, getting on her knees. He could no longer hear the music then—they were far away—just the white noise in his head, a string between the noise and the feeling of her warm mouth around him, her tongue and a slight nibble that he found both painfully self-conscious and unbearably good, so much so that James put his hands on her shoulders and pushed her mouth off him just in time, the wet mess remaining on his pants, far from her face looking up at him, the chewed lipstick on those thick lips. He looked upon the strangest grin, a smudge of destruction and shame and pride.

James backed away, the two of them returned to their own bodies, their hands doing snaps and buckles and putting themselves away as easily as they had served themselves up just a few minutes before.

James wanted to be heroic, to apologize, to beg forgiveness, to swear it off forever, but he said nothing, only felt the walls around him tilt and whirl ever so slightly. They walked back to the club together, but a half block before it, still in the shadows of the alley, Emma stopped.

"I've got to meet some people," she said. James wondered if he should kiss her. Before he could decide, she reached into her pocket, and James felt a tingle of curiosity: What else did she have to offer? Was it not over? Then she pulled out her phone and ran her fingers over its face. She backed away, typing and waving.

The club was still full. James felt he had been away for days, but it had been less than a half hour from the air to the joint to the girl's mouth around his cock.

Ana appeared beside him, carrying two plastic cups of beer. What surprised him was the calm he felt and how recognizable it was. He had almost forgotten, in his time with Ana, that he had always been a liar, that he had gone from bed to bed in one night on several occasions and looked women in the eye with ease. Just washing a few key body parts and carrying a toothbrush in his backpack had been enough to get him through university. He was good at this.

What he wouldn't consider (until morning, oh, morning) was how refined Ana's sense of him was. What did she know, or fear, about this part of James, that had been lying dormant for all those years?

"Were you smoking a joint with my subordinate?" Ana shouted over the music, smiling, passing him the beer. James relaxed. Her face was dancing with drunkenness. He had not seen her so loose in weeks, or longer. If he was honest with himself, that static between them had been crackling long before Finn arrived. James took the beer and drank it in one sip, washing away Emma's taste. Then he grabbed his wife by the waist and kissed her. Those hipbones against him; her familiar mouth, welcoming, and a wave of loss smacked him, broke his grip on her. The band was louder than it had been, but sadder, too, filled with urgency.

"Careful," she said, as he lurched apart from her, brushing the droplets of beer that had splashed on her wrist.

"What about Finn?" Ana asked suddenly.

"What about him?" shouted James.

"We should get home."

Both of them drained the plastic cups. James made a gesture to throw his on the ground, but Ana intercepted, depositing them both in a recycling bin as they pushed through the crowd.

They were close enough to walk home, through city streets full of people shouting for no particular reason, into phones, at each other, at cabs roaring past.

"I need to go in here," said James, under the glow of the 24-hour drugstore sign.

"Can it wait until tomorrow? I'm so tired," said Ana, realizing how true that was, how she felt that her skin had separated from her flesh. Inside, the aisles were painfully bright, but quiet. Ana followed James silently.

"Here," he said, pulling a small brown stuffed dog from a rack of animals. "What kid doesn't want a dog?"

"That's what we came in here for? It's two in the morning."

"We're a block from home," said James, paying in a great clattering shower of coins.

"Yes, but I'm tired," said Ana, the drink thickening her voice. Back outside in the cloud of yelling youth, she added: "And where the hell did you go anyway? I was waiting for you. Your little girlfriend looked crushed that you left her."

James gripped the dog tightly by the neck. "What girlfriend?"

"Ruth. Why, is there another one?" Ana laughed, and the arrogance of James's question seemed to distract her from her irritation. She put an arm through James's as they turned on to their block, toward the brothel house, where candlelight flickered in an upstairs window. As they got closer, Ana realized it wasn't candlelight, but the blue flutter of a television set.

"It's nice you got him that dog," she said. "You're a good doggy. A good daddy, I mean." And she was laughing like a lunatic again when James unlocked the door of the house. There was Ethel sleeping on the living room couch, a magazine and a green throw blanket covering her body, and the quiet hum of a house in order singing along beneath his wife's drunken laughter.

* * *

Ana felt the burn move down from her head to her fingers where she clutched the car door handle. She closed her eyes as if to keep every possible orifice sealed, afraid of what might escape.

"I'm sick," she moaned.

"You're just hungover," said James.

"Ana sick?" asked Finn from the backseat. The high pitch of his voice felt like a letter opener inserted into Ana's ear, cleanly slicing her head in two.

"No, I have a fever," she said. James placed a hand on her forehead, which was slick, warm.

"Yeah, maybe," he said. Then, to Finn: "It's when you don't feel good because you drank too much."

"Does he need to hear that?" asked Ana.

"Drink juice?" asked Finn.

"Grown-up juice. Ana's sick today." He beeped the horn. "Isn't that what Michael Jackson called it, when he drugged those kids? Grown-up juice?"

Ana swallowed; steel wool taste.

"Jesus Juice!" said James. "Jesus Juice! Can you imagine? Bringing Jesus into that shit?"

They were in the very center of the highway, surrounded on all sides by cars, lane after lane of indistinguishable noise and speed. The scenery beyond the cars repeated: mall, massive concrete industrial building with a parking lot as big as the building, then another mall. There were no mountains, no sign of water. Any trees they passed were as trim and contained as if they had been unwrapped from cellophane yesterday. The highway continued like this, without a rise or a curve, on and on for almost an hour.

James had considered his actions, all through the night, his drunken sleep broken by waves of possibilities. What shape would he lend to this transgression? He composed a partial confession in his head, a general unburdening without detail: "Something happened last night. I stopped it before it went too far." He couldn't imagine Ana seeking more information. She was not a woman who needed to know. And how would it make him feel, what would it relieve him of, really, this rubbery admission? And then there was the possibility of silence, which was sitting with him this morning like a gray, furry egg in the pit of his stomach. In exactly the way of love songs, he found himself unable to look at his wife. He could not meet her eye.

Well, the truth, then: "A girl gave me a blow job last night." What could Ana possibly say? In all the scenarios he played out in his head, she did what she did best—she left.

Right after James moved into Ana's apartment, when she was amassing a wardrobe of blazers and carrying around a gigantic black leather Filofax, James had run into an old girlfriend in a bar. That night Ana had stayed home to get up early for work, but James was barely working then, teaching just one unpopular class, on Aristotle. The small, dark club had no chairs and a band, two guys, one on bass, one on guitar. It sounded awful, and drinking more didn't alter that fact. Then Catherine appeared, oh Catherine with the baby bangs and the cigarette tongue, and the T-shirt spilling over with flesh right along the pink scoop neck. As a girlfriend, she had been dumb but untroubled, up for anything in bed. She was a type of girl that James was always meeting, with a clerical job in an art gallery and ideas the size of peas, which she reiterated up against the bar: "I'm doing these paintings about the body, uh, about how men were always painting the body but now, like, I'm a woman painting the body..." He had nodded and imagined peeling off her T-shirt, getting her to bend this way and that. A few more beers and she was running her hand along the inside of his thigh (Did she remember how that killed him, or was it a generic move, available to all? He decided not to be bothered either way.), and then they were upon each other in the bathroom. He was actually fucking in a bathroom stall! The thrill of fulfilling this cinematic objective lasted for about eighteen seconds, and then he began to question the initiator. Only an artist as bad as Catherine would fail to recognize this event for the creative cliché it was. And also, in fact, uncomfortable—she was a little tall for him—and when he glanced down and saw the cigarette butt floating in the yellow water of the toilet, James had to close his eyes to finish.

When he got home, Ana was asleep. James was wearing the paramedic shirt he always wore in those days. He buried it at the bottom of the laundry basket.

After a long, scrubbing shower, he emerged and stood naked above his new girlfriend asleep on the mattress, the first real bed he had bought in his adult life, after years on futons on floors. And she had helped him achieve this milestone. He took in the exposed brick walls of the loft and Ana's briefcase leaning by the door, her red leather gloves across the top, the empty fingers flopping gently. He could feel in that moment that they had already begun their ascent, that they were unmoored and lifting toward adulthood, and she had chosen him to accompany her, he who would have stayed on the ground, in the filth, forever. She had chosen him, and he had rewarded her with this, the crassest kind of betrayal, one involving toilet paper and an unsigned band.

And so he woke her, and confessed every detail, and wept and wept, naked on the bed. Ana lay frozen, nodding from time to time. He told her he was filled with shame, that he had always been filled with shame, and that he needed her to remind him to be good. Ana lay there, expressionless, asking only one, unanswerable thing: "What do you mean?"

The sun broke through, and Ana rose for her shower. When she came out of the bathroom, she was already fully dressed and made up.

"If it matters to hear me say it, I would never do it again," said James from under the duvet, as Ana gathered her keys, put on her jacket. She thought of her mother, of the weeping. She had no memory of her father leaving, just her mother flailing in his wake.

She turned to James.

"Okay," she said.

Because it seemed appropriate, James nodded fiercely.

He spent the next days trying to revive Ana. Her eyes flattened, and she would go for hours without talking, even as they continued their routine as if nothing had happened. From the moment they awoke, James talked. He talked through her silence at breakfast, her quiet sips of wine at the pub after work. "You picked the wrong guy if you think I'm going to run out of things to say," said James, folding laundry and talking about baseball, C. S. Lewis, Rodney King. He thought she was weighing whether or not her "Okay" was sincere, and that was when he knew that he could not have a life without her, that such a future would be entirely without purpose. So he talked, hoping some of his words would hook and reel her in.

Ana had arrived to him, at age twenty-six, exhausted by the needs of those who claimed to love her. She no longer wanted to be tired out by the folly of others. James knew how her father had vanished literally, and her mother vanished nightly into the drink. He knew her teenage days stopped at 10 p.m., when she shut her door and put on headphones to drown out the rattle and rant of her mother on the telephone or cackling in the living room with a new friend. And in the morning, when the sunlight hit the African violets, Ana felt optimistic again and was eager to bring her mother back to the world, carrying her a tray of Tylenol and tea.

Later, Ana tended to boys who loved her only part of the time, too. She might stitch a torn sleeve, or show up on the doorstep with the right album, but even a fuck in some vacationing parents' bedroom was never enough to keep the full attention of these sleepy-eyed lovers. They left.

But James would be present. James wouldn't take advantage. James promised to fill this vacant building from which all the people who had promised to love Ana had fled. He knew that she couldn't sustain any more betrayal. And three weeks after he had sex in the bar bathroom, he awoke to Ana's eyes on him. They were her real eyes at last. "Never again," she said, and James held her so tight he left a faint yellow bruise on the back of her left shoulder.

This was their covenant, then. It seemed to James that there were things he needed to keep from her, and that she had asked him to do so, in fact. And now, driving to his parents' house, he tried to convince himself that not telling her about his weakness and terrible mistakes was a gesture akin to love. He told himself this while attempting to ignore the rotten stench floating up from his guts.

"Where doggy?" asked Finn.

"He didn't come with us, Finny," said James. Ana opened her eyes, saw a mall before her, closed them again, her headache rotating.

And then it began. Finn started to snarl, and the snarl begat a kind of bark that was actually a cry, a sob, a wracking of body, a flailing of legs, small, strong feet pounding into James's back as he drove.

"Dogggyyyyy!" he wailed through a wall of sobs and screams.

"Finn, don't kick me! I'm driving!"

A huge truck went by James's window, too fast, too close. He swerved, and bodies thrust forward and back.

"James!" said Ana, clutching her side.

"Doggyyyy! Want him! Want him! Want him!"

Ana's stomach bounced up and down. She put one hand over her belly, one on the top of her head, holding both in place.

"Doggyyyy!"

"Make him stop," whispered Ana.

"What?"

"Make him stop!"

"Doggyyyy!"

"What can I do?" shouted James.

"Just do your thing! Just do it!" Bile rose in her throat; she choked it back.

"Finny—just stop it. We'll get the dog later," shouted James.

Finn seemed to regard the words as a challenge, ramping up the volume, the kicking. James felt Finn's snot and spit flying in droplets through the car.

James took the next exit, following the signs to Tim Horton's.

"Are you coming?" he asked Ana from the backseat, unstrapping the flailing body. She nodded, trying to unlock the door.

"Drugstore," she said, feeling her throat, parched and burning.

"Maybe you could fucking help me," he said, but Ana didn't hear him.

They split off from each other, then, Ana retreating to the relative calm of the small pharmacy in the strip mall. She bought a box of cold medicine, throat lozenges, a large bottle of water.

While she thumbed through a magazine, the pictures shifting and sliding in front of her eyes, James guided Finn into the handicapped stall at Tim Horton's. There was no hook for Sarah's diaper bag, a pink-and-blue-striped tote with a small, tasteful label on the pocket: YUMMY MUMMY. James placed it far from the sticky floor surrounding the toilet.

Finn was calmer. He stood, puffy and shellacked with snot, pulling at the toilet paper roll, pointing at random, vaguely disgusting objects that James had never noticed existed in a bathroom stall. "What's that?"

"A wad of toilet paper someone stuffed in the lock."

"What's that?"

"It's called graffiti."

"What's that?"

"It says: 'Blow me.' "

"Ha!" Finn laughed.

Without a changing table, James was reduced to pulling off Finn's Pull-Up as he stood, which meant shoes had to come off, which in turn meant he was standing in his stocking feet in the sticky circle. James located the wipes, which had been left open, and had become dry and useless.

"Wait here." At the sink, James tried to dampen a wipe with water. It began to disintegrate in his hand, forming small globules.

A man entered the bathroom and nodded, began peeing in the urinal.

"What's that?" cried Finn from the bathroom at the sound of the urine rushing with the force of a shaken beer can being dumped down a sink.

"It's someone..." James hesitated. The man's girth had not escaped him, nor the fact that he was wearing a sleeveless jean jacket with no shirt underneath. The word "peeing," which sat on the edge of James's tongue, didn't seem adequate to the task, suddenly.

"Going"—he considered the word—"urinating."

"Tinkle?" shouted Finn, who had flung open the door of the stall and stood naked below the waist, his pants around his ankles, Spider-Man socks pulled up around his calves. He glanced at the man. "Giant go tinkle?"

"Yes," said James, entering the stall quickly and shutting the door. He wiped the boy with a paper towel.

"Do you want to try to pee in the toilet? We should get moving on this issue."

Finn looked alarmed.

"Toilet?"

"Don't the big kids at daycare use the potty? Big kids go peepee in the toilet?"

James was speaking in a tiny voice, trying not to be heard by the giant, who washed his hands at the sink, though James realized the giant could easily peer over the stall if he were so inclined.

James whispered again: "Let's go pee in the toilet. Maybe later we can buy you some underwear."

"Spider-Man underwear?" Finn had seen this in the mall with James only a few days before. James marveled at his powers of recollection.

"Sure, sure," said James. "Want to pee in the toilet? You can sit."

Finn looked at the toilet, frowning. He shook his head.

"Another time," said James, strapping the Velcro on Finn's sneakers that matched his own.

The urinator left the bathroom, and James hoisted Finn to the sink to wash his hands. James took small pleasure in depositing the wet diaper in the garbage and wiping Finn's face clean with a paper towel. He exited like a victor, pink diaper bag slung over his shoulder, the giant glancing his way with a manly nod as they left the restaurant.

When he got to the car, Ana was in the front seat, staring at the row of garbage and recycling cans in front of the car.

"Thanks for your help back there," said James, strapping Finn into place.

Ana said nothing.

"I can't do everything," he said, backing out of the space quickly.

Ana reached down between her legs and into her purse. The dog in her hand was small, brown, not unlike the one James had bought Finn. She turned and held it out for Finn, who grabbed it, as if starving.

James looked at his wife. Her head was turned so he couldn't read her expression. He had a strange thought: Now the dog

James had bought was second rate, older and lesser. James had been elbowed aside.

"Now he's going to think if he cries, he gets what he wants," said James.

Facing the window, Ana said: "God forbid."

James took the beer, because he was offered the beer, and because it was his father doing the offering. His parents had switched roles in old age: His father fussed and hovered while his mother sat with Ana and talked to her about budget cutbacks at the library. James's father looked like a peer of Finn's, in a canary yellow polo shirt so silly it must have been purchased by his wife. He passed drinks around the room with the gentility of a maid.

"Two hands," said James offhandedly to Finn, who drank his juice from a real actual glass, slowly, wondering at the adult item in his hands.

"I should have looked for one of those—you know. What are they called, Diana? With the lids?" asked James's father.

"Sippy cups," said James's mom, who then turned to continue her real talk with Ana.

"That's right. Mike's girls always leave a few behind, but I don't know where they went."

"He's happy to use a cup, Dad," said James. Finn looked at James.

"Where Dad?" he asked. James braced himself.

"He's not here, Finny," he said. This sufficed somehow. Finn put down the juice on the coffee table and began to move about the room, scrutinizing each piece of furniture, the wall, as if he were in a museum. James's father passed his son a look of sheer sadness.

"He's not used to such a big house," said Diana, directing the conversation back into a foursome.

Finn ran his hands along the couch, which was glistening black leather and made James think of a bear's gleaming fur, a hunter's prize. The scale of the entire house left James woozy. Even the double garage had rounded arches above the electronic swing doors. The living room with the airplane hangar vaulted ceilings was punctuated, precariously, by a fan that appeared to be dangling down from a thin string. It was never turned on, because it was never hot between these walls; the air was entirely still and perfect. Warm in winter, cool in summer. From the living room, James looked up at the wraparound second-floor balconies. All the doors were shut. The house contained rooms that James had never set foot in. His parents had purchased the place when James and his brother were in university; bizarre timing, as both boys pointed out. James was at his poorest then, taking the train to the new house on the weekends with his laundry. At dinner, he complained of the price of utilities and the gouging landlords in the city. His mother was sanguine: *You wanted to live in the city, you live in the city!* His father, though he had worked downtown for thirty years, retained a deep fear of the unknown pockets that existed in between his train stop and the office tower, four blocks away. He had once seen a man casually walking along, carrying a package close to his chest. When he got closer, Wesley saw blood escaping through the cracks between the man's fingers. Bleeding, the man had swooned, smiling a little, as if he'd seen a pretty girl. He fell to his knees not a foot from Wes Ridgemore. When the police officer arrived, he told Wesley: "Stabbing. Happens all the time." And this was where his son wanted to live.

On his way out the front door at the end of those university weekends, James's father would take his son aside, place a bundle of twenties in his hand, rolled up to look smaller than they were.

"Diana, don't we have those puzzles? Didn't Jenny leave a couple?"

"In the basement, I think," she said. Wesley pushed himself up from the couch, struggling a little against the bursitis, the sciatica, all the rest. He froze for a beat halfway up and steadied himself, like a diver on a board. James averted his eyes. There were disk issues, James recalled. He had not asked after these issues in a while and now felt too ashamed to draw attention to what he didn't know.

Diana's eye makeup was blue and a little thick, like crayon filler in a few creases. But otherwise, she was perfectly contained, upright in her kitten-heeled shoes and flesh-colored stockings over her slightly rounded ankles. "Elegant" was the word she was going for. It was how she'd described Ana when she first met her: "A smart dresser. Elegant." This was possibly the only judgment she had ever voiced around James's biggest choice. Diana was fundamentally, agonizingly private. What had happened in Belgrade that brought her here was never discussed. James had tried, question upon question, and the answers were always the same: "It was a long time ago. It doesn't concern you. It's over." But James could piece together something, a shape. He knew that she was five in 1941 and so must possess some memory of the Luftwaffe bombs raining down. But how, exactly, had her parents managed to get her out, through fascist Italy and Switzerland to the new world? Was there a priest? Were there false documents, illicit favors? Did money change hands?

He looked at her. She was talking. He remembered her saying to him, at thirteen: "I came because my family died." Died. Not killed. As if old age had gently carried them away.

She met Wesley while working in the sock department of a clothing store. She had become a librarian late in life, through hard, private work, but why this pull toward books? James wondered. She was a woman entirely uninterested in stories. Sitting on the edge of his bed, upright in the darkening room, she would shut *Narnia* and say to her sons: "You must know this is only fantasy. Enjoy it as such." She dragged James away from gulches crossed by children in the night and lions waiting and closets that led to forests, dragged him away and back to his bedroom with its glow-in-the-dark globe, his window overlooking the pebbled driveway.

"So," said Diana. "You are playing at parenthood."

Ana filled her mouth with water, thereby volleying the non-question to James. Her body was grateful not to be in the car anymore but had retreated to a hum of discomfort centered in the back of her head.

Ana could see James flushing, reverting to guttural teenage responses. "Not really. Maybe. I guess so," said James. Diana stared at him, her eyelids vanishing.

"It's very strange, isn't it, a child with no relatives? In this day and age, it's possible to trace anyone. I've never heard of such a thing," she said, something faintly foreign in the phrasing if not the accent.

Wesley placed three wooden puzzles on the floor. James recognized them from the toy stores in his neighborhood: new but designed to look old-fashioned, with Depression-era line drawings of little children (Dick and Jane?) running and fishing and becoming obsolete, their socks drooping around their ankles. His parents must have kept them around for Mike's children. Finn dumped them out, one by one, the pieces scattering on the carpet.

"Do you think about hiring a detective, to see if there's anyone else?"

"We were stipulated in the will. They didn't want him to go to anyone else," said James. He tried to sound certain, but the questions brought more questions: What if, right now, the grandparents were packing their bags? What if there was a knock at the door, a phone call, a letter? Family wins in these situations. Blood wins.

James looked at Finn, and then at Ana, who was not looking at anyone. He suppressed a sudden swell of tears.

Wesley nodded, saying, "Yes, of course," at the same moment that Diana cried out: "But it's absurd. You must know this." Ana nibbled from a glass bowl of mixed nuts, as if by keeping her mouth full, she was excused. They tasted stale. Ana felt James next to her giving off heat, like a planet imploding.

"They were optimists, your friends," said Wesley. "They saw something in you."

"But can you imagine it, entrusting your child to two people who have never changed a diaper? Am I right, Ana?" Diana turned to Ana, who put down the peanuts slowly. "Do you have any experience with children? I had the impression you two did not even want children."

Ana was surprised by the question. The holidays and evenings they had passed in one another's company had run on the momentum of the quotidian: the mortgage rates, the garden, the traffic problems.

"It wasn't about want," she said. Then, to James: "You never told them?"

James rubbed his hand across his forehead.

"We can't have children," said Ana.

Wesley reached a hand down to the floor, as if searching for something in the carpet. Diana didn't blink.

"You waited too long," she declared. "It is not your fault, of course. This is how it is here."

Ana could feel each one of her particles circling, trying to remember where to land.

"Jesus, Mom. It's nobody's fault," said James.

"In a cosmic sense, certainly, but medically, the doctors must have given you reasons. There were tests, am I correct?"

"It's personal, Mom," said James tightly.

Finn tired of the puzzles and began circling the room like a shark, pulling at a coffee table book, pointing at a vase of hydrangeas.

"Don't touch!" called James. "Gentle!"

"Diana, tell them about the cottage," said Wesley, nervously redirecting the room.

"Ah, yes. We might go to a new cottage this year with Michael and Jennifer," said Diana. "In Quebec, while workers renovate the other one."

"You hate cottages, Mom," said James.

"Michael said there was a high-quality washer and a dryer."

Ana watched Finn carefully and tried to make sense of her anger toward James, the sensation that she might just pick up the table lamp beside her in one hand and crack it down on James's head, watching pieces fly across the room, hair and blood clinging to the ceramic edges. What was the thing she wanted him to say to this woman?

He was not going to rescue her, so she tried: "I..." said Ana above Finn's babble and Wesley's murmuring to him. Heads turned.

"It was a difficult time for me," said Ana. "But I don't think about it anymore."

"Because you have the boy now," said Wesley conclusively. "It makes perfect sense."

Ana shook her head. "No, no, it's not that—"

"We don't really have him," interrupted James. "It's probably temporary. It depends on Sarah—"

The ramble was halted by Finn's squealing car sounds as he raced two coasters along the floor.

Diana stood, clearing James's empty glass and drifting on her stockinged legs to the kitchen. Her heels left half-moon indentations in the carpet as she walked.

Ana needed for Finn to stop his wailing so she could make sense of the chaos, locate exactly the source of the slight. She knew that a moment had passed, and they had all survived it somehow. But then she glanced at her husband, who looked wild. He was red-faced, his hair strangely mussed.

Ana stood and turned to the kitchen, feigning an offer of help, though there was never anything to do.

"This is nice," said Ana, picking up a small glass from the window ledge. It was a little bigger than the lid of a shampoo bottle, and covered in tiny painted flowers.

Diana wrung a sponge at the sink. She placed it in its dish and looked at Ana. "Oh, yes, that's Wesley's. A tea glass from Tunisia."

"Tunisia? What was he doing there?" Ana had only one image of Wesley spanning the years, courtesy of James: in a windowless office, with a giant ledger open in front of him, like Bob Cratchit.

"There was a business opportunity," said Diana. "We actually considered moving there at one point. Can you imagine? James and Michael with their blue eyes."

"Why didn't you go?"

"I don't think I would have been functional there," she said. "Water?"

Ana nodded, and she drew them each a glass of water from the tap. They stood, sipping.

"Did you see there will be a new development? Condominium tower. Right by the train tracks," said Diana.

"We came the other way."

"I hope it means we can get more funding for the library," said Diana.

They finished their water and smoothed their skirts, but as they were walking toward the door, Ana stopped: "What did you mean, functional? If you don't mind my asking."

"Ana," she said, a quick, deep-voiced response that suggested Ana was right to press further. "It's difficult to be a mother." She paused. "Don't tell James I said that."

Ana shook her head.

"It is more than just giving up your freedom, or your marriage, in many ways. It's a loss of an idea of who you are. And they will tell you: 'Oh, you get an abundance in return, you get it back, it's simply different.' But that's not quite true. What is true is that you are altered, and I suppose it depends who you were to begin with, if you have the kind of genetic structure that can withstand such change. Does it make sense?"

"I don't know. Maybe," said Ana, caught in Diana's unyielding gaze. "Did you feel like you'd been changed enough already before you had kids? By the war?"

Diana flinched and looked away, and Ana recognized a misstep on her part. They would remain in the realm of abstractions.

"Perhaps in some way," said Diana. "I sympathize with you. I can't say I regret my children. Of course I care for them. But I do sometimes wonder what was lost to me."

Footsteps outside the door passed, and Ana felt as if she was about to be caught in something illicit. James would never believe this; he always said that his mother had locked away the sentient part of life. She had once cut her hand on a can opener and strode into the living room where the boys were playing, a newspaper wrapped to her wrist, blood speckling the ground behind her. "There has been an accident," she announced like a town crier, before dialing a cab with her other hand. Wesley loved to tell this story, but James didn't see it as valor, the way his father did. He saw it as a way of defying her family, announcing that they were, for her, not a source of comfort. There was nothing she could possibly need them for.

And now this confession and warning by the kitchen door. What was Ana to do with it? The illness in her head bloomed.

The door swung open, and Finn stood at their knees.

"Hungry," he said. Diana moved to meet his hunger. Cupboards opened and drawers rattled and food came forth for the boy, pieces of cheese cut in tiny squares, which he placed in his mouth with chipmunk propulsions, humming cheerfully, oblivious to the eyes of the women. Ana watched her mother-in-law, imagining that she was seeing in Finn her own son in a different kitchen, and she, a young wife forever new in a foreign country where the cheese had the consistency of soap.

Ana looked upon the boy and rooted around for some kind of feeling. It was there, but not the texture or the size she sensed was required. Still, she could feed him if he was hungry. Not all women could do this. The apartments of Ana's youth had empty refrigerators, still slimy from the previous tenants, burned-out bulbs. As a teenager, she was often a dinner guest in the homes of her friends. Ana loved these evenings, reveling in the overflowing plates of chicken and bowls of vegetables, quietly taking in the large families with their regular seats at the table, the mother and father like dollhouse figures that had been placed at either end. (Who were those friends? What were their names? Ana had lost all of them, like a bough shedding ripened fruit, as she moved from school to school.) And then, out of fairness, she remembered sitting next to her mother in their favorite restaurant, against the banquette, while the waiter flirted with them both. And Ana drinking her Coke, nestled against her mother's arm, and the two of them content in their quiet.

There had always been food. A bagel wrapped in a paper towel stuffed in her backpack. The remains from the doughnut store, or later, the catering company where she had worked as a teenager. Sitting on the couch late at night, eating pasta salad from take-out containers with plastic forks, her mother telling her about her Ph.D. that she would never finish. Poetry.

"I'm not feeling too well," said Ana, and Diana nodded, as if it were a given.

"Come, Finneas," said Diana, extending a hand. Finn got up from the table and walked past her hand, toward Ana. A small strand of snot joined his ear to his nose, like a purse handle. Diana reached out with a Kleenex and wiped it away.

"Up," said Finn, his arms extended to Ana, his face tired.

Ana nodded at him. Diana said softly: "Ana, he wants you to pick him up."

"Oh, of course," said Ana. She bent and pulled him up, his legs tightening around her waist like a spider trapping a fly, but his hands on her neck were loose and soft. Ana rubbed his back, felt the warmth of him bending into her, his sweetness drowned out by her sadness, her humming knowledge that hers was not the body he needed, that they were caught together in this web of compromise. A smell of orange cheese in her throat.

Ana lay in bed with the lights out, trying to still her head, which seemed to keep pushing away from her, as if trying to unscrew itself. The fever came quick and angry, leaving her drenched and shaking under the duvet.

James came in with aspirin in one hand and a tall glass of iced juice in the other.

"Turn out the light," she said, but there was no light on.

Finn stood in the frame of the door, staring. James wondered if he could yet recognize other people's pain. His friends at daycare broke skin and bled and it interested him. He informed James of these accidents, the stickiness, the hidden possibility that a body could just leak itself dry.

James tried to imagine what played over in Finn's head from the twisted wreck of the car: the empty face of his father, with a small scar by his lower lip. Finn had woken up screaming only that one time. His nights were deep and long. He was not yet haunted, James thought, but it would come.

Ana moaned slightly in the dark and James straightened the duvet at her shoulders. He looked over to see Finn reaching out a hand in front of him, as if trying to touch something. His hand extended into space made James think of Sarah, reaching for the boy as he toddled across the room, the two of them laughing, and Finn reaching her to place his own small palm between his mother's clapping hands, which would still and hold him.

James took Finn gently by the shoulder, moving him out of the doorway, shutting the door behind them. Finn resisted.

"Ana," he said. "Want Ana." He slipped behind James, knocked on the door, loudly.

"Finn, she needs to sleep. She's sick," said James.

Finn banged on the door. "Ana! Ana! Come play!"

James picked him up, and he went soft in his arms, put his fingers in his mouth and began sucking.

James carried Finn downstairs and settled him on the couch. He sat beside him, stroking Finn's forehead, the boy's furrowed brow.

James was used to being a study in contrast to Ana: He didn't mind mess, could sleep in knotted bed sheets until Ana, annoyed at the lumps, roused him in the dark, smoothing and tucking. But he was struck now by the sensation that he had turned into his wife, and knots were digging into his skin. Marcus. His lost job. And upcoming losses were queuing for him, too: Finn, who might be taken back or away, and his wife, who was always leaving, and now had good reason to do so. Soon his mother and father would corrode with illness and then he would be alone, a childless middle-aged man, bald and suspect.

Oh, he missed them all, even Emma, young Emma and that fleeting moment of debauchery that might be his last. In a few years, she would lose her glimmer, and her love of risk, and become a mother to somebody. Getting older was infuriating. He needed the steady footing of his youth, the certainty of opinion, and it was gone. James took a deep, quivering breath.

On this note of self-pity, James turned to the window and saw Chuckles pulling in with his other car, not the SUV but a white van, planks of wood sticking out the back, dangerously untethered. He was taking up two spaces again, leaving a huge gap on either side. His silver SUV was parked up the street.

James placed a throw pillow under Finn's sleeping head and stood up. He strode toward the door.

Chuckles had not moved from his van. He sat shuffling papers and smoking when James appeared at the window. In his anger, James had failed to put on shoes and stood now on the road in a pair of dark blue cashmere argyle socks. He rapped on the glass with his knuckles. As Chuckles rolled down the window, he seemed to take in James from the top of his head—the thinning hair slightly shining with wax, the ironic beard, the expensive untucked button-down shirt in a grayish pink—and then stopped at his feet. James, too, looked down then at the dumb, dog-snouted, shoeless appendages and thought: *Disadvantage.*

But oh well, he was in it now, hot with rage. Up close, James was surprised by Chuckles's face. He had pcitured him as a kid, a know-nothing just out of trade school. Yet up close, the face was lined and browned, as if from some stain, like the hands of a leather dyer. And the guy was bigger, too, than James had supposed, as often seemed to be the case at moments like this, he noted to himself. And also, Chuckles looked angry. This anger, located mostly in the sneer of Chuckles's lips, snuffed any small hope in James that this might go a different way (A surprise friendship from across the divide? A human interest story on the local news?). No, Chuckles did not like to have his paper shuffling interrupted, or his cigarette. This much was clear.

But what else? What next? James was now upon his enemy empty-handed, without a plan. His entire body tingled. He would, then, improvise.

"Sorry to bother you," he said, a phrase that he knew did not match the previous furious shoeless strut across the street, the door slamming and knuckle rapping. James's voice, too, wasn't quite as loud or manly as he'd anticipated, but instead sounded, even to his own blood-rushed ears, like a little French schoolgirl buying a croissant from a friendly baker. It was in this dulcet tone that James delivered his kicker: "You're taking up two parking spots. Do you think you could move up?"

Now James waited. The truck leaked a prickly odor of cigarette and rust. Chuckles took one final drag and James waited for the Bazooka Joe finale, the stream of smoke blown in his face. Instead, Chuckles turned and exhaled on the passenger seat.

Then he turned back to James and said: "You the guy who left the note?" His voice was firm, with a vaguely Godfather-ish tinge.

Did he? Did he leave it? James hurried through his thoughts. If he answered yes, then that door might open and James might get picked up by his belt loop and hung from the branches of the nearby oak tree. If no, then James had officially slapped down his admission to an amusement park only for pussies, where the rides were slow and low to the ground and the seatbelts thick and castrating. He made a quick decision.

"Yeah, that was me," said James.

Chuckles's eyes narrowed. "Why didn't you sign it?"

"What?"

"Why didn't you sign it?"

James considered this question and how it firmly located

him on the wrong side of reason. If he had signed the note, he would not be here now. The whole thing could have been resolved at the kitchen island over one of Ana's perfect espressos. But no, he had not put his name on it, had, in fact hidden, once again, behind his little pen and his paper, his tiny ideas, his life of distant reportage.

James elected not to answer the question.

"The point is, you have a garage, and we don't. Why don't you use it?" His squeak grew fuller, if not deeper, and the little French girl in him whined: "Show some respect for your neighbors! Show it! Show it!" The last words sputtered and landed on a face, one that was suddenly up against James's, a large hamburger face attached to a larger neck and a body that had exited the car so swiftly, James had barely seen it happen. Chuckles was wearing steel-toed work boots as tall as downhill ski boots, and one of them was on James's right argyle foot, grinding down.

"Respect this, cocksucker," said Chuckles, not living up to his nickname, grinding James's right foot like it was an unsnuffable cigarette butt. James closed his eyes and let the heat pour over his toes, smelling Chuckles's meaty breath, waiting it out.

His work done, Chuckles stepped back and slammed his door shut. He leaned against the car, crossing his arms as James limped slowly into the road, backing away.

"It's"—he squeaked—"about...courtesy!"

Chuckles barked a laugh and shouted: "This is what you have to worry about? Don't you have a fucking family, cocksucker? Go worry about your family!"

"The social contract!" called James, limping toward the island of his porch, where he leaned on a post to straighten up, trying to keep his crippled foot tucked beneath him. Something moved in the picture window, a blur of blond hair. Finn had not been sleeping, then. James shut his eyes against that reality.

"Have a nice day, cocksucker!" yelled Chuckles as James opened his door, suggesting that he, James, had earned his own nickname. Cocksucker and Chuckles: the sitcom no one wanted to see.

The orange tin bird that Ana had hung in the center of the door swung on its discreet nail.

Inside, James turned the lock and inserted the chain. He hobbled to the living room and immediately saw Finn, rigid and upright on the couch, staring at him.

"Who that guy?" said Finn, pointing out the window, a look of grave concern on his face. "Who?"

James sank down next to Finn, his foot throbbing. "It's no one. It's a guy. A neighbor," he said. Finn looked down at James's foot and made a sound like a lion tearing meat. "Grrr!" he said. James tried to smile, but pain shot through his leg. At his wince, Finn returned to his look of fear.

"It's okay, Finn," he said. And he tried to conjure up some of the anger that had taken him over there in the first place, but he couldn't touch it. "I did a stupid thing."

Finn looked at him. "Why?"

In lieu of answering that particular question, James echoed something he'd seen a large purple puppet utter during a children's show on the same public television station that had fired him: "'It's not right to fight. It's better to use your words.'" Finn had a look of incredulousness on his face that struck James as extremely mature.

James picked up the remote control and found an attractive

young Asian woman in a cape and bodysuit singing a song about recycling. The effect was instant; Finn turned to stone, mouth slack in the television's glow.

Grasping the handrail, James pulled himself to the bedroom, opening the door to the strange midday darkness of the ill. Ana rattled in her chest as she slept. The room smelled of sick breath and orange juice.

James clumped past the bed to the bathroom. He turned on the light and shut the door, perching on the edge of the bathtub. He pulled his sock from his foot. The sole of the sock was thick with dirt, specks of mysterious gelatin and baby stones. His toes, as they emerged, were grotesque, red and swelling before his eyes like sea anemones. Only the little one looked undamaged and pale up against its expanding siblings.

"Ana," he whimpered. She would know what to do: ice and peroxide and bandages. But she remained in her bed, burdened by her own illness. She was dreaming of the Max Klinger painting on Mike's coffee table; she could hear the crunching of the grass as the man stole away, baby in arms. She could feel the mother breathing, but not waking. She tried to rouse her, to step into the painting from the outside and shake the mother awake: *Tend to your disaster!* she wanted to scream, but she could not make a sound, and she could not wake herself, either. She was trapped in the four borders of the gray and white idyll.

"Ana," called James, but softly, too, wanting her to sleep and wanting her to wake and care for him, wanting it both ways, always, again.

Halloween Day

ON HALLOWEEN MORNING, Ana left for an early meeting while the house still slept.

James awoke to Finn next to him in bed, wide-eyed.

"Hey, man," said James, reaching for him. "How long have you been there?"

"Long."

After breakfast, James wedged Finn into his panda suit, slipping black rain boots over the paws. The suit was too fluffy and the boots too small, and Finn looked like an inflated toy from the knees up.

"Too tight!" said Finn.

James went to the kitchen for scissors. He removed Finn's boots, and the boy sat on his bottom with his legs in James's lap expectantly.

"This will be better. You can just put the legs on the outside of the boots...." James strained as he cut open the bottom of the panda suit, aware of the blades slicing close to the small toes in their bright red socks.

James put a ski jacket over the top of Finn's panda suit. At every house, the boy stopped, running up strangers' staircases to examine pumpkins on stoops. James dragged his injured foot, trying to keep up.

A paper skeleton attached to a door made him scream: "Dead!" And then he laughed. James called Finn back, calming him, then watching him sprint away again.

Finally at the door of the daycare room, James released Finn, and the boy ran as if unhooked from a leash. Colored pictures of bats lined one wall; white paper ghosts made of tissue paper balls hung from the ceiling. Across the room, Bruce, two silver hoops replacing the gold ones, smiled his mournful, supportive smile and waved at James.

As he waved back, James's BlackBerry beeped. The sound had become less and less frequent over the past weeks. Exiting the daycare, James looked at it: *Fun night. Going to The Ossington @ 10. Halloweeeeeen. Em.*

He walked to the row of cafés, selecting the one with the unflattering mirror above his bald spot. James left his hat on and ordered a coffee and sank into a chair at the window. With his laptop open, he became one of several men gently clicking away. Then he pulled out Finn's picture, the mouthless boy floating in space. He stared at it for a long time. He wanted to hold Finn, wanted his body close to him.

Then he began to write. It made no sense, what he was writing. There was no money in it. There was barely a story. But he felt clear. He was writing at last. And he continued to write and, in doing so, forgot about Emma and the green door that held her in, just across the street from where he was writing his confession.

Leaving the café, he deleted her text.

On the walk home, James, tingling with accomplishment, stopped in a small CD store, a place where he had spent a few hours a week only a decade ago. He didn't recognize the name of one single band in the window. It had happened, then; he was not just outside the loop, the loop was unrecognizable to him, a new shape entirely.

The girl behind the counter was difficult to take in all at once. She had a metal stud in her chin, another in her lip. Black eyeliner seeped into her acne. She wore black leather cycling gloves.

To this, James posed the question: "Do you have any children's music?" She smiled, then, not bored, not angry, but young, very young and pretty under the armor.

"Sure. Follow me." The children's section was small, a single row underneath CONSIGNMENT.

"These guys are awesome. Local. This is a compilation, money goes to fighting poverty or something." She pulled discs out one by one.

"I'm looking for a specific song. It has the word 'light' in it."

The girl laughed. "That's all you know? Who wrote it?"

"That's what I'm telling you. I don't know. This kid I know keeps requesting it. A song about light."

"Man! That's insane!" Still, she divided the row into two stacks and handed James half. They put their legs out in front of them, the discs in between like they were dividing Halloween candy. "Light... light..." she muttered. At the end of ten minutes, they each had three discs with songs containing the word "light" in the title.

"Thank you," said James, pulling himself to standing.

As she bagged the discs, she said from her black chapped lips: "Thanks. That was fun, sir."

Ana had missed three days of work. This long an absence was unprecedented, a fact underlined for her by others several times during the day. In a meeting, Christian's small, loud greeting: "Nice of you to join us. How was Aruba?" But the evidence against Aruba was in the looking; Ana was pale, thinner. The skin around the bottom of her nose glowed, ravaged and peeling, its redness unsuccessfully damped down by copious amounts of foundation and concealer. But even tired and only slightly recovered, Ana fell deeply into her work, investigating soybean seeds spliced in laboratories, impervious to disease, and twice as expensive as regular seeds. *Genetically modified.* Ana typed the phrase eight times in one hour.

As a researcher, Ana could pluck the legal issues from any subject she was assigned like a butcher removing the feathers from a dead chicken. But the substance of the question only appeared to her when she stopped to blow her nose. She thought of the wands the doctors had put inside her, the confidence that her body could make something of itself. The doctors were certain that life could be inserted, removed, that pieces could be implanted in other people's bodies, in other people's lives, and that this future was something everyone could live with. But she had heard the weeping woman in the room next to hers at the fertility clinic, absorbing the bad news of another wasted round of carefully placed embryos. Ana was suspicious.

She had consented to the treatments, but had she ever really felt the need, the urgency? She couldn't remember. James had felt it. He was rushing to the petri dish; he was desperate to keep existing. *Maybe that's the difference between us,* she thought.

At four o'clock, Rick Saliman appeared in her doorway.

Sitting himself down without invitation, he said: "Croissants. Café au lait. St. Laurent Boulevard. Bagels." Ana nodded. She had long ago realized that speaking as little as possible around Rick was the best strategy. He would simply pile on top of her words anyway. "Have you ever been to Saint Joseph's

Oratory? People throw down their crutches and crawl to the top of the dome on their knees." Rick was enormous. He crossed his legs in the little chair. Ana felt as if a dinosaur had entered her office.

"I've never been there," said Ana.

"To Montreal?"

"No, the Oratory."

"Me neither," he said. "We need bodies in Montreal. They're struggling since the restructuring."

"Bodies?"

"Your body, Ana. Would you consider it? They're desperate for a first-class researcher. A transfer? Not permanent, just six months or so. Unless you wanted it to be permanent."

"I don't—"

"It's a given that you're beyond capable. But you're also mobile. With James working on his book, no kids—it's an opportunity."

"Opportunity" was another word for "chance." Ana felt that she had a very close relationship to chance these days. Futures kept raining down on her like cold hard pellets, scattering this way and that. She was not sure which way to look anymore. She liked the idea of making a decision one way or another. She liked the idea of croissants and a city without her childhood in it.

"Can you outline in more detail—" she began.

"The proposal. Of course," said Rick. "I'll e-mail it to you this afternoon."

He stood up, broadening as he did.

"I can't say this officially, of course, but I believe this is the fastest way to equity partnership for you," he said. "I think you could expect that within a year, pending review."

Ana nodded. This was what she had wanted. It looked duller up close.

"You've been away," said Rick at the door.

"I've been sick." Ana said it quickly.

"Nothing serious, I hope?" The inquiry was a rough, ill-fitting effort, a delicate glass object in a big hand.

"Just a cold," said Ana. But his point had been made. The afternoon cleaning Sarah's house; the illness. These were to be the last absences. She was being as measured and monitored as a parolee. She needed to be in the chair.

At 5:30, as the room darkened, Ana turned on her desk lamp and watched the man in the tower opposite hers reach around to turn off his computer. He buttoned his coat and flipped up the collar. Then, with his hand on the door and his back to Ana, he froze for a moment, as if steeling himself. He stood like that for long enough that Ana felt embarrassment and looked away, checking her e-mail for the first time in an hour.

Subject: *You should know*

She clicked.

I'm writing you this because I think you deserve to know. Your husband is not a good man. Ask him about the girl in the black coat. Your being made a fool of. I think you deserve to know but Im sorry to tell it to you like this.

Signed,
A Friend

Ana's practical sense took over even as her emotions drained out of her body. She checked the return address—a 1234

Google account. Garbage. Then she read it again, annoyed by the spelling and grammar. For all the appearance of intrigue, it wasn't much of a mystery, really, she thought, as she fumbled for her coat, her fingers sticking on the buttons, her breath short.

Where did Ruth sit? she wondered. She came out of her office. Most desks still had people at the helm, bent and clicking keyboards, murmuring into headsets. A few were in the process of gathering their things to leave. She gazed across the room to the small, exposed cubicle in the center. Ruth's cardigan hung over the back of her chair, but her lamp and computer were off. The girl was gone.

A hand touched her elbow.

"Who are you looking for?" asked Elspeth.

Ana shook her head, offered a smile. "No one. I think I should go."

"Lucky you," said Elspeth. "I'm here all night. I just lost one third of my team."

"Who?"

"Do you remember that blond girl? Sort of pointy?"

"From the party."

"Right. Erin. She quit. She's pregnant, so she quit. Can you imagine? The arrogance! She's going to lose her mind. She has no idea what's in store."

Ana nodded. She began to cough violently, retreating to her office. She found her briefcase and, turning out her light, stopped and looked again out the window at the office opposite hers. She half expected the man to be standing there still caught in his reverie, but the lights in his office were out. Ana clicked off her own.

She decided to walk home, in the direction of the hospital.

Ana couldn't see the need for drama, for the rush home in the taxi. This uninvited e-mail would not ruin her plan for the early evening.

The sun had set, and once in a while she passed an office worker in costume: A witch carried a briefcase in one hand. A man in a suit wore devil horns.

The lobby of the hospital was crowded with people in face masks, and at first, Ana thought this was simply a part of Halloween. Then she realized they were real; was there a new infection for her to be afraid of? She couldn't muster anxiety over theoretical viruses, even when the security guard insisted she accept a squirt of hand sanitizer. In the crowded elevator, every person but Ana had a white cotton mask across the mouth, staring straight ahead. Ana coughed. Around her, eyes cringed.

Ana found Sarah's room easily. The other beds in the ward were empty; one was stripped to the mattress, another was missing an occupant but maintained the veneer of a dorm room, with magazines caught in the sheets and photos taped above the bed. Fresh flowers sat on the bedside table.

Sarah's table was empty.

Ana's eyes followed the path of the tube jutting from Sarah's neck collar to the machine, blurting its rising and falling noises. Her jaw hung open, dry at the corners. But the stitches were gone, leaving a web of pale red lines.

Ana removed from her bag the two framed photos of Finn she had taken from Sarah and Marcus's house those weeks ago. She placed them on the table next to the bed, adjusted the pictures so Finn was facing Sarah. Ana pulled a chair from the wall and moved close to the bed. It wasn't only work that had kept her from the hospital until now. What she had feared the most was exactly what she felt, finally sitting next to her friend: that Sarah was a sign of Finn's future sadness. This barely breathing body was an absence that Finn would have to endure, and Ana and James would never be enough to soothe that agony. All the warm rooms and square meals would never stand in for this body that made him, that loved him from that first breath.

Ana smoothed the sheet by Sarah's face, pressing down on the cool mattress. She remembered the warm chaos of Sarah's house, the dirt and disorder and Sarah's huge, unplugged laugh. She wanted to tell her about the madness in her own life, but it was nothing compared to the madness that was waiting for Sarah if she awoke. She should tell her about Finn instead. But there was too much to tell, and around her, from the hallway, the murmurs of the ill.

Instead, Ana whispered: "I can't do it." And then: "I don't want to do it." And then: "I miss you."

She leaned down and left a small kiss on her friend's forehead.

"I'm sorry," said Ana.

A nurse entered, black hair in cornrows.

"Are you James's wife?" she asked. Ana startled at the familiarity, wiping her eyes.

"Yes."

"She's doing much better," said the nurse. "Look." Ana looked down at the bed. The second finger on Sarah's right hand moved slightly, as if beckoning her. Ana gasped. The finger went flat again.

"She can hear you. At least, I think she can, and so does your husband," said the nurse. "Your husband was right to hold off on moving her into long-term care." Ana absorbed this information. She was quick to cover up her confusion—decisions, life-changing decisions had been made, and Ana, once again, not consulted.

"When was he—how often is he here?"

"He's here every couple of days," she said. "It does help her."

Ana nodded. She pulled herself to a standing position, still nodding. The nurse suddenly seemed to realize that she may have betrayed a secret and mumbled a few incomprehensible words before rushing from the room.

Holding herself steady, Ana closed the door hard. Her vision blurry, she banged into the nurses' desk on her way down the hall, and a plastic pumpkin came tumbling to the ground. She kept walking.

James took the call as he walked toward the daycare. He had a video camera in one hand, the cell in the other. Doug announced himself in his usual way: "Jaaaaaames," he said.

"Hi, Doug."

"How goes it? You didn't come to dinner."

James was tempted to scurry for an excuse, but he didn't. He thought about the CDs at home for Finn. He wanted to see if they could find the song. "Yeah, sorry, man. Ana's been sick. It's busy."

He shouldn't have worried; that part of the conversation had been pretense. Doug said: "I have a proposition for you." The words came at him in the same kind of indecipherable rush that his firing had: "We're doing this doc and we need a producer." James was nearly at the daycare. He could hear the shouting of children in the yard, mismatched sounds of terror and laughter.

"You know what? I can't talk right now—"

"Don't you want to hear what it's about? You'll love this—"

James stopped him. "I'm picking up my—I'm picking up Finn right now. It's Halloween. So can I call you back tomorrow? Is that cool?" The shrieking got louder. "Doug, you know what? You're going out on me. This phone is shit. I'll call you tomorrow. Thanks for thinking of me, man."

Finn had his coat over his panda suit. He was waiting at the door for him, vibrating with excitement.

"Camera!" he called, pointing at the camera. James took his hand. They walked along the street quietly.

After a block, James said: "You know, I used to have a job. That's a little factoid about me that you may not know." He cautioned Finn to look both ways at the crosswalk. They continued on.

"I don't know if I really want that job anymore. But today I was thinking: A camera is a very useful thing. Beautiful even. And I can't think of anyone I'd rather make a movie with. Do you want to make a movie?"

Finn looked up at him and nodded.

"Let's make a movie," said James.

All the way home, James took footage of Finn. Finn ran up staircases. Finn sat on a manhole. Finn kicked at leaves. He stopped every few minutes to look at James's footage, entranced by his own image in the camera's small window.

But when they got to the park, Finn stopped suddenly.

"What now?" he said.

James put the camera down on a picnic table and stood next to Finn, both caught in the camera's square eye.

"Now this!" And James beat his chest and began yelling up to the sky. "RARARRARA!" A few trick-or-treaters ran past, giggling, trailed by a mother who glanced at James nervously. James jumped up and down. "RARARARARRR!" he screamed. He made gorilla sounds, scratching his armpits and leaping in the air. Finn looked up at him, grinning. "RARARA!" said Finn. He beat his own small hands against his panda chest and ran around James in circles. "RARARRAR!" he called, too, circling and circling and circling.

Halloween Night

IT HAPPENED BECAUSE the door was open. The sun had just set and the trick-or-treaters arrived immediately, released with the darkness. A baby butterfly in the arms of her father. A trio of Chinese kids on the verge of adolescence who hadn't bothered with costumes.

"Do a trick," James demanded. The kids looked at him blankly. Finally, the tallest one began singing "Happy Birthday" in a thick accent. James cut him off.

"Never mind. Forget it." James handed each of them two miniature chocolate bars from a blue glass bowl.

The doorbell kept ringing. James decided to prop it open with a chair, leaving the bowl of candy on top.

"Ready!" said Finn. It was true. He stood in front of James, arms at his side, grinning broadly, his face shrunken by the fluffiness of the panda hood. The legs hung over the boots, raggedy and odd.

"I've got to take a leak. I'll be right back," said James.

Finn hopped on the couch and stared out the window at the creatures on parade in the falling dark. James was gone for less than a minute—forty seconds? Thirty seconds? He would be asked for the exact number of seconds several times. He zipped up his fly as he emerged from the bathroom below the stairwell. No, he had not washed his hands, because he was rushing, because he was aware of the boy alone.

"Ready, Freddy? Let's get some loot!" He emerged into the living room to find the white leather couch empty.

"Finny?" called James. He moved quickly through the rooms, his eyes landing on the open front door. A Spider-Man appeared in the space, his finger on the bell.

James shoved past him and onto the porch.

"Trick—"

"Just take it," said James. He looked down at a mother on the sidewalk.

"Did you see a panda? I can't find my—there's a boy—he's two—" The woman shook her head.

"Your son?"

James didn't answer. "He's in a panda costume—" James said this as he walked backward into the house. "Finn! Finny!" He began opening cupboards, closets. Without hesitating, the woman followed James inside.

"When did you last see him?" she called to James, who had sprinted up the staircase. The woman crouched down, checking under the couch. Spider-Man, a few years older than Finn, opened closets and cupboards, too, following James's lead.

"I'll check the basement. Is your wife here?" the woman called up the stairs. James peered down at her, a stranger with a kind, unyielding look, the firmness of a beloved librarian.

"She's on her way home from work. Yes, yes, check the basement."

She did that, too—How long? How long these footsteps?—and returned to the main floor.

"Upstairs again," said James. He led her up to the long, dark floors of the hall, into the white bedroom.

The woman said: "You have a beautiful home. It's so clean!"

Then she put her hands to her mouth. "I'm sorry. That was inappropriate."

"It's fine." James had a sensation in his stomach of bread leavening, something expanding, moving up into his chest.

Spider-Man followed, homing in on the guest bedroom that was only half transformed into a child's room. He picked up Finn's Moo blanket, twirling it around by the head. Quickly, his mother pulled it from his hand and laid it across the quilt.

"I'm calling my husband," she said, pulling a cell phone from her jacket.

James nodded. Finn could not be found. The house was stuffed with his absence. James could smell him, peppery and sweet; he could hear him howling outside to come back in, straining at the windows. He put his hands out for his hair, his warm skin—and then dropped them to his sides.

James ran outside, jogged up the street calling: "Finn! Finn!" Small children moved aside, and he leaned down, walking crouched, trying to see their faces, to see through the masks and hoods. None was Finn. James went the other way, south, weeding through the bodies. He was out of breath, sweating in the cold. None was Finn.

James ran back to his porch, certain Finn would be there, waiting, but there was only a man on the front steps, hulking and peering through the open door. Chuckles. Spider-Man clung to his leg.

"My wife called me," he said.

A stream of fairies and princesses moved up the stairs. The sun had set now; the sky was black. The trick-or-treaters wore bright armbands on their wrists and ankles. Some waved glow sticks, artifacts from parties James had once attended. Spider-Man passed out candy from Ana's bowl.

James could not meet Chuckles's eyes. He began to speak, tumbling: "He was here. I went to the bathroom—"

"Do you have a picture?"

James nodded. He floated up to the guest room and took the photo of Finn with Marcus and Sarah that rested on the bedside table, a boy being hugged on both sides by his mother and father. He glanced at it, at the breadth of Finn's smile. He went into the bedroom and grabbed his camera, too, with the footage from the afternoon.

Chuckles said nothing about the parents in the picture.

"My buddy's a cop. Hang on." He dialed his cell phone, speaking into the earpiece that was permanently clipped to his skull like a hearing aid.

On the street, Sandra Pereira, whom James now knew to be Chuckles's wife, was standing at the center of a circle of adults. Chuckles handed her the photo. They glanced back at James, fear bouncing back and forth between them. They looked focused, ready, as if they had been practicing for this. Sandra returned to James on the porch and drilled him: *What was Finn wearing? How tall? How heavy? Where did he like to go?*

James pressed a button on his camera, and they watched Finn on the small screen, jumping and yelling in his panda suit, bouncing in the leaves. Chuckles appeared and watched, too. Sandra put a hand on James's shoulder and squeezed.

James turned off the camera and went through Sandra's questions, one by one. He knew every answer.

The buzzer was broken. Ana knocked loudly. No one came to the door. She stood on the porch, glancing at the stained seats from the car, wondered if there was a key hidden inside one of the tears. Then she tried the handle of the door, and with a turn, it opened.

The shoes remained in their jumble. Today the hallway smelled of vinegar. She moved up the staircase, hand on the loose rail. She could hear the explosions, the sound of gunfire and battle. She knocked.

"Come in!" a voice called. Ana opened the door. Charlie's roommate was on the couch, console in hand, thumbs flying. Charlie sat next to him, attached by a cord to his own plastic box. He glanced at her once, blankly, then again with recognition. Startled, he dropped the box.

"Ana!" He stood.

"No! Chuck! Keep going!" shouted Russell, grabbing for Charlie's box, trying to work two of them, one in each hand.

"What are you doing here? I mean, it's fine, it's great—"

"I wanted to give you something," said Ana.

"NOOOO!" Russell shouted. "NOOOO!" His forehead was slick with sweat.

"Okay, this is—the kitchen's a mess—" said Charlie.

"Should we go to your room?" He opened his eyes wide, nodded. Ana followed him down a corridor.

"Sit down," he said. The bed, tidily made, filled almost the entire room, so Ana sat on the edge of it. A white curtain covered the window. Charlie grabbed a wadded T-shirt and tossed it into the old armoire.

"You don't have much stuff," said Ana.

"Really? I always feel like I have too much."

He stood in front of her and then sat down. They were shoulder to shoulder, as if sitting on a bus. Ana reached into her purse and pulled out a brown paper bag.

"Here," she said. Charlie removed a black notebook. He flipped through its empty lined pages.

"Thank you. I'm not sure—what made you—"

"I saw it. I don't think you should get a BlackBerry. I think this is better."

Charlie laughed. "A one-woman campaign against technology."

"It's also a bribe," said Ana. "I might be going away for a little while. I'm not sure. I want you to take care of my mother. Will you do that for me? Will you just keep an eye on her until I get back?"

"Of course," he said. "I'm always looking out for her, Ana. Even if you didn't ask me, I would." He tried to catch her eye, but she was gazing at the curtain. "Where are you going?"

Ana saw upon the white canvas of the curtain faint lines like rivers, crossing and cutting.

"I don't know," she said. She could feel Charlie's arm near hers, the fraction of space between them. She could imagine her hands on his neck, the roughness of his jaw. She could feel it without doing it, even the aftershocks, the mess. And then she thought: *No, it's not true: In fact, you don't know how this will turn out.* She had always tried so hard to anticipate every step before it landed, but now she didn't even know who would be in her home, or where that home would be. And that thought set her freight-free.

Ana stood.

"Thank you," she said, turning for the door.

"Ana, wait—" But she was gone, through the battle and the electronic bloodshed, past the man on the couch who was wailing now as if he were injured.

Outside, she moved fast through the trick-or-treaters. The

sounds of fireworks had begun, explosions in the distance, some nearby, but untraceable, popping from alleys and behind cars. The sky, far away, was streaked hot red.

James knew Finn's height, his weight, the color of his socks. He repeated these things.

Ana turned onto their block. She watched a man and woman walking quickly, knocking on one door and the next, like urgent trick-or-treaters without a child. Then she saw the crowd on the sidewalk in front of the house, James in the center. She sped up and then slowed down. Should she rush toward this dark thing in front of her? *Yes,* she decided. Finally, *yes,* and she broke into a jog.

Ana was next to James. He looked at her blurrily.

"You're the mother?" asked Sandra.

"What?" asked Ana.

"Yes. Basically," interrupted James. "Finn is—I can't find him."

Ana blinked, took in this information. "When—"

"About forty-five minutes ago. I don't know. An hour. They're looking."

"Who? Who are these people?" asked Ana.

"Neighbors, I guess," said James.

Ana went inside the living room and saw a man in construction overalls on the phone. Chuckles looked even browner against the white furniture. He held out a hand. "Mario Pereira," he said. His hand was gentle in Ana's. "Pleased to meet you. My buddy's a cop. They're on their way."

"Cop," Ana repeated, letting the blunt magnitude of the word settle. "When are they coming? Did you look everywhere?" But Mario had turned, was speaking into the Bluetooth, passing on the color of Finn's boots.

James followed Ana as she moved through the house, bending to peer below tables, into cupboards.

"He's probably hiding in the basement," she said, trying to coax the words out normally.

"People are looking," said James. He corrected himself: "We have looked."

Outside the kitchen, the porch lights flooded the yard. Ana and James saw it as if for the first time. The workers had finished. The limestone pieces fit together like the jagged countries on a map. The knee-high grasses around the perimeter swayed.

But there were two people in the backyard, strangers, a young couple in their twenties.

Ana opened the French doors.

The girl, wearing a loosely knit hat topped by a large pink flower, rushed to Ana, grabbed her hand.

"We'll find him, don't worry," she said. "I'm Erica. That's David. We rent the apartment next door."

"Yes," said Ana. "I've seen you. Thank you." David was shaking James's hand. James was looking over his shoulder, eyes on the tall grasses swaying.

"We looked in every inch of this yard," said Erica quietly. "Several times."

James walked around them, off the limestone and into the garden.

"Dude, he's not here," said David. The bored, rock star voice struck James as untrustworthy and he kept moving, pushing apart the grasses, squatting in the shadows. Nothing.

He sprung up and left the two of them, rushing inside. All

the doors were open in the house, front, back. A chill had entered the house.

"I'm Sandra Pereira, Mario's wife." She extended a hand, and Ana thought quickly: *I have shaken too many hands today*—but the hand landed, instead, on Ana's shoulder. The woman's voice was grave: "The police are here."

The police were a young man and woman, almost as young as the couple in the backyard. They looked awkward in the white club chairs opposite Ana and James. The woman sat right on the edge, her ponytail swaying.

"When did you last see your son?" asked the male officer.

"He's not our son. We're his guardians. His father died." James was growing angry at this question, the complication in it.

"You adopted him?"

"No, not yet," said James. Ana absorbed the last word of the sentence. Everything had been decided somehow, when she wasn't looking.

"His mother's in the hospital. You can call his social worker if you want," said Ana.

James blinked at her.

"It doesn't really matter right now. The main thing is, we need to find him," he said.

Ana was scrolling through her cell phone for the number of Ann Silvan.

"Here's the social worker's number." She handed the phone to the woman cop.

"Ana..." said James. Her trust in authority made James's stomach churn. In the look on his face, pained and nauseated, Ana saw suddenly what he was afraid of, saw holes that they might slip inside, court rooms, a boy removed. But had she not recognized this possibility when she handed over the number? Perhaps she had. Perhaps she was orchestrating a quick, swift conclusion. Was she now this kind of person? But no, she told herself, I just want to do it aboveboard. I just want to be honest.

And James next to her could feel her cycling through these thoughts, could see her abiding every formality, filling in every blank, and he loathed her, he loathed her. She was risking everything.

They sat there as the police officers spoke, and both Ana and James silently arrived at the exact same thought, bristling with shame: *I am not sure what I am capable of anymore.*

James said the things he had said several times in the past hour, perfecting his description of Finn. Each time he said it out loud—the panda suit, the black boots, the yellow-and-gray-striped T-shirt underneath—the horror grew a little more pronounced. Finn became smaller, farther away from him. The outside became darker.

"What do you do in cases like this?" asked Ana. "How will you find him?"

"We'll engage all resources, ma'am," said the woman cop. The woman cop spoke to Ana, and the man to James.

"What does that mean?"

"We'll need to interview you both," said the male cop.

"Now?" asked James. "I need to look. I need to be out there."

In concert, the cops' faces had narrowed from sympathetic to something distant, aloof. This shift began around the time James had mentioned the fact that they weren't Finn's parents. Ana saw them through the eyes of the police. She saw the house, white and empty (the housekeeper had come; it was so damned *tidy*), the childless couple within it, tourists to parenting. What had they done to deserve this boy? What did they know of little boys? She thought of Marcus, young and at the hands of his father, the scar below his lip. She thought of unknown little boys lured to drainpipes by bearded men. She saw James at the bottom of the ladder of images just because he was a man with a beard sitting next to his barren wife.

"Do we need to get a lawyer?" she asked. "I'm a lawyer. I can make a call."

James turned to her. "What? That seems a little premature."

"We're not arresting you," said the female cop. "We just need some information."

"I think we should get a lawyer," said Ana. "I'll call Elspeth. No—I'll call Rick."

"What are you talking about? Ana, my God." He turned to the officers, both of whom had assumed a studied blankness. "We're happy to talk to you. We're doing it right now."

Ana said nothing.

"If it's all right, I'll talk to you in the kitchen," said the male police officer, standing. James followed him.

"Can we shut the door?" The officer looked around for a door.

"Open concept," said James. He led him to the breakfast nook by the garden, where two people continued to search behind plants that had been searched behind already.

The officer took out a small notebook, clicked his pen. James began to sweat, rivulets from his Adam's apple down to his chest hair.

The officer asked him the time, the outfit, the names of friends. James moved through each question dully, feeling the water seeping through his shirt, approaching his sweater. His beard began to itch from the sweat.

"So he's your nephew?" said the cop.

"No. He's the son of a friend who died. His mother's in the hospital." The cop nodded, wrote in his blue scratch.

"And is everything okay with him here? Any fights or anything out of the ordinary this morning?" The bluntness of the question surprised James. He expected it to be gently bracketed: I'm sorry to ask you this, but...

"Yes. I mean, as okay as it can be. His father died. He's living with strangers...." The cop paused, began to write.

"Don't write that down. We're not strangers. You know what I mean. We're not family. We're not his real family. But we love him like he's our real family. Please don't write the word 'strangers'—I—" James was exploding with the need to get out of the kitchen, on to the streets. He could find him, he was certain. Finn would want to be found by James. He would rise like a gas from the cracks in the sidewalks, pull himself up from the gutters where he was hiding, and make himself solid and seen for James. "Please let me go look for him."

The woman cop grinned at Ana, like a girlfriend happy the husbands have left the kitchen.

Ana found the constant shifts in the woman's demeanor ridiculous, something studied on television. She craned her neck and saw James facing the cop across the nook table far away. They could be two guys waiting for the coffee to drip, except for the cop's bowed head as he wrote.

"When did you last see Finn?" asked the cop, still smiling.

"This morning. No, last night. I was gone before he got up."

"So your husband got him up?"

"Yes."

"He fed him, dressed him, took him to school?"

"He doesn't go to school. He goes to daycare three days a week. James took him."

"We'll need to get the number of the daycare." The cop clicked her pen, flipped open a rubbery notepad like a small medical chart. She wrote something, shielding the paper from Ana. "So Mr. Ridgemore took him to daycare. Does he do that most days?"

"I told you. Three days a week."

"I mean, he's the one who gets him up?"

"I have to be at work very early. James works from home."

"What does he do again?" She asked this in a false voice, the "again" a silly little effort at intimacy.

"He's a writer."

"Lucky you. Husband does all the hard stuff, huh?" She smiled. Ana wanted to snap off her teeth, one by one.

"Did he call you today? Tell you anything about the boy?"

"Like what?"

"Did they have a fight? Anything unusual?"

"No. I don't think I heard from him today." The cop raised her eyebrow.

"Really? I got two kids, eight and ten, boy and a girl. If their dad's with them, I'm calling every ten minutes: How are they? What'd you screw up? What'd I miss?" She was grinning. "They go to my mom's after school. We never had to put them in daycare. We're lucky like that."

Ana said nothing, attempting to dissect this line of questioning, wondering if it was a strategy of some kind, or if the strain of contempt was how mothers were expected to talk to one another.

The cop held her gaze steady. After a moment of silence, she said: "Is there anything you want to say that you can't tell me in front of your husband?"

Ana's disdain for this cop and her simple view of the world

rose up in her throat: The beautiful house must have the dungeon in the basement. The beautiful wife must barely survive the monstrous husband.

"There's nothing I can't say in front of him."

The woman cop looked at Ana expectantly. Ana was meant to crucify him now, and she could have. She thought of the e-mail, and the secret visits to Sarah's room. But she said: "James is a good father to this boy."

The cop nodded. She didn't write anything in her notebook.

"You should write that down: He's a father to that boy. He would never neglect him. He would never hurt him. This is a freak occurrence, something that must happen every Halloween. Children try to get candy, they try to make their way without their parents, right? That's what kids do."

"Absolutely, Mrs. Laframboise. Is there someone we can call to corroborate your being at work today?"

Ana found Elspeth's number on her cell phone and handed it to the cop.

"Now please," said Ana. "Can you stop talking and find him?"

Voices echoed up and down the street: "Finn! Finn! Finn!" People whom James had never seen before were crouched next to cars, banging on doorways.

James saw Chuckles's shadow looming, black on black night. He went to him.

"We've checked every house on that side of the street where people are home," Chuckles said. "We need to finish this side, then cross over."

They were in front of the brothel house. The windows were dark, almost invisible. An empty cat food tin, congealed, lay on the patchy grass by James's foot.

"I think this house is a brothel," said James. "I think there's sex trafficking going on in there."

"What the hell are you talking about?" said Chuckles.

James shook his head. He sounded insane. He always sounded insane around this guy. "Ah, fuck! I don't know. I have no idea what I'm talking about." He went to the door and banged hard. No answer. He banged again. Chuckles stood behind him, saying nothing.

"Come on!" James kicked at the door, and his swollen foot shot heat up his leg. "Fuck! Motherfucker!" He jumped up and down on his good foot, grabbing at his damaged toes.

Chuckles stepped in front of James and rang a doorbell.

"I didn't see the bell," said James.

The door flew open. A warm yellow light flooded the stoop, and churning music escaped, accordions and guitars and incomprehensible foreign moaning. A young woman with thin brown hair stood in front of them wearing sweatpants with the word "Juicy" crawling up one thigh.

"Yes?" she said.

Chuckles was forceful: "We're looking for a kid. A kid's missing. He's almost three, blond. Have you seen him?"

She peered behind the men, at the police car down the street.

"You are missing a boy? Lots of kids come to the door tonight but I don't have candy. I don't know. My English not so good. I sorry. You are police?" she said.

"No. He's my son," said James, not tripping on the word. "We're just trying to find him. You're not going to get in trouble."

"No trouble. I have papers. I am legal. You want to come in?"

James nodded. He moved inside and stood in the living room

while Chuckles wandered through the rest of house. If the girl objected, she said nothing about Chuckles's explorations.

The living room contained nothing but an old couch, pink and faded. Books and notebooks lay scattered across the floor, English language textbooks, books with titles in unidentifiable, swirling script. On the fireplace sat a row of empty wine bottles enclosed in candle wax. The thin curtains were nailed to the windows, above the molding.

"You live alone?" asked James, scanning for nooks and crannies and Finn inside them.

"No. We are three girls, all from Georgia. We come as nannies but it doesn't work out for us. Now we are students. I am legal. My friends are not here." She looked at him, squinted. "You live on street also, yes? I see you. You want one drink?"

"No, thank you," said James. After months of speculating, this reality seemed worse somehow: There was no one to be liberated here, no Russian pimps, no gangsters. Just girls. Pretty girls. Students who didn't mind a little squalor and couldn't take their garbage out on the right days. Girls he would have tried to fuck two decades ago.

"Sit, please," but James could not. He stood in the middle of the room, smelling something pungent, the music loud enough to block his thoughts.

"What do you do?" she asked.

"Do?"

"For job."

James looked at her. "I'm unemployed," he said.

She nodded. "Is very difficult time. Economy."

Chuckles appeared.

"I don't see anything," he said.

"You, sir, you want drink?" Chuckles glanced at James.

"No thanks, lady."

James reached into his pocket and held up the photo of Finn, Sarah, and Marcus. The girl took it in her hands and held it close to her face.

"He is very beautiful, yes." She passed it back. "Wait here." She disappeared through a door. James avoided looking at Chuckles, knowing the relationship couldn't sustain too much extra meaning.

The girl reemerged, swiping her hair from her face. She held out a photo: a young girl, the hostess, only a few years ago. She sat on her knees between two boys, each on the edge of adulthood, wispy facial hair and acne. Above them stood her parents, tall and unsmiling. A Christmas tree covered in tinsel took up the background. The father's downward smile matched his mustache. The mother had one arm on the girl's shoulder, the other dangling uselessly at her side. They all wore cheap-looking sweaters. The photo was glossy, with fingerprints on the edges.

"This is my family," said the girl. "My brother was hurt. You know about the war?"

James stared at that arm, that hanging arm.

"Of course," he said. "What happened?"

"Oh, is grenade, you know. He is different now, but he is fine. It is a miracle."

Chuckles cleared his throat.

"Is sad, yes. But my parents are still in Georgia. This is good news. And I think they will come here, and stay on this street. You can meet them."

James imagined this, all the Georgians in his white living room, Ana passing flutes of prosecco to spill on their polyester sweaters.

"I hope I do meet them," said James. "Thank you." Chuckles could sense that James was unable to move now; he put a hand firmly on the center of his back, guiding him to the door.

To the girl, Chuckles said: "He's at number ninety-four. Come by if you hear anything, please."

She nodded, pushing her hair behind her ears.

"Yes, I will," she said at the door. "Yes, we are neighbors. So I will look for the boy."

The girl stood in the doorway with her arms wrapped around her torso, watching the men, one supported by the other.

They completed the street, door to door, ahead of the police, their pleas generating alarmed faces and offers of help. Neighbors put on their coats and followed them. Mothers stood on porches and watched them walk away, teary, grasping their children's hands.

James crossed the street and continued south, banging on doors, while Chuckles stayed a few steps behind him, working his cell phone.

Finally, it was too late for trick-or-treaters, and the children vanished from the streets. Pumpkins were extinguished. At the top of James and Ana's block, a police officer ran a piece of yellow tape between two stop signs. No cars were permitted to drive on the road, and people gathered under the streetlights, organizing into groups to descend onto the streets beyond. A few of the adults were in costume. One middle-aged man was trailing mummy bandages. Ana, staring through the picture window, her arms wrapped tight around her body, recognized the mother of that new baby. She was dressed as Pippi Longstocking. The woman walked from car to car, peering in windows, the wire in the wig of red braids holding them in the air like smiles.

It had been nearly three hours.

James's foot was throbbing, his stomach churning with hunger. He was far from home, so far that he couldn't imagine Finn could have made it through the traffic alive. But he had no thought of stopping. Finn was somewhere, and he would find him.

Suddenly, Chuckles cried out. James turned. Chuckles was close behind, running, holding up his phone. His face was alight.

"Get home!" he yelled.

James broke into a run on his beaten toes. He tried to push aside the thought of the worst ending, ignoring the distant wail of an ambulance. It could not go that way, back to the morgue, back to the drawers in the bottom of a city hospital.

Then Sandra was coming toward him, jogging past the skinny Victorian houses, deking between the hovering people.

"You didn't answer your cell phone!" she called.

"I didn't hear it—" said James, and then he saw her face: joy. "We found him! We found him! Come home!"

He limped and dragged as fast as he could until he reached his house, the picture window framing a crowd of strangers. In the center, Ana. And Finn, his head buried in her shoulder, the panda hood slack around his neck.

James pushed through the wall of people.

"He was in Mario's van, can you believe it? He fell asleep in there," called Sandra to his back.

"Oh my God, I left it open. Jesus Christ..." said Chuckles somewhere in the din of voices. But James couldn't answer. He looked at Ana, and he could not identify the expression on her face.

"Finny," said James, moving his own body around both

Ana's and Finn's, collecting their bodies in his arms. Somehow, in the crush of limbs, Finn shifted and came apart from Ana, attaching himself at James's neck. James took in his scent, the warmth of him, and the two stood separately, breathlessly.

"Don't ever do that again," whispered James. "You scared us so much. You scared us to death."

"Okay," said Finn.

When James lifted his head from the boy, Ana had already moved across the room and stood talking to the police officer.

The crowd began to thin. The young couple from next door waved as they left.

"I can't thank you—" said James, and Sandra shushed him, taking her husband's hand. Their son, the boy in the Spider-Man costume, grabbed the final handful of candy from the blue glass bowl.

The bath was hot with lavender sweetness. James used Ana's special bubble bath. He rubbed the washcloth over Finn's shoulders. The boy did not feel fragile to him. *This is new,* thought James; he had always worried he would break him.

Ana sat on the toilet behind them, holding a white towel. James glanced at her and thought, *Ah, there's the broken body.* Her thinness shocked him.

He returned to Finn and began his patter: "What's the boat do? Does the boat go *pshew*?" James picked up a yogurt container, flew it through the sky.

Finn squealed. "No! That's airplane! Boat stays in water!"

"Ah, like this?" said James, driving the yogurt container along the side of the tub. *"Vroom, vroom."*

"Noooo!" Finn was laughing now, his shoulders sprinkled with soapsuds. "That's car!"

"Oh, I see," said James. "This is a boat. Delicious!" He pretended to eat the yogurt container. Finn could barely control himself, laughter pealed out of him. James glanced at Ana. She wasn't smiling.

"Finn show you," said Finn. He dropped the container on the water's surface. It floated. "See?"

The phone rang. Ana handed the towel to James and left the bathroom.

James finished the routine: the small toothbrush, the Pull-Up, the flannel pajamas covered in monkeys.

He sat on the bed and read to Finn a book about a mole looking for love. He laid the boy down, moved his hands along the sides of the body as if encasing him in a tomb. Then he leaned in, nose to nose.

"You can't go anywhere without me, or without Ana," said James. "Do you know that now? I was so worried."

Finn wriggled his arms out of the quilt and reached for James's face.

"Okay," he said.

"What were you doing anyway? Why did you leave?"

A look moved across Finn's face, inquisitive and pained. James braced himself. "I look for Mommy," whispered Finn.

James's throat constricted. He put his hands on the boy's face. He kissed one eyelid, then the other. "Yeah? You thought she was outside?" he asked. Finn nodded.

"I go home now?" he asked.

James took his hands from Finn's cheeks, pulled at his beard.

"I don't know, Finny. Your mommy's really sick. You might have to stay here with us for a long time. Would that be okay?"

Finn searched James's face. He didn't reply.

"We would love to have you. We would be—honored to have you live with us," said James. His voice dropped to a whisper. "We could have this extraordinary life. We can do anything. I think it's possible." He stroked his arm.

"I go home," said Finn.

James pulled the boy from the mattress, engulfed him. He assumed Finn was crying, but when he placed him back on the bed, he saw that he was wrong; only James had been crying.

With his head on the pillow, Finn's eyelids fell, and he was asleep.

Ana was sitting in the kitchen nook, surrounded by dark windows. Her hands were clasped in front of her on the empty table.

James filled a glass with red wine.

"Want one?"

Ana shook her head.

He stood at a distance, leaning against the island in the middle of the room.

"Who called?"

"Ann. The police called her," said Ana. "She's coming by in an hour."

James stared at her. "Did she say anything? Does she think it's unsafe here for Finn?"

"I don't know. She said it was procedure."

"Procedure." James paused, sipped his wine. "Fucking bureaucrats."

Ana could not look at him. She could feel him standing there with Finn on his side. Their allegiance was suffocating. It had filled the house, crowded her out.

"I don't know if I can do this," said Ana. She felt strange as she spoke, dry.

James put down his wine.

"What do you mean?"

Ana looked out the window.

"I don't want to be a mother," she said blandly. James breathed. He saw her suddenly as something barely held together, like a stack of sticks that happened to be piled up on the chair. She was a liar. There was a lie in their house. Anger welled up in him.

"Why did we spend two years with your legs in the goddamned stirrups then, huh? Why did we spend thirty thousand dollars? What the fuck are you talking about?"

"*We* didn't spend it. *I* spent it. It was my money," said Ana. "You wanted me that way."

James stared at her. "You don't get to say that."

"I don't? What do I get to say, then?" Ana turned from the window and locked James's eyes. "How about: Who are you sleeping with? Or who did you fuck? Was it in the bathroom at the club, like last time? Was it that classy? Or is it something real? Is it love, James? Are you in love with Ruth the Temp?" The word "love" was twisted and wretched.

Then she turned back to the window.

"Never mind, actually." Ana continued, in the same blank voice: "I'm not sure what I'm looking at. I recognize this house. I think I do."

"Ana..." said James. "Ana, it was nothing. And it wasn't Ruth. This girl—this woman I used to work with—not even sex, I swear—"

She waved her hand. "I don't want to know," she said.

James stammered, "What do you want me to say?"

"You never asked me what I wanted. We just kept moving somehow. We were grabbing at things as we moved along, and it seemed like the right moment, so we grabbed at a baby. But what if I never wanted that?"

"Don't conflate this. You're angry—"

"Yes, I'm angry," said Ana. A blackness rustled in the yard.

"You did want a baby, you did. We both wanted it—"

"No," said Ana. "I was relieved. I was so relieved. I went up to Lake Superior and I stayed in that hotel—"

"When you lost the baby—"

"But it didn't feel like a loss. It felt like a reprieve."

James shook his head. "Don't say it—"

Ana continued: "And a woman—if you're a woman—you can't say that out loud. Did you know that? You cannot say it—" Ana began to weep. Her body rippled, her face went liquid. James stared at her. He had not seen her cry in years. "Because it makes you monstrous. To not want to be a mother is a monstrous thing for a woman. It's grotesque."

"Don't cry, Ana, please," said James. He leaned across the table toward her, reaching for her hands. She kept them at her sides, hidden.

"Being with you was good for me because it was like being alone. You—you were your own planet. I could just watch you from down here. But now—you're something different. You're so small now," said Ana.

James bent his head. He knew this was true; something had broken off from him, some potency that they had both pretended was not required. But what it had been replaced with was better, he thought, what it was replaced with was Finn. He, James, had in him the possibility of something hallowed.

And then—the alley—the girl—

He expected the explanation to come up in him, to tumble from his lips, but there was nothing. He struggled: "I'm not good at being old, Ana. I don't feel old, but I'm old, and I hate it," said James. "I don't know why I do the things I do. Nothing is wrong in my life. Nothing is wrong. We have everything. We even have a kid now."

Ana shook her head. "You have a kid. You're the father," she said, rising to her feet.

He grabbed for her, knocking the glass of wine. It fell from the table, shattering on the tile.

"I wanted it. Ana, I wanted to be a father. I need it—"

"What do you think it's giving you, James? Wisdom? It doesn't change who you are."

"It does, Ana."

Ana shook her wrist free of James's hand. "It was a great gift they gave us, really, these people we didn't really know. The ultimate audition."

She began pacing the room. She was still wearing her work clothes, and her black stockings made no sound as she moved back and forth, never glancing at him. She stepped through the wine, leaving footprints.

"Watch the glass," said James.

The wine spread across the floor, and suddenly, as if emerging from the dark puddle, James saw a future without Ana in it. He could call Doug about a job. He could sacrifice something. For the first time, he could see himself with Finn, two guys in a crowded apartment. Elsewhere.

It was ruthless in this way, the shift. It started only with this image, this ability to see a life even if it did not exist, like one of Finn's picture books, like a segment for his TV show. It gathered momentum.

"Do you love me?" asked Ana.

She could not mean this, thought James, she could not be serious that, in the end, he had to choose. When he considered the question, he knew the answer, he knew it by its weight, the scales of history upon it. The entire past of them, the creation of them, the idea of them, bore down upon him. But he could not answer.

Ana had her own picture in her head: the whiteness of a bed.

"You love him more," she said. James crumpled against the wall and slid to the floor, his feet out in front of him. His head slumped. Now he was crying, and Ana remembered: James is a crier. Ana knew that this was the kind of useless detail she would carry with her forever, long after they ended.

"It's okay," said Ana. "I don't know if I love you anymore, either."

James shook his head. "I hadn't answered yet," he said.

"Oh, James," said Ana. "You did. You answer it all the time. And it's okay. We're not enough. It's too weak, this life we made. It can't carry what we're asking it to carry." She crouched, ran her fingers over his slumped head: "It's okay. It's okay."

"Ana..."

She began to pick up the broken glass. She made a stack of it on the counter. She took a piece of newspaper from the recycling bin and wrapped the glass in it.

"You are so careful," he said.

She nodded, her hand on the newspaper, pressing down, feeling a slow searing pain in her palm.

As she did this, James came behind her with a cloth and

began wiping up the wine, all of Ana's dark footprints vanishing.

By the time Ann Silvan arrived, Ana had showered. They sat on the couch, side by side, Ana's hair dripping down her neck, onto the collar of her sweatshirt. They answered more questions. Ann smelled of dinner. She apologized for not coming faster; her own daughter was ill from Halloween candy. Her demeanor had changed. She was warmer, less wary. Something had been proven in the handling of the averted disaster. They were publicly competent at last, but privately ruined.

James took her upstairs to look in on Finn. Ann Silvan went to the edge of the bed and leaned over his gently sleeping form. She didn't wake him. She said she would return in the morning. She told them the police were not concerned, that everything was routine. She told them not to worry.

Ana took almost nothing from the house. A large suitcase stood in front of James's desk, where their printer sat. James leaned in the doorway as she ran off her ticket.

Down the hall, Finn napped.

"What about your books?"

"Don't need them."

It was the first time she had entered the house in a week, but she'd been in his dreams so much lately that her actual presence made James feel like he was asleep. He was exhausted; sleep came in quick furious bursts, electric with Ana, and then he'd wake and stay that way until the sun came up, looking at his empty room, his empty house.

She had been living in a downtown suite that the firm owned and working until one or two in the morning and then collapsing into bed. Only when James asked her about the hotel did she realize she couldn't describe a single physical detail of where she'd been sleeping. Maybe wallpaper?

And now she was going to live in another hotel suite in another city.

"You'll need your winter jacket," said James.

"I shipped it."

Seeing him made her angrier than she had expected. She didn't flick aside her anger, either, but kept it close, her eyes down, pushing past him with her suitcase jostling his body.

"I'll take it," said James.

"Don't," she said. They collided a little, disentangled, and made it downstairs with Ana carrying the bag.

"Ana..." said James.

He shadowed her as she did one final sweep of the house, picking up a few letters and a reusable coffee mug. She considered the mug, then put it back down on the edge of a bookshelf where it had left a brown ring. She called a taxi on her cell phone, giving the address with the prickly awareness that she might never say it again.

In the living room, James moved in front of her. "Ana, I'm sorry. I said this in my e-mail: It was nothing, a drunken grope—I was going to tell you—I was even writing it that day...."

Finally, she looked at him, scanning his face angrily. James was relieved to have her eyes; it seemed like progress somehow. "So you get to shed your story and I get to carry around forever a picture of my husband getting blown by a twenty-year-old or whatever it was?" said Ana. "I don't want your confession. That's your burden."

Ana walked past him, kicking at the mess on the floor, the toys and dirty clothes. The entire house smelled like blackened banana. She opened the door. Leaves spun on the pathway outside.

James suddenly moved in front of her, slamming the door.

"Let me go," said Ana.

"Ana, I've—been thinking...." He moved to grab her arms, then thought better of it and clasped his hands together. "Here's the thing: We don't have to live here, right? We could move to one of those small towns outside the city, with a big yard. People are doing that now. We could scale down. Maybe I could do something totally different, get into my music—you can take the train into the city. I'll look after Finn— just simplify, right? Just get back to the land—"

"We were never on the land, James." Ana tried to get past him.

"But we could try it. We could leave and really try being a family—"

Ana threw her hands in front of her face and yelled: "I don't want it! I don't want to be raising everybody!" Her jaw clenched. "What if I had gotten pregnant? I'd be here, at home, glued to a baby, and where would you be? Off with some intern?"

"I would never do that to you."

"But you did it." She wiped her nose with her sleeve. "For one night, you did what you wanted. You're always the one who gets to be free."

"Okay then, let's go back. Let's go backward. We'll be like we were before, but with Finn—"

"And have more brunches? And go on more holidays? And all the time, you'll be thinking: My empty wife. My poor empty wife. The one thing you need, the one thing that will make you grow up, I can't give you. Do you forget that? Do you forget that I don't make babies?"

"Neither do I! I can't make babies either, you fucking idiot!" James yelled. Ana went for the door, opening it. Again, James slammed it shut, blocking it with his body.

"Don't go—I'm sorry—don't go—"

"Let me go."

"Don't go—" Ana opened the door, and James slammed it again, louder. Ana breathed heavily.

"Ana, look at me." She wouldn't, her eyes fixed on floating space. "Don't leave. You're always leaving—"

The sound of fist on wood was a dull whack that left no mark, but James pulled his hand away and swore. Shreds of skin flapped from his knuckles, tiny white sheets. Blood seeped onto his wrist. They both looked down at the useless hand.

"What are you doing? What are you doing?" Tears were streaming down Ana's face. "I can't help you."

She opened the door at last, and he followed her, the blood from his hand seeping down his arm now. "Ana!"

The taxi idled outside.

Ana managed to carry the suitcase, and the driver met her halfway up the walk, grabbing one of them, glancing at James with suspicion.

At the same time, Ana and James heard it: Finn crying, distantly, through the open door.

"Ana—" said James, straightening, clutching his ragged fist.

"Go get him," she said, and she meant it.

But James stood on the walk as the driver loaded her bags, and Ana climbed in. He stayed there as she shut her door, and the car pulled away. Only when he couldn't see it anymore did he turn and stagger back to the house and the boy waiting for him.

December

ANA HADN'T HAD much to unpack. The movers had brought a few more suitcases and boxes. She had taken a junior suite, not because it was cheaper, but because she imagined something sparser and more monastic than the Grand Suite option. Instead, rooms were opulent in ambition, but cheap in materials, with yellow throw cushions in the tones of a fast-food restaurant occupying all the extra space on the couch and the wing chair. A miniature Christmas tree sat in a bucket next to the kitchen table.

On a Saturday afternoon a month after her arrival, Ana sat on the edge of the couch, looking at the tree, decorated in gold balls. She felt tired and light, but not sad.

She had done it in such a way as to never have to see them. She had left the car. Everything else could be dealt with later, in six months, when she would decide whether or not to return. She didn't miss any of her things. She felt that she was readying for something and wondered if this was how James had felt all those years, waiting for their baby—the great, exhilarated anticipation.

She put on her scarf and jacket, took her bag. The door was hollow and caught on the rug behind her.

"Good night, *madame,*" said the doorman as she passed through the lobby.

"Bonne soirée," she replied.

Ana went to the gym and ran farther than usual on the

treadmill. Her body was getting stronger. She had put on a little weight, and with it came a sensation of being rooted, heavier in her feet. She liked the new curve of her hips.

After her workout, Ana sat in the steam room, something she had only started to do in Montreal. There was one woman in the room with her, concealed by puffs of steam. At one point, she shifted to reveal a long, vertical scar along her chest plate, and then vanished in the heat again.

After showering, Ana applied her makeup carefully. Half the guests would be francophone, and though her French was rusty, it was passable, and she had found herself enjoying speaking it, even when she struggled for the right word. She felt as though she were leaving everything, even her tongue.

The party turned out to be dull. By dessert, Ana had stopped listening to the conversations around her, gazing instead out the large paned windows at the frosted streetlamps, wondering why there was no music playing.

A man in an elegant suit switched seats with a colleague in order to sit next to her. He spoke English and asked her the same questions she was always asked: What did she think of the city? Was she cold? Was she following the government corruption scandal? His name was Richard, and he had a practiced intensity, locking her gaze. As he filled her glass, Ana assessed the gray hair, the weathered but moisturized face and tidy nails. He was a type. At the end of the evening, she gave him her number when he asked for it.

The first date, Richard picked her up in his car. He took her to dinner at a restaurant in Outremont, ordering in his perfect French, complimenting Ana on her own efforts. Afterward, she went back to his apartment in Old Montreal, a prewar loft now walled with glass, with views out to the skyline.

The sex was another foreign experience. She hadn't slept with that many people, really. She was suddenly acutely aware of how her body had changed; only James knew what she really looked like, who she had been when she had been her physical best. As Richard pulled down her tights, Ana imagined the pale blue veins in her legs. He kissed her neck and shoulders, and she saw the skin on her elbows thinning, puckered. But Richard murmured worship about her body: "You're gorgeous," he said, gripping and smoothing, and she let herself fall into him. He was forceful, too, and the staged roughness turned her on. She came with stuttered breath, but then he glanced at her with a triumphant gaze that made her look away.

Ana went through the courtship with the fascination of an archaeologist at a dig. *This was here, all this time, and I didn't know!* She thought of him as her first adult boyfriend.

Richard sent flowers and took her to the opera, where the heels pinching her feet didn't stop her from luxuriating in the music. He would vanish for days into his work, and that was fine. She could do the same, and he said nothing. Once, he went away to Florida for a weekend of golf with old friends. There was no talk of fidelity or future. A fifty-three-year-old man without any children spoke to long-ago decisions, not to be reopened. He never asked her why she had no children, and at first, this silence was emancipating.

And there was much silence between them, which Ana had thought she needed.

One night, Richard cooked her dinner, and they had sex, furiously, on his bed. It was only ten o'clock, but Richard lay sleeping, shirtless with a chest of gray hair, arms like a starfish. He slept in this odd way, totally untroubled. She felt a pull of longing for James, an urge to share her strange new reality with him. She knew James would find Richard outrageous; corporate and trivial. This comforted Ana somehow, for part of her agreed.

She had awoken that morning feeling that she had left a piece of herself somewhere, the way she imagined a heroin addict might feel joining the sober and straight life. This, she realized now, was how it felt to be bound to James. Their past, known only to them, could rear itself anywhere, even here, in the bedroom of another man.

Ana pulled on her underpants and went to the window. Below, on the cobblestone streets, snow lay shining, inviting in the streetlamps. She put on her skirt and her boots, washed her face in the bathroom. In a week, she would see her mother for Christmas. She had booked a hotel. She wouldn't call James, not yet.

She left Richard sleeping.

The cold was still shocking to her. It had begun to snow, large, fat flakes that melted on Ana's face.

She walked quickly, crunching in her boots past Christmas lights in trees. Illuminated wreaths hung from the streetlamps on Sherbrooke.

She heard the choir before she reached the church, which was modest, its stained glass clouded with dirt. They were having a rehearsal, starting and stopping, with laughter in between. Ana stood and listened until the singers fell into one another and the music rose, draping her body.

She stood for a long time in the snow that made equal the sidewalks and the shrubs, shrouding the skyscrapers. She listened to the strangers' voices calling *glory, glory* through the trees of the city where she now lived.

* * *

Finn had a candy cane in one hand. A crowd of people waited outside Sarah's door. Suspense bounced back and forth between all of them.

Finn stood on James's feet, clutching James's pant leg with his free hand, looking up at him.

"Let's dance!" said Finn.

"Shh," said James, reaching down to rub Finn's head.

The young doctor with her hair tightly pulled back was speaking. The content of her speech mattered less than the way she was saying it, which was hot and breathless. She had not learned to mask that yet. She was thrilled.

"MRI indicates complete brain function," she said.

"Complete?" asked James.

"Extensive therapy will be required. Hers is a serious brain injury, but she's extraordinarily lucky." James tried not to roll his eyes at the word "lucky."

"James! Dance!" said Finn, hopping up and down on James's feet. James put Finn's candy cane in his coat pocket so they could hold hands.

"Has he been in to see her yet?" asked the doctor.

James shook his head. "We were waiting. I was waiting to talk to you guys...."

With both of Finn's feet on his, and their hands clasped, James began to waltz Finn around the corridor, singing: "Dance me to the end of love. La la, la la, la la..." Finn laughed. The doctors watched and waited. Finally, the routine was done, and they went inside.

Sarah looked as she had looked for the past fifteen weeks, but her eyes were open. It startled James, as though the glass eyeballs of an animal in a museum diorama had moistened. A patch of white gauze on her neck covered the hole where the tube had been. She had been liberated from the machines and brought back to a private room, which was suddenly quiet. She didn't move her head to look at anyone in the crowd that had gathered.

His hand in James's, Finn walked slowly toward his mother. A doctor moved a chair to the bed's edge. Halfway there, Finn stopped, looking up at James with an expression of great concern.

"It's okay, Finny," he said. "She's sick, but she's going to get better. Do you want to say hello?"

"Yes," he said.

James lifted him and put him on the stool. He looked down at Sarah. The marks of the stitches of her face had faded to pale shadows. Her hair was covered with a kerchief, pink and black, a gesture for Finn, James noted to himself; someone tried to cover her trauma so Finn wouldn't be frightened.

Finn was silent, staring down.

"Say something, Finny," said James quietly.

After a long pause, in his small voice, Finn said: "Mommy, hello."

Sarah remained unmoving.

"Lean right over her," instructed the doctor.

James tried to show the boy how to lean over the bar's edge, and in helping him, James was close to Sarah, too, with Finn at her face and James at her torso, when the flicker happened. Sarah turned her head slightly, and the mother and son saw each other. It was palpable, this act of seeing. The moment of recognition consumed the room like a back draft of fire bursting through a doorway.

She opened her mouth, and the voice was rough and wooden: "Hi, love," she said.

"Mommy," said Finn, and he dropped his head onto her chest. Sarah's eyes filled with tears.

James began laughing. Even as he pulled back and leaned against the wall, watching the two of them hold on to each other in disbelief, he could not stop laughing.

Late Spring

ANA STOOD BY the open door of Charlie's office. She could see him, bent over his computer, his dress shirt untucked. She knocked lightly.

Charlie looked up and, at the moment of recognition, beamed.

"Ana," he said. They went toward each other, extending hands, then fell into an awkward hug. Ana let herself be enfolded, breathing in the scent of Charlie's neck.

"How are you?" she asked, pulling back. They stood close together in the small room.

"I'm okay." He smiled. "Are you back for good?"

"I don't know yet."

"James has been in to see Lise a few times," said Charlie. In their e-mail exchanges, Ana had given no details about why she had left. But it was clear that Charlie knew. She realized he was telling her about James's visits for a reason; he was counseling her like a chaplain, nudging her toward her husband. "He brought Finn."

Ana raised her eyebrows. "I didn't know that."

Looking at Charlie, hands in his pockets, grinning and blushing before her, Ana realized that whatever live current had been between them was snuffed out now. Ana saw Charlie's youth, which had seemed at that last meeting in the bedroom such a thrilling unknown, as a liability. Her age was the same. The simple fact of time apart had broken their pull.

He was the smart young man taking care of her mother, ushering her through these last years, to the upcoming. That was all, and comforting in itself. She was another daughter of a patient, shackled by duty and love.

"How is she?" Ana asked, but the answer didn't really matter. It was always the same: a little worse.

Ana asked after Charlie's lethargic roommate and was pleased to hear he'd found work and had been separated at last from his couch. Charlie was going home soon, he said, to be with his parents for a week, out west. Ana described Montreal, the mountain in the middle of it, and the spring changing the trees.

She hugged him again quickly and turned to leave. She was almost out the door when he said her name.

Charlie went to his desk and pulled a CD from a drawer.

"I've been hanging on to this for you. It has the original of that song you liked, from that night at the bar." Ana looked at the cover: *Lone Justice.* Lots of eyeliner on a pretty face framed by tendrils of blond hair.

"I got it used. No one's really buying CDs anymore. You can get anything," said Charlie. "It's the last song."

"Thank you. That's very sweet," said Ana, slipping the disc in her purse. She was grateful for the reminder of that beautiful song, and that evening she had needed so much, during the autumn of Finn.

In her room, Lise sat in a chair. Someone had placed plastic flowers on the dresser, of no determinate type, which had accumulated a thin layer of dust. Ana wiped the leaves with a Kleenex.

Lise's recognition seemed to be moving in and out today, like a kaleidoscope brought to full length, then collapsed, then back again, over and over. "How is James?" said Lise, pushing her hair (slightly dirty, Ana observed) behind her ears.

"He's all right," said Ana, sitting on the edge of the bed. "We're not together right now."

Lise nodded. Ana tried to interpret the nod: Maybe James had told her mother of their breakup, or perhaps she was remembering Ana's explanation in the fall, or at Christmas. She wondered what James's version of events would sound like, but her mother would never be able to recount that conversation to her, if it had happened at all.

"How's your father? What's his name?"

Ana laughed. "Mom, I haven't heard from him in years."

"Yes, I know. But what's his *name*?"

"Conrad."

"Yes, Conrad," said her mother. "Conrad." A wide look of pleasure came over Lise's face, and she grinned. "Oh, Ana. We were at the beach. It was a very white beach, so hot that when I came out of the water, I couldn't walk on the sand because it burned my feet." Ana didn't know where her mother was in this memory. Perhaps somewhere in Greece or Italy, years before Ana was born, when her parents were skimming the globe together.

"Did Dad carry you across the sand?"

Lise laughed. "Oh, no. I waited in the shallow part of the sea until the sun set. We both did. We sat down on our bums in the water and waited for the sand to cool."

Ana squeezed her mother's hand. Lise looked at her, and Ana could see the memory vanishing.

"I'm having a good day," said Lise.

"Yes, I think you are."

"Who are you?" The question would never cease to take away Ana's breath.

"I'm your daughter. I'm Ana. You're my mother."

"I know that," said Lise, snappishly. Then she sighed: "But not a very good mother."

"You did the best you could."

Lise looked over Ana's head, toward the window, which was open, letting a warm breeze move across them both.

"I loved Conrad," said Lise.

She looked back at Ana. "Oh my," she said, as if startled by what she saw. Ana knew that she was always being seen anew by her mother, which might have been liberating, but somehow felt exactly the opposite.

Lise searched her daughter's face and said, finally: "What are you so afraid of?"

Ana didn't know how much meaning to ascribe to this question and suppressed the sensation that she was being had, searching for profundity where there was none. Any revelations were just the brain seizing and releasing, and not her mother at all. She tried to believe this.

"Do I seem afraid, Mom?"

"I loved being your mother," said Lise. Ana nodded, bracing herself.

"Don't be afraid," said Lise, loosening her grip on her daughter's hand. "Don't be so afraid."

James finished with the sunscreen and stood back to admire his handiwork. It was one of the first days hot enough to require lotion. James was now learning about Finn in spring, and what he needed: hats and sunscreen, water bottles and sandals.

Finn smiled up at him. James reached out and rubbed a white splotch from the boy's nose.

"Ready, Freddy," said Finn.

Sarah was sleeping upstairs in her bedroom. The day she came home from the hospital, six weeks earlier, James sat in the back of the medical van with her while Mike and Jennifer looked after Finn. Under the rim of her baseball hat, Sarah frowned at the fuss, but when they hit a speed bump and her wheelchair shifted lightly in its locks on the floor, she looked terrified. James moved into the house that day, without any discussion.

He had a few things in the spare room. During the day, he took Sarah to her appointments and Finn to daycare. Then he met with Doug at his offices, polishing a script for a new documentary about the politics of traffic.

The cat, returned from the house next door, lay on the pillow beside him while he slept. James was constantly rubbing fur from his mouth. When Finn and Sarah were asleep, James stayed up late with his laptop and the cat, fiddling with footage of Finn on the new editing software he'd bought.

His own house, his house with Ana, sat empty several blocks away. He was glad not to be there. For the first weeks that Ana was gone, friends had come by, not knowing what to say about the split. James fielded many calls, and a lasagna. People were sympathetic, but no one really knew what he had lost. He was now carrying sadness, the man who had never tasted of it, whose parents were alive, whose mother had survived carnage and spared him its description, refusing to burden him with even a single image. He knew now why she would die with that war inside her. He knew what it was to pretend anything for a child.

Sarah was like a dimmer switch slowly being turned to maximum, getting brighter every day. But there were ugly moments, too, bursts of anger followed by tears, and collapse. James took over then, cleaning the kitchen and bathing Finn, putting him to bed. But most nights, Sarah tucked him in alone, and James could hear her, singing: "'You are the light in my dark world...'" The great mystery of the light song was solved—it turned out to be a song by an obscure eighties cow-punk band that even James had never heard of.

James brought his guitar over from the house and learned the song in a few minutes from the Internet. But Finn was indifferent to James's performance. It turned out he cared about the singer, not the song.

When she was recovered, James would have to go. He couldn't imagine returning to the house. Maybe Ana would come back from Montreal and want to live there. She had revealed no plans. The e-mails between them were polite; unadorned information traveling between machines.

"Ready, Freddy," said James, picking up the bag containing a Mexican blanket and plastic containers of snacks. Finn put his hat on without a fight.

James was anxious to get Finn to the park and catch the good early afternoon light for his filming. The night before, Sarah had invited some former colleagues over for dinner. James had done the cooking so Sarah could rest and be ready. It was a gentle evening (everyone was afraid to be raucous, afraid of Sarah's new softness), but after Finn went to sleep, James, Sarah, and the two high school teachers drank a glass of wine in the living room, and Sarah told the story of Finn's birth.

James was determined to take this story back to Finn.

James locked the door behind him, and they headed down the street.

"You lead the way to the park," said James, and Finn ran ahead. He was three now and had a good sense of direction.

In the distance, James saw a woman clutching a large bouquet of pink flowers. Finn stopped in front of her, and she crouched down, pulling him toward her. James picked up speed, his heart pounding. Since Halloween, he was prepared at any moment for rescue—and then he saw the woman rise. Finn turned and came running back toward him.

"Ana! James! It's Ana!"

James felt short of breath. She got closer. Her blond hair was longer and her face a little rounder. *My Ana,* he thought. *My wife of a different substance. My vapor wife.* But she was really there, watching him. He ran his fingers rapidly across the raised scar on his knuckles.

She stopped, across from him but still far away. "Hi," she said.

"You're here," said James.

"I'm sorry. I should have called. It was spontaneous. I wanted to see Sarah, but I didn't know—"

"Let's go to the park now!" said Finn, tugging on James's sleeve. "Come! James! Come to the park! Ana!"

Ana stared at James. Bats flapped inside her torso.

Ana gestured at Finn, running ahead again. "You're going out."

"I promised him. We're working on this movie and…" James rubbed his face, fumbling in Ana's presence.

"Should I go to the house? Is Sarah there?" asked Ana.

"She is, but she's sleeping. She won't get up for another couple of hours."

"Oh," said Ana, looking down at the flowers in her hand. They seemed suddenly ridiculous.

"Do you—you could come to the park with us, and then, you know—come back after..." James had wondered how he would feel at such a meeting, and now he knew: He was famished for her. He didn't want her to go yet. He needed to show her that he was not the bleeding mess she'd left in November, and that even then, he hadn't been the mess she'd presumed. He wanted a chance.

Ana smiled. "I'll come," she said.

Finn reappeared and chatted as the three walked to the park. He and James had banter: "Tell Ana about the goose at the farm." "It had a bad foot!" said Finn. "Tell Ana about your favorite color." "Green!" "What things are green?"

Ana was impressed. He had found his gift. For the first time, she didn't feel excluded. It wasn't her failure; it was their victory.

She thought suddenly how in all their time together, there must have been a moment where that other life would have been possible. If they had been able to have a child easily, or accidentally, then maybe the propulsion would have kept them aloft. They would have been like everybody else, never looking down because they wouldn't have had to. But without either of them noticing, that moment had passed. Motherhood had passed. They got this instead.

Ana felt the sun on her face and heard the sounds of other people's children, and she didn't want to mourn anymore.

She stood back, holding the pink flowers and James's bag as he pushed Finn in the swing. Then his phone rang, and he called to her: "Can you take over?"

"Sure, sure," she said, putting the bag on a bench.

"Higher, Ana!" cried Finn as Ana pushed him, glancing at James, pacing under the tree with his phone. She startled at the sight of James's arm in his T-shirt, the twist of muscle and lean forearm. She knew every inch of that arm and felt like she was seeing a part of her own body that had been hidden away under a cast for months.

"It was Doug," said James, putting his BlackBerry in his pocket, returning to take over. But Finn had found a daycare friend and was immersed in sandcastle building. Ana and James sat on a bench, side by side.

"You look good," said James.

"So do you. No more beard." James touched his chin.

"Do I look younger?"

Ana laughed. "Not really. Sorry."

"Dammit."

Finn was placing twigs in the castle, making arms or antennae.

"How's Sarah?"

"She's a miracle patient. The brain just kicked in. Where the connections were damaged from the accident, her brain made new connections. No one really knows why."

Ana nodded. "I do."

"Why?" asked James.

"She needed to get back to Finn."

They watched him frowning while he built, as if everything depended on the height of this castle. He worked so earnestly that Ana felt like applauding. Maybe he would be an engineer, she thought, like his father.

James looked at her looking at Finn. She was smiling at first, and then she tilted her head, and it was as if she was looking through Finn, and through all the children in the playground, and through the parents, too, spectral along the park's edges. She was looking ahead of them all, into old age and after, as if she had set her eyes on what was waiting there and made peace with it. And James wanted to be with her while she went, weakening and old, to where they would all end up, the parents and the children. He wanted her, wanted her under his fingernails, in his mouth.

"I'm so sorry," he said.

"I am, too. James, I—"

"Watch!" Finn shouted. He lifted his fists and pounded his castle, over and over. Then he looked at them and grinned.

"We had a marriage," said Ana, eyes on Finn.

James said: "I know."

"Don't forget. It wasn't just accumulation. It was sacred."

James nodded vigorously. "I know."

"I miss that the most," she said, moving her foot back and forth in a straight line in the grass. "That's what it is to be married: You offer up your life, and the other person takes it. I miss that offering."

James sat very still. "I miss it, too."

Their bodies leaned toward touching.

Then there was Finn, jumping in front of them. "Up! Up! Let's make a movie!"

Ana and James stood, following Finn to his favorite tree. When they got there, James laid out the Mexican blanket.

"Do you want to stay for this?" he asked Ana, breathing in, waiting for the answer.

Finally, she nodded. "If you don't mind."

"Of course not," said James.

He set up the camera on a tripod. Finn knew what to do, lying down on the blanket, perfectly framed by the camera. Then

James lay down next to him, and Finn put his head on James's chest.

"Ana, you come, too," said Finn.

Ana stood to the side, next to the camera, another eye on the scene.

"No, no. You do your thing. I'll just watch for today." She sat down on the grass.

Finn pointed at birds in the sky, singing nonsense.

"Ana, can you press Record?" asked James. Ana did so, then sat down out of the frame, crossing her legs.

James could see himself and Finn in the camera's display square, against the red blanket.

"Story time," said Finn.

"Are you ready for it? This one's about you," said James.

"Meeeee!" squealed Finn. James wanted Finn to know that he was keeping the information that Finn would require. And for this, at least, Ana might be proud of him.

He began: "You took so long to come out that your mother nearly went mad. In the fifteenth hour, she was on her hands and knees, and she kept saying: 'Tell me what to do. Tell me what to do.' And your dad laughed about that later because, you know, she never wanted anyone to tell her anything.

"'I'm done,' she kept saying. 'I can't do it.' She was thinking: 'Women do this? My mother did this? My grandmother? It's impossible that women should have to do this!'"

Finn curled closer to James, his head rising and falling with James's breathing.

"She turned onto her back, and the midwife put the long plastic arm of a machine on her belly. She was ten basketballs huge, because you were in there. I knew her during this time, and this part is definitely true: She couldn't even see over the top of her belly to her feet. And the machine beeped, and the midwife said, in this really strange voice: 'Now, Sarah. Now we have to push. There's something wrong with the baby's heartbeat.' Your mom had been feeling so weak, so tired, but she heard that sentence and everything changed. There was just a second then where she glanced out the window, and you guys were so high up in the hospital, she could see the towers of the city, blinking in the darkness, all lit up like it was any other night. And she thought: 'Okay now. Okay.' "

Ana watched them, Finn protected by James's arm.

She could remember all of it, the great love they had once. It streamed past her, the limbs and the warm pockets of it, even the brutality, the smell of it. She could see it all, from every angle, like she was turning over an artifact in her hand. She did not know yet if something new was growing in its place, if the stone was going to warm and reshape itself. She closed her eyes, tried to see the earth giving way, but she saw only whiteness, so well cultivated, so pointless. She opened her eyes.

Finn looked up at James, telling his story.

"And she screamed, and she pushed. She screamed like she wanted to wake the city. And your dad said that no human had ever screamed like that before. It made his ears ache, he said. It shattered windows. People cowered and hid, and other people came out of their houses, onto their porches and sidewalks, trying to make sense of what was happening. But it worked. You pushed yourself out of her body. She called you, and you came to her sound."

Reading Group Guide

1. How do you understand the meaning of the novel's title?

2. In what ways is this novel informed by its setting in a major city? What might the author be expressing about modern urban life?

3. Ana asks Sarah how she knew she wanted a child. Whose side of the ensuing exchange made the most sense to you? Why could Ana not be honest with Sarah about when, or if, she herself "knew"?

4. How does James's behavior upend (or conform to) conventional notions of masculinity, at work, at home, and with Finn? In what ways does Ana challenge the concept of femininity? How do these shifting gender roles affect the story?

5. At certain points, both Ana and James find themselves acutely aware of their age. What triggers this awareness in each of them? What does this awareness mean to each of them?

6. Neither Ana's nor James's mother quite fits the picture of a conventional mother. Can you see people you know in either of them? In what ways?

7. Is it still a social taboo for a woman to resist motherhood? How does Ana experience society's attitudes toward women who aren't mothers? Is it possible for a female character to be sympathetic if she rejects motherhood?

8. How does Finn's sudden presence in James and Ana's relationship foment marital discord—or does it? To what extent is their marriage affected by parenthood?

9. What do you make of Ana's relationship with Charlie? What draws her to him?

10. The final scene of the novel involves James telling Finn (and Ana) a story. How does this closing story-within-a-story relate to the novel as a whole?

11. What do you think the next chapter in life will be for Ana, for James, for Finn, for Sarah?

Acknowledgments

The epigraph is from the poem "Filling Station" by Elizabeth Bishop, in *The Complete Poems, 1927–1929,* by Farrar, Straus and Giroux. The snatches of lyrics about rockin' leprechauns are slightly misquoted by James from Jonathan Richman's "Rockin' Rockin' Leprechauns" (from *Rock 'n' Roll with the Modern Lovers,* 1977); the phrase "Dance me to the end of love" is from Leonard Cohen's "Dance Me to the End of Love" (from *Various Positions,* 1984). The line "A naked woman my age is just a total nightmare" is from Frederick Seidel's poem "Climbing Everest" (2006). The book from which James reads the lines "The world can only change from within" and "When you are present in this moment, you break the continuity of your story, of past and future" is Eckhart Tolle's *The Power of Now* (1999). And Marvin Etzioni generously agreed to allow us to quote some lyrics from Finn's beloved song "You Are the Light" (1985).

I am indebted to my gifted U.S. editor Emily Griffin, for her patience and needle-in-the-haystack attention to detail. I am very lucky that the first draft of this book was shaped by Lara Hinchberger at McClelland and Stewart (a special thanks for lending Ana some most personal details about plastic flowers and loss). I'm especially grateful to Jackie Kaiser, who is part agent, part editor, all kindness.

I want to sincerely thank the Canada Council for the Arts for giving me the time to sit in a room of my own.

ACKNOWLEDGMENTS

I wrote much of this book trying not to stare out the window at the Carso that surrounds the United World College of the Adriatic in Duino, Italy. Thanks to the people we met in this otherworldly place, especially Annemarie Oomes and Filippo Scalandi.

Thanks to Maryam Sanati, Stephanie Hodnett, Kate Robson, and Andrea Curtis for editorial guidance and emotional endurance. True friend Celia Moore put me in touch with Dr. Asrar Rashid, who provided medical insight. Alisa Apostle, Alison McLean, and Mercedeh Sanati all submitted to my brain picking on law and finance when they had much better things to do.

Writing is a family pastime, whether the rest of the family likes it or not. My parents, Gary and Cindy Onstad, have always been supportive, but they also understand that a writer's favorite phrase is: "We'll take the kids." Thank you both.

Those particular kids, Jude and Mimi, are the source of this story and all that's meaningful. Thank you for your patience with the closed door.

And I thank my husband, Julian Bauld, who gave me the title, and the reason, and lives closer to art than anyone I know.

About the Author

KATRINA ONSTAD is an award-winning journalist whose work has appeared in the *New York Times Magazine,* as well as in the *Guardian* and *Elle.* She has been nominated for the Giller Prize and a National Magazine Award. She is a culture columnist in the *Globe and Mail* and lives in Toronto with her family. Visit her at www.katrinaonstad.com.